# What the critics are saying about...

## Tales from the Temple I

**4 Stars!** "Entertaining, highly sensual and thoroughly enjoyable…a great selection of stories." - *Page Traynor, RTBOOKclub*

**4 ½ Roses!** "…one of the most erotic anthologies that I've read so far…" – *Mireya, A Romance Review*

**5 Hearts!** "…first-rate…No dragging, no slow spots, and not one story that does not live up to the others…a must read!" - *Sara Sawyer, The Romance Studio*

## Tales from the Temple II

**4 ½ Stars!** "This anthology overflows with high class sexual tension. The short format will satisfy those looking for a quick, hot read."

*Reviewed by Suzie Housley for RTBOOKclub*

"…starts with a bang and never fizzles out. Each story is great in its own right, but put together makes one awesome read…a perfect way to showcase some of Ellora's Cave's top talent…not to be missed." - *Tina Burns, The Road to Romance*

**5 Blue Ribbons!** "This hot and passionate collection displays several styles which prove the versatility of the genre and provide great delight for readers." – *Daria, Romance Junkies*

## Tales from the Temple III

**5 Roses!** "...sure to delight readers..." – *Jackie, A Romance Review*

**"5 Hearts!"** - *Angel Brewer, The Romance Studio*

**4 Blue Ribbons!** "...will leave you panting for more. I liked all of the stories in the anthology and found each to be unique in its own way." – *Julia, Romance Junkies*

## Tales from the Temple IV

**4 Stars!** "Six extraordinarily talented authors bring you exciting and sizzling love stories in this awesome anthology...a purchase you'll be pleasantly pleased with." - *BJ Deese, eCataRomance Reviews*

Available June 21st

Available September 22nd

Available December 21st

# Ellora's Cavemen

## Legendary Tails I

ELLORA'S CAVEMEN: LEGENDARY TAILS I
An Ellora's Cave Publication, March 2005

Ellora's Cave Publishing, Inc.
1337 Commerce Drive, #13
Stow, OH 44224

ISBN #1419951513

ISBN MS Reader (LIT) ISBN # 1-4199-0153-2
Other available formats (no ISBNs are assigned):
Adobe (PDF), Rocketbook (RB), Mobipocket (PRC) & HTML



Edited by *Raelene Gorlinsky*.
Cover design by *Darrell King*.
Photography by *Dennis Roliff*.

## Warning:

The following material contains graphic sexual content meant for mature readers. *Ellora's Cavemen: Legendary Tails I* has been rated E–rotic by a minimum of three independent reviewers.

Ellora's Cave Publishing offers three levels of Romantica™ reading entertainment: S (S-ensuous), E (E-rotic), and X (X-treme).

S-*ensuous* love scenes are explicit and leave nothing to the imagination.
E-*rotic* love scenes are explicit, leave nothing to the imagination, and are high in volume per the overall word count. In addition, some E-rated titles might contain fantasy material that some readers find objectionable, such as bondage, submission, same sex encounters, forced seductions, and so forth. E-rated titles are the most graphic titles we carry; it is common, for instance, for an author to use words such as "fucking", "cock", "pussy", and such within their work of literature.
X-*treme* titles differ from E-rated titles only in plot premise and storyline execution. Unlike E-rated titles, stories designated with the letter X tend to contain controversial subject matter not for the faint of heart.

# ELLORA'S CAVEMEN: LEGENDARY TAILS I

**The Changeling**

*By Callista Arman*

**Breaking the Rules**

*By B.J. McCall*

**Abduction**

*By Lynn LaFleur*

**Dark-Pilot's Bride**

*By Cricket Starr*

**The Windsday Club**

*By Charlotte Boyett-Compo*

**Manacles of Love**

*By Elizabeth Lapthorne*

# THE CHANGELING

**Callista Arman**

# Chapter One

*His mouth covered her nipple, sucking hard through the white linen barrier. Her body arched into his heat, even as her mind struggled to resist. He was an outcast. She was the daughter of his enemy.*

*This was his revenge.*

*Rough fingers branded her bare thigh, delved in her curls. They invaded her pussy, smeared her moisture over her clit. Her breath came in mindless little puffs as he circled her sensitive nub with his strong, calloused fingers. Fire sprang to life in her belly. It streaked through her veins, igniting longing in every fiber of her being.*

*She bit her lip, lest she shame herself by begging for more.*

*"Open yer legs wider, lass."*

*"Nay," she whispered. It was her last bit of pride that spoke.*

*His fingers entered her slowly, twisting and flexing, causing her to gasp from the exquisite pleasure of it. A rare hint of a smile crooked his lips. Then his hand withdrew, leaving her empty.*

*Catching her wrist, he tugged her to her feet. "Undress, lass." His eyes, dark and sinful, dared her to refuse.*

*She obeyed with shaking hands. She'd never been completely unclothed in the presence of a man, and now…*

*His dark gaze never wavered as her garments slid, one by one, to the rough-hewn plank floor. She shivered, but 'twas not fear that caused her to tremble. Nor cold.*

*'Twas anticipation.*

* * * * *

"Do you think we should lower our prices?"

Raye MacLeod rocked her hips into her husband's forward thrust, doing her damnedest to ignore his whispered question. It was *so* not in tune with her fantasy.

"Well, do you?"

She opened one eye.

Ian supported his lean body on rigid arms, looking down at her. A frown creased his brow as his hips rocked. "A ten percent cut might give us the edge we need. On the other hand…" He withdrew until the head of his cock teased the outer lips of her pussy.

Raye grabbed his ass, pulling him back into her body. "I can't believe you're asking me this right now."

"It's been on my mind."

"Can't it wait?" Raye squeezed her eyes shut, desperate to recapture the intensity of her fantasy. A fantasy in which Kieran MacKenzie—dispossessed laird of Clan MacKenzie and owner of the biggest, baddest cock in all of medieval Scotland—deflowered Tess, the virgin daughter of his most hated enemy.

It was a scene from Raye's favorite erotic romance, *Highland Passions*.

Ian slid back out. "The ad copy's due at the printer's this afternoon."

Raye's hopes for a climax melted like her fading daydream. Okay, so after five and a half years of marriage, sex with Ian was a bit routine. That was only to be expected. But did he *have* to bring up the café right now? She'd been so close to coming. Damn it.

Kieran MacKenzie would *never* talk business during sex.

"If we don't do something to lure our clientele back," Ian said, "we might as well not open."

"Okay, okay." Raye's last twinges of arousal vanished. She and Ian had sunk their life savings into Coffee and Scones, a trendy coffeehouse on the edge of the historic district. The Scots theme had been Raye's idea—Ian had suggested Caribbean jungle décor. They'd done great for a couple of months, until the national chain Star Coffee opened a mega-café less than a mile away, right on the corner of Broad and Main. *With* a parking lot. Just like that, Coffee and Scones' bottom line had turned a bright, ugly red.

If Ian and Raye couldn't steer some thirsty traffic through their brass-handled front doors, they were headed for bankruptcy.

"Yeah, we'll have to lower our prices," she said.

"What do you think about a buy-one-get-one-free day for the college crowd?" Ian asked. He dropped his head into the crook of Raye's shoulder as the tempo of his thrusts increased. "Maybe I'll even break out my grandfather's bagpipes."

Raye groaned, but not from pleasure. She loved everything Scots—her husband most of all—but Ian had absolutely no talent on the pipes.

"We want to attract customers, not drive them away," she told him.

Ian chuckled.

She nuzzled the side of his neck. "Forget the bagpipes. But you *could* dress up in the Highlander's costume I bought you."

He grunted. "No way. I am not wearing a skirt."

"It's a kilt, not a skirt."

"Same difference." A fine tremor rippled through his body. "God, Raye, I'm getting close."

He stopped talking then, thank God. Raye concentrated on matching the rhythm of his deepening thrusts. A mildly pleasant sensation washed through her, but it was nothing like it used to be. When she and Ian first got together, he'd given her one shuddering orgasm after another. But now…

Now she needed daydreams of Kieran MacKenzie to help her come.

She sifted her fingers through her husband's dark curls. It was too bad she couldn't get off without a fantasy. Closing her eyes, she tried to lose herself in the feel of Ian's cock sliding inside her. A few thrusts later, she gave up. It just wasn't happening.

Tess never had this problem with Kieran in *Highland Passions*.

But Raye wasn't married to a medieval Highland warrior. Not even close. Ian was an accountant. But right now, his wire-rimmed glasses were far away on the dresser and his button-down shirt was on the floor. With the leading edge of his orgasm sharpening his features, she could almost imagine the passion of his fearsome Scots ancestors burning in his veins.

His eyes glazed. His arms flexed around her and his torso went rigid. Then he came alive, pumping into Raye's pussy with short deep, thrusts, groaning her name as the pleasure poured out of him. Then his arms gave way and his full warm weight collapsed on her, pressing her down into the mattress.

Raye kissed his neck and stroked his sweat-slicked shoulders, but she couldn't repress a tiny sigh. Why was it the man could always come, no matter what? It was just not fair.

Ian rolled to one side and flashed her a lopsided smile. "Sorry you didn't make it in time," he said. "Want me to finish you off with the vibrator?"

Raye angled up on her elbows and peered at the clock. "No. We'll be late opening if we don't get out of here soon." And God only knew they couldn't afford to miss a single customer.

"Later, then." Ian pushed off the bed and strode toward the bathroom.

Raye watched him. Her husband had a nice ass. He was tall, too, which was a plus, and his torso was solid, but not overly muscular. Not so long ago, just the thought of getting her hands on Ian could turn her on like crazy. Now she spent fourteen hours a day on her feet, selling designer coffee. She'd choose an hour of sleep over an hour of sex any day of the week.

But to be truthful, an hour of reading beat out either of those options. No matter how stressed out she was, a well-written erotic romance always made her feel better. Especially when the hero was Kieran MacKenzie.

Ian turned on the shower. She toyed with the thought of joining him. She could talk him into that orgasm he'd promised her. Or…

She opened the night table drawer and slid out her dog-eared copy of *Highland Passions*.

*The hunger in Kieran's gaze set Tess' heart pounding. Belatedly, she questioned the wisdom of coming to him in the abandoned cottage. She tried to cover her nakedness with her hands.*

*Kieran caught her wrists and spread her arms wide. "Nay, lass. I'll not be allowing ye to hide. Ye belong to me now."*

Raye gave a little sigh. *Ye belong to me now.* How incredibly romantic. What would it be like to belong to a man like that? Smiling, she turned the page.

*Kieran flung off his plaid. Tess nearly lost her breath at the sight of him. His strong arms were corded with muscle and sinew. His chest was broad and muscular, cruelly marked with what looked like an old knife wound.*

*Her gaze dropped. Sweet heaven! The kitchen girls hadn't been exaggerating. Kieran's cock was enormous.*

*"On the bed, lass."*

*She could do naught but obey.*

* * * * *

"Hey, chica, what've you got under there? A porn magazine?"

Raye's head jerked up as she shoved *Highland Passions* onto the shelf under the counter. "Angie. Sorry. I didn't hear you come in."

Raye's best friend drummed her French-manicured nails on the counter. "Don't see how you could have missed the racket. You've got more bells on your shop door than Santa has on his sleigh."

"Yeah, I know. Ian put them there so we could hear the door open if we're in the back."

Angie smirked. "In the back doing what?"

"Not what you're thinking, that's for sure."

"Too bad. Is your yummy husband back there now?"

"Yeah."

"Well, why don't you just corner him behind a stack of boxes and—"

"Oh, right."

"Why not? You guys used to be wild. Remember that time at the lake, back when you were dating?"

"It's not like that anymore." Raye scowled as she served up Angie's regular jolt of caffeine—Edinburgh Roast, black. She looked up to find her friend regarding her with a sympathetic expression.

"Want to talk about it?"

"Nah. I'm good. It's just..."

"Just what?"

She leaned her elbows on the counter. "I love Ian, don't get me wrong."

Angie raised her plucked eyebrows. "But?"

"But he's so *easygoing*. Sometimes I just wish he'd, you know, be more macho. Take charge." Raye shook her head. "He asks my opinion on everything."

"I thought you liked that about him."

"I did. I mean, I do. Sometimes."

Three sugars plunked into Angie's coffee. "And other times?"

"Other times I could just scream. Some days I'd sell my soul for a guy who calls the shots."

Her friend snorted. "You'd hate that."

"No, I wouldn't. I'd love it." Raye nodded toward the pastry case. "You want anything with your caffeine?"

"Yeah. The chocolate-dipped scones look good. I'll take two."

"I don't know how you manage to stay so skinny," Raye groused as she deposited the pastries on a plate.

"It's in the genes. What do I owe you?"

"Forget it."

"No way. You can't afford to give away your inventory."

Raye sighed. "I hardly think two scones are going to make or break our bottom line." She paused. "Did you pass Star Coffee on the way over?"

"Yeah."

"Packed?"

"To the gills." Angie glanced at her watch. "Oh, shit, it's almost nine and I can't afford to be late for work—*again*." She headed for the door.

Raye stared at the empty café for a beat, then pulled out *Highland Passions*. She could almost feel Kieran MacKenzie's Scots brogue tickling her ear.

*"Ye are a dream, lass."*

*Kieran pressed a hot kiss just below Tess' ear. She trembled. He'd spread his plaid over the straw-filled mattress. The wool, still warm from his body, scraped her bare skin, sending a jolt of hot pleasure to the sweet place between her thighs. He kissed the base of her neck. The rough stubble of his beard scraped her tender skin. His hands covered her breasts, lifting one, then the other.*

*He watched her face as his thumbs passed over the sensitized peaks. "Ye like that, don't ye, lass?"*

*"Aye," she gasped. Her hips lifted in invitation. He pulled her close, his large hands positioning her body for his invasion.*

*A quiver of apprehension shook her. His cock was so big, so hard. The serving girls giggled that Kieran's rod was the largest in all of Scotland. Looking at it now, Tess was reminded of her father's favorite stallion.*

*Sweet heaven! Would Kieran's cock fit her virgin passage?*

"Oh, don't worry about that," Raye murmured aloud. "It'll fit. It always does. Just you wait and see."

She shifted, suddenly warm. And horny. Her thighs were wet beneath her tartan plaid barista skirt. Dazed, she looked from her book to the door leading to the café's back room. Ian was in there, glued to his laptop, trying to chart a course through a sea of red ink.

She glanced toward the street door. Not a customer in sight, and there wasn't likely to be one before lunch. And even if someone *did* come in, there were all those bells on the door to let her know.

She stowed *Highland Passions* under the counter. Quickly, she undid her apron and tiptoed toward the back. When she reached the door at the rear of the sales area, she paused. There weren't any windows in the storage room, and making love under glaring fluorescent lights didn't seem too sexy. Backtracking, she snagged a votive candle from a sales display and a lighter from the drawer near the register. Thus armed, she pushed open the door to the back room.

Ian's back was toward her. He hunched over his secondhand desk, tapping on his laptop keyboard, bills and other papers scattered all around. Raye lit her votive and placed it on a stack of boxes. Then she flicked off the lights, leaving only the glow of candle flame.

Oh, and the glow of Ian's laptop, too. She hadn't considered that.

His head swiveled toward her. "What—?"

She draped her arms over his shoulders from behind and summoned her best provocative whisper. "Forget the quarterly reconciliation. Let's make love."

He turned back to the screen with a noncommittal grunt.

She slipped open the top two buttons of his shirt and slid her hands inside. His bare chest was warm under her cool hands. She pressed her breasts into his back and swirled her tongue into his ear.

He shrugged, as if trying to shake off a swarm of gnats. "Not now, Raye. I'm posting bills."

She raised her head and focused on the screen, then wished she hadn't. Last quarter's losses were worse than she'd thought. Add that to what they already owed…

God, she'd do anything to forget what a mess they were in. Even for a few minutes. And she knew just how to do it.

"You can take five." She eased Ian's glasses off his nose and dropped them on the desk. "Come on, let's do it."

Ian frowned at her. "Here?"

"Sure, why not?"

"Well, for one thing, this is a glorified storage closet. For another, we're supposed to be open for business."

"This is our slow time. Besides, we'll hear the bells if anyone comes in." She dropped to her knees and began unbuckling his belt.

"We just fucked this morning."

"So?"

"So, that wasn't even three hours ago."

"Well, I didn't come."

"You could have," he said, defensiveness creeping into his voice.

She unbuttoned his pants and tugged down the zipper. "I'll come this time."

"Raye…"

She slipped her hand under the waistband of his boxers and closed her fingers around his penis. Even semi-hard it filled her hand. Ian' equipment wasn't as impressive as Kieran MacKenzie's monster of a cock, of course, but her husband really had nothing to be ashamed of. The thrill of doing it in the café, with the front door unlocked, caused a streak of arousal to shoot through her pussy. Moisture creamed her thighs.

This was going to be good.

And it was, for about two seconds, until Ian caught her hand and eased it away from his crotch. "Look, Raye. This isn't a good time. I'm trying to figure out which distributors we're going to pay this month."

"Screw the distributors," Raye said, shaking free of his grip. She sat back on her heels and started unbuttoning her blouse. "Better yet, screw me." She looked around for a likely spot. "Over there. On that crate of napkins."

A thrill jackknifed through her as she pictured herself with her plaid skirt bunched at her waist, her legs wrapped around Ian's hips. Kieran had made love to Tess like that, on a window seat in Castle Dunhardie. Anyone could have caught them.

"And maybe..." she breathed, getting caught up in the fantasy, "maybe you could talk with a Scots brogue."

"I'm from Cincinnati," Ian said. "Not fucking Edinburgh."

"Just pretend," Raye said, slipping her blouse off her shoulders. "For me."

His gaze narrowed. "Does this have something to do with that book you're always reading?"

"No," she lied. She undid the front closure on her bra and lifted her breasts, offering them to him. "Please?"

He looked down at her for a long moment, then stood and zipped his pants. "Button your shirt, Raye. I told you, this isn't a good time."

She felt like she'd been slapped. "You're turning me down?"

"Of course not. We'll do it later. Come on, get up." He grabbed his glasses off the desk and put them on.

Raye rose slowly, hugging her open blouse to her body. "You'll be lucky if there is a 'later'."

"What the hell is that supposed to mean?"

"What does it sound like? Maybe I'm sick of being your blow-up doll. You know, it's no thrill being screwed by someone who's not there."

Confusion flitted across his face. "What do you mean 'not there'?"

"Not *with* me," Raye said slowly. "Not paying attention. You're on autopilot every time we make love, Ian. You might as well be jerking off. All you think about is this damn café."

His jaw hardened. "If I don't think about the café, we'll be in bankruptcy court. Grow up, Raye." He dropped into his chair and swung toward his computer.

Red blotches crowded Raye's vision. "Don't you turn your back on me, Ian MacLeod! We started this fight and we're going to finish it."

He gripped the mouse and scrolled down the page. "I didn't start this fight, Raye. You did. And I have no intention of continuing it."

# Chapter Two

"I don't know, Maggie. Maybe Ian just doesn't love me any more."

Raye sank onto a padded stool behind the counter at Highland Magick, the shop next door to Coffee and Scones. The proprietor, Maggie Dunstan, was a plain, elderly Scots woman with neat white hair and half-moon reading glasses. She looked like anyone's grandmother, but even so, Raye had always thought there was something a little odd about Maggie. Something witchy. Ian insisted it was just Raye's overactive imagination.

Maggie patted Raye's hand. "Och, lass, come now. That lad loves ye. I can see it in his eyes."

Raye shrugged.

"It canna be as bad as all that," Maggie said gently.

"It is," Raye said. "I think…oh Maggie, I'm afraid Ian and I just don't click any more. We've grown so far apart. I don't know if we can put things back together."

The old woman clucked her tongue. "Ye canna be giving up on yer marriage, lass."

"What marriage? Ian and I barely talk anymore, except about the café. And he's hardly ever interested in—" Raye shut her mouth abruptly, heat flooding her cheeks.

Maggie just chuckled. "So it's like that, is it?"

"Like that and worse," Raye replied glumly.

"Dinna worry, lass. Your man will come around."

"I hope so."

Maggie set her walker in front of her and pulled herself out of her seat with arms that seemed remarkably strong for a woman well past eighty. "Will ye watch the shop for me a spell? I feel the need to stretch my old limbs. I'll take myself next door for a cup of your fine coffee."

Raye set her purse on the counter. Watching Maggie's shop would hardly be taxing. Highland Magick, with its moldy collection of old books and second-rate artwork, attracted even less business than Coffee and Scones. The strange thing was, Maggie never seemed to have money problems.

Ah, well. Maybe she did mail order.

Maggie settled her tartan shawl about her shoulders.

"Wait," Raye said. "It's slipping." She reached over the counter to adjust Maggie's shawl. As she drew her arm back, her elbow connected with her purse, toppling it over.

*Highland Passions* spilled onto the counter. Before Raye could cram the battered volume back into her bag, Maggie scooped it up.

She held it at arm's length. "Oh, my, my, my."

Raye stifled a moan of embarrassment. Kieran MacKenzie appeared in naked glory on the cover, the hilt of his sword barely covering his legendary family jewels. He stood on a rugged Highland hillside, dark hair whipping about his neck. Castle Dunhardie, his childhood home, perched on a faraway cliff just beyond his left shoulder. His eyes were dark and tortured, but his chin was set with his determination to regain his stolen birthright. Tess clung to him, red curls tumbling down her back, big boobs bursting from a gown far too skimpy for a Highland winter.

"Och, what a fine laddie this one is," Maggie said. "I'm thinking *his* lass has no complaints in the bedroom."

Raye covered her shocked gasp with a cough. "No," she croaked. "She doesn't."

"A shame he isna real," the old woman said softly, glancing at Raye.

"I wish," Raye said.

"Do ye now? Do ye truly wish to have this man for your lover?"

"Yeah," she said. "I do." She touched Kieran's image. "He's brave. Strong. Searching for the right woman to heal his tormented soul." A sigh escaped her lips. "And his body… What woman wouldn't want a man like that?"

Maggie bright gaze rested on Raye. "Wishes hold power, lass. They shouldna be made lightly. Sometimes they bring things we dinna expect." She looked down at Kieran MacKenzie, then said, "Do ye mind if I borrow your book? Just for a wee bit? I'm thinking this lad would be a fine companion for my coffee break."

Raye nearly choked. "But that's…um…not your typical romance. It's…" she lowered her voice, even though there was no one in the shop but the two of them. "*Erotica*. I don't think…"

Maggie chuckled. "I'm an old woman, lass, but I was a young wife once, and I havna yet forgotten it." She slipped the book into the pouch attached to her walker. Helplessly, Raye watched her shuffle out of the shop.

It was hard to imagine Maggie perusing *Highland Passions* over a cup of coffee. Still, a woman would have to be dead not to enjoy reading about Kieran MacKenzie. And Raye had a feeling that old as Maggie was, she was far from the grave.

Deprived of her reading material, Raye settled on Maggie's stool. Highland Magick was a tiny shop, smaller even than Coffee and Scones. Books lined the walls from ceiling to floor, and Raye would be willing to bet money not one was less than fifty years old. A distinct moldy aroma clung to the shelves. The subject matter was entirely Scottish—history, castles, art, folklore.

One tome, larger than the rest, lay on the counter by the register, as if Maggie had just been reading it. It was bound in cracked green leather, its engraved gold title barely legible.

*Changelings.*

Curious, Raye opened the cover, taking care not to crack the aged pages inside. The book was typeset in an old-fashioned font that exuded an air of mystery.

Intrigued, she started to read.

*Changeling: a faerie being who takes the place of a human, often a child. It is empowered by an ill wish. The switch comes at dawn, accompanied by the laughter of the fairy folk. The household does not know the change has taken place, as the Changeling takes the appearance of the beloved. This is a false visage, however. The glamour of the faerie folk obscures the Changeling's true features.*

*Soon, however, the faerie will make itself known. A Changeling plays magic on the pipes or fiddle, ensorcelling all who hear it. It bewitches all it touches. Its hunger is extreme, and can never be sated, for a Changeling has no soul.*

*To rid your home of a Changeling, you must…*

Raye looked up from the page as the door to Maggie's shop opened, admitting a middle-aged couple who were probably Maggie's only customers for the day. Raye shut the book and rose to greet them, a bright smile plastered on her face.

* * * * *

*Would Kieran's cock fit her virgin passage?*

*Tess shuddered at the thought.*

*His mouth covered hers in carnal possession, allowing her no quarter. Tess' maidenly fears whipped to full fury, like leaves caught in a gale. Rough lips plundered, demanding entrance. This was not the gentle kiss they'd shared in the garden. That kiss had been but a lure—Tess realized that now. He'd been hunting her, like a doe or a vixen, and now she was in his power. He would have her now, whether she wished it or not.*

*She wished it.*

*He staked his claim to her body, his mouth brazenly erotic on hers. His kiss kindled a fire within her and fanned the flames until she thought she would be consumed with wanting him. Sweet heaven, how she loved it! Moisture gushed from her core as Kieran's tongue mastered hers. Before the sun rose, his cock would master her pussy.*

*She mewled deep in her throat. Kieran's hands roamed her shoulders, breasts, and buttocks, and none too gently. He shifted, coming over her, the straw ticking of the mattress rustling under his weight. His enormous cock probed her slick folds.*

*Fear blossomed, setting her heart to pounding. How could she take the biggest cock in all Scotland?*

*"'Twill hurt," she whimpered.*

*"I'll nay be denyin' it, lass," Kieran replied.*

*But his rough voice was oddly gentle.*

"Are you coming to bed?"

Raye's head jerked up. Ian stood in the doorway, arms crossed over his bare chest. He was wearing the bottoms of the pajamas his mother had bought him last year for Christmas. Not a good sign. He usually slept naked.

With a smooth motion, she flipped *Highland Passions* closed, cover side down, but not before he saw it. His lips thinned, but he said nothing.

She sighed. She wanted to work things out, like Maggie had urged, but Ian had barely looked at her after she'd gone back to Coffee and Scones. They'd eaten dinner separately, closed up late, driven home in silence. Inside their tiny apartment, Ian had headed for the bedroom while Raye had fled to the living room, to take refuge in *Highland Passions*.

She cast a surreptitious glance at the book, wishing Ian would leave so she could continue with Tess and Kieran's first sexual encounter. There was no way Raye could read about Kieran thrusting his massive cock into Tess' virgin pussy while Ian stood there, watching her.

She shifted in her seat. "I'll come to bed in a little while."

Ian's dark eyes regarded her steadily for another couple seconds. "It's past midnight, you know. We have to be up at five."

"I know what time we have to be up."

"Good night, then." He disappeared down the short hall into the bedroom.

Raye sighed. Ian was right. If she didn't go to sleep soon, she'd never drag herself out of bed in time to open the café. She flipped over her book and ran a finger over the picture of Kieran MacKenzie.

The biggest cock in Scotland would have to wait until morning.

# Chapter Three

Raye rolled over, her mind dimly registering the fact that Ian was no longer in bed.

The shower was going at full blast. Damn. That meant it was somewhere between five-ten and five-fifteen. She could set her watch by her husband's morning routine. She rolled over and pulled the pillow over her head. God, what she wouldn't do for another hour of sleep. She lay there, motionless, until Ian cut off the water.

That was when she heard it. Female laughter, coming from the bathroom.

What the—? Raye sat up. Was Ian listening to the radio in the bathroom? He'd never done that before. Disconcerted, she swung her legs over the side of the bed and padded to the door.

The laughter came louder. Not one woman, but several, whispering and giggling. There were words as well, but for the life of her, she couldn't make them out. It was almost as if they were speaking in another language.

A creeping sense of foreboding slithered down Raye's spine.

She gave herself a mental shake. It had to be a radio. Some foreign station, though God only knew why her husband was listening to something like that. He preferred classic rock.

"Ian?"

No answer.

She put her hand on the doorknob. "Ian?"

The laughter stopped, leaving nothing but silence.

Odd. Very odd.

Raye turned the knob and pushed the door open. Ian stood in front of the sink, a towel wrapped around his waist, frowning at his electric razor. There was no radio in the room, at least not as far as she could tell.

"Did you hear that..." The question died on her lips as he turned toward her.

For one suspended moment in time Raye could do nothing but stare. There was something different about him. His face was the same, yet not. His handsome features were sharper, his dark eyes lit with an odd glow. He seemed taller, somehow, and broader. Had Ian's muscles always rippled over his chest in such a sensuous rhythm? She'd never noticed. Glistening beads of water clung and slid on his pecs and abs. She watched a drop flow into his navel, then lower, toward the bulge under his towel.

"Ian?"

His dark eyes raked over her body. A tight, almost painful smile touched his lips. He set the razor on the vanity and took a step toward her.

"I would have ye now, lass. Strip off that gown."

Raye gaped at him. She must have tried a thousand times to get Ian to role-play a scene from Highland Passions. And just yesterday, in the storage room, he'd flatly refused to fake a Scots accent. He just wasn't interested in spicing up their sex life that way.

At least he hadn't been.

She couldn't believe he'd changed his mind. She needed to hear it again. "What did you say?"

"Ye heard me," Ian growled. "Strip."

A tingle of arousal teased her pussy. "Now?" she asked, her pulse speeding up. "Are you sure? We have to leave for work in a few minutes."

"Lass, yer not going anywhere—except into my bed."

His hands came down on her shoulders. Exerting a steady pressure, he walked her backwards, out of the bathroom. Toward the bed.

Moisture trickled down Raye's bare thighs. "Okay," she said, her voice suddenly high.

The back of her legs hit the mattress, and she went down, sprawled on her back. Ian towered over her, the expression on his face an exquisite study of pure lust.

*Oh, yes!*

"I'm going to mark ye as my own, lassie. By the time I'm through with ye, ye'll nay be moving a muscle without remembering who yer master is."

She giggled. The macho talk turned her on like crazy. Ian didn't go for that, either—she could hardly believe he'd created this fantasy for her now. Maybe it was his way of telling her he was sorry they'd fought.

He stood at the edge of the bed, his hot gaze roaming her body. "I told ye to strip," he said, his voice taking on a hard, delicious edge. "I'll tolerate no disobedience."

Gathering the fabric of Raye's nightgown in his hands, he ripped the garment from neckline to hem.

Cream gushed from Raye's pussy.

Ian loomed over her.

A hysterical giggle bubbled into her throat. "This is crazy," she said.

"What man could remain sane when faced with yer beauty?"

Raye gaped at him. Kieran MacKenzie had said those exact words to Tess. How had Ian…

"Have…have you been reading my book?"

His gaze raked her body, his eyes darkening. A sound Raye could only describe as a growl ripped from his throat. "Ye are a dream, lass."

*Oh, God.* Kieran had said *that* to Tess, too.

Raye's heart stuttered. It was utterly insane, but lying here like this, with Ian's broad body filling her vision, it was almost like Kieran MacKenzie had come to life.

She swallowed hard. Maybe she'd read *Highland Passions* one too many times.

Ian straightened, his hand moving to untie the towel about his waist. Raye's gaze followed his movements, her breath suspended, waiting for the tented terrycloth to drop. Was it her imagination, or did Ian's hard-on seem a bit larger than usual?

The towel fell to the carpet.

*Oh. My. God.*

Raye's heart nearly stopped beating.

She had to be hallucinating. Either that, or her husband had been responding to enlarge-your-penis spam ads behind her back.

Ian's cock was fully twice as big as it should have been. It was longer than her longest dildo, and she was sure her thumb and middle finger wouldn't come close to touching if she wrapped her hand around it. And the head… She swallowed. The plump, glistening head was almost the size of her fist.

*Holy shit.*

There was no way that thing was going to fit inside her.

The bed dipped under Ian's weight as he came over her, his enhanced penis prodding Raye's thigh. She burrowed into the mattress, not sure if she was really up for a round with Mr. Supersized Schlong.

"So bonny." Ian wrapped a lock of Raye's hair around his finger. "'Tis the color of…" He frowned.

Raye held her breath. Tess' hair was red and glossy her own was frizzy and brown.

"…of a freshly plowed field," Ian finished.

*A freshly plowed field?* In *Highland Passions,* Kieran MacKenzie had likened Tess' abundant red curls to a wildfire. But of course, that didn't fit. And besides, maybe Ian hadn't read that passage.

His gaze dropped to her tits. "Yer breasts are like…er…" He frowned again. "Like ripe tangerines."

She glared up at him. Honestly. Was that the best he could do? Kieran had called Tess' breasts "ripe melons, sweet as summer honey". Raye's boobs were by no stretch of the imagination melon-sized, but *still.* Tangerines? Come on.

"Ye are enough to drive a man to the edge of reason." Ian bent his head and sucked her nipple into his mouth.

*Whoa.* This was more like it. Desire sliced through Raye's stomach like the blade of a finely honed dirk. Her fingers curled in Ian's hair, anchoring his mouth to her breast. It had been months—no, *years*—since she'd felt this turned on.

Ian left one nipple and turned his attentions to the other. His hand slipped over Raye's belly, traveling toward her drenched pussy. She wiggled her butt, tilting her hips into his hand. His long fingers entered her, twisting and pulsing. A series of spasms exploded in her vagina.

She moaned when his thumb found her clit. Moisture gushed from her core and dribbled down her butt crack. The sheets were drenched. She was going to have to change them, but she didn't even care.

Ian bit softly on her nipples, first one, then the other, never once breaking the rhythm of his finger and thumb. Raye clutched his shoulders. She was getting close, so close, and she knew when she came, it was going to be good. She ground her hips into his hand.

"Oh, God, yes, Ian. *Yes*. Harder."

Normally, Ian responded to her demands. Not this morning. As if triggered by her plea, his hand slid from her body. An instant later, his mouth left her breast. Raye cried out as her climax receded.

"Come back," she begged. "I was so close. Why'd you stop?"

"Stop?" He chuckled. "Ah, lass, we've just begun."

His strong palms stroked the sensitive skin of her inner thighs. He pressed her legs apart and hitched them up on his shoulders. Raye sucked in a breath. Ian hadn't gone down on her in ages. Her last thought before his tongue touched her was that it had been far, far too long.

She shuddered as he ate her out. Her hips jerked when his lips caught her clit. He teased the sensitive kernel with his tongue, then drew the hood over the head and suckled. His fingers kneaded her inner thighs, then slipped into her pussy, flexing and twisting.

Pleasure built. Ebbed. Built again. Ian doubled his efforts, driving her higher. Her hips rocked to accommodate his rhythm. Her head tossed back and forth. She was on the plateau, that excruciating place where everything felt so good, yet it wasn't enough. She was lost in a swirling, tumbling world of sensation, fulfilled and yet bereft at the same time. The end was coming, though. Just a few seconds more…

"Oh, God." Raye fisted her hands in Ian's hair and held on. Her hips jerked. Mewling sounds came from her throat.

Ian's head lifted.

"Nooooo!" Raye cried. "Don't stop! Finish me off."

He came over her. "Aye, I'll finish ye, lass. I'll fill yer sweet cunt with my hard cock."

His cock. *Shit!* She'd forgotten about his monster cock! She wriggled, trying to move back on the bed, but she didn't get far. His arms surrounded her like a vise.

"Ian, I'm not so sure…"

"Quiet, lass."

"Look, time out, okay? Let's talk about this. What did you take to get your penis to grow like that? How long is it going to last? Because I'm not sure I want to screw until it goes back to normal."

He sank one knee firmly between her thighs, opening her. "Quiet," he repeated. His voice was firmer now, as though he expected her to obey.

Was he nuts? Reading about Kieran's mastery of Tess in *Highland Passions* was fun, but Raye had her limits in real life. "Listen, Ian—"

He silenced her with a kiss. He rocked atop her, supporting himself with rigid arms, the head of his cock hot on her pussy. His hips moved again, and the shaft invaded her vagina. Just an inch, but she already felt full to the brim.

She tore her mouth free. "Ian," she whispered. "It's going to hurt."

He chuckled. "I'll nay be denyin' it, lass."

*Damn.* He must've read the consummation scene in *Highland Passions*. Not surprising, considering how dog-eared the book was. No doubt it had fallen open on precisely that page.

Ian kissed her again, easing another inch into her body. Raye forced herself to relax. After all, Tess had submitted to Kieran's amazing cock, and look what had happened. She'd come her brains out.

Another inch. There was a burning pain, but also burning streaks of pleasure. She clung to Ian's shoulders.

"Almost there, love." His fingers teased her breasts, momentarily distracting her. Then, with a swift jerk of his hips, he plunged in to the hilt.

She was skewered. Impaled. Nearly split in half. Utterly and completely possessed. Ian lay still for a moment, his forehead pressed into the crook of her neck. "Damn me, lass. 'Tis been years since I've had a virgin, and never one so tight."

And then he started to move.

Sweet God in heaven, it was incredible.

Every thrust was bliss. The huge head of his cock stimulated nerve endings Raye never knew existed. It was as if her entire vagina had tuned into one big G-spot.

She cried out. Ian increased his rhythm, sliding in, then out, pushing her higher. She clutched the bedsheets, her breath coming in gasps and moans. She tried, but it was impossible to move with him. The pleasure was too much. It was as if he'd taken over her body, commanding it to a fever-pitched response. She was at the crest of a tidal wave, hanging above the dark depths of a rolling sea, ready to plunge into the unknown.

Her brain ceased to function. She was a being of raw, aching pleasure, living only for the thrust and drag of the enormous cock inside her. She moaned again, a long keening sound.

"That's it, lass. Let it come. Let it come hard."

The wave broke, hurling her over its leading edge. Her heart pounded. Blood rushed in her ears. Her inner muscles clenched in an exquisite spasm.

Raye's scream echoed off the walls as she plunged into a wild sea of sensation. Ian pounded inside her, driving like a man possessed. Her orgasm seemed to go on forever. Wave after wave of sharp bliss spiked through her body, rushed through her veins, until she was sure every cell in her body was saturated with it. Ian's body went tense. His cock hardened inside her, triggering a second spasming orgasm in Raye's sensitized pussy. He cried out, his hot cum shooting into her.

She clung to him as his rhythm slowed, catching her breath as he caught his. Finally he lay limp, crushing her into the mattress, still semi-hard inside her.

She smiled, smoothing his damp hair off his forehead. "That was incredible," she whispered. "We should do it again sometime."

He raised his head a fraction. "Och, lass, ye dinna think I'm through with ye yet, do ye?"

Raye's eyes widened. Ian was staying in character, even after that amazing climax? And he wanted to do it again, right away?

Apparently, whatever enhancing formula he'd taken hadn't worn off.

He levered himself up, and with one strong hand on her waist, rolled her onto her stomach. "On yer hands and knees, lass."

*Oh, boy.* Doggie style was her favorite. How would it feel with Ian's enhanced cock?

His palm came down on her ass, hard, the smack going through her like a lightning bolt. "Higher, lass."

She gasped, totally turned on. She pressed her forehead to a pillow and wiggled her ass in the air. "Fuck me, Ian."

"My pleasure, lass."

He gripped her hips and drove home in one long, hard thrust.

*"Oh, God."*

He set a fast pace, hips pistoning, fingers gripping her hipbones so tightly she was sure he would leave bruises. She didn't care. The pain added an incredible edge to her pleasure, and Ian's cock—well, there just weren't any words to describe it. He fucked her hard, his balls slapping against her pussy with every thrust, his fingers exploring the crack between her ass cheeks. Another wonder—Ian usually avoided her anus. Now he was fingering the puckered opening like a pro.

The sensation was amazingly erotic. "Yes," she moaned. "Oh, yes."

His finger slid into her hole, pressing and rotating, a counterpoint to the rhythm of his cock in her pussy. Raye lifted her hips, and a second finger joined the first, causing a brief dart of pain as the knuckle slid past her sphincter. The discomfort vanished when his fingers flexed inside her. Every nerve ending in her body shuddered with pleasure as her climax careened toward its peak.

She nearly laughed out loud. When was the last time she'd come twice in one lovemaking session? Too goddamn long ago, that was for sure.

She screamed when the orgasm hit. Ian kept his cock and fingers pumping, triggering a series of aftershocks. She rode each one out, gasping and moaning, her pussy milking his incredible cock, her anus contracting around his fingers.

Finally, he left her body and eased her down onto the pillows, where she lay limp, sated, and exhausted. Ian nestled beside her. They lay like that for what seemed a long time, until Raye summoned enough strength to open one eye.

The bedside clock shone with a disapproving red glare. 6:57.

Shit.

They'd missed opening the café. Reluctantly, she rolled over and poked Ian. He didn't budge.

"Ian! Get up! We've got to get to work."

He opened one eye and looked at her. "Work?"

"Yes, work. We were supposed to open at six. It's almost seven. That new girl we hired is showing up at eight."

Ian gave her a blank look.

"Hello?" she said. "Coffee and Scones? Remember?"

Finally, understanding dawned. "Ah, yes. The café." He smiled, as if expecting a prize.

Raye heaved herself out of bed, ignoring her protesting muscles. Ian had really worked her over. She smiled, replaying the scene in her mind as she went into the bathroom and started the shower.

A minute later, he joined her.

She gave him her brightest smile. "That was fantastic," she told him. "*You* were fantastic."

"Ah, lass, 'tis you who are the special one." He gathered her in his arms, holding her while the water sluiced over their heads. His cock grew had again—*again!*—prodding her stomach.

In *Highland Passions,* Kieran and Tess had done it under a waterfall. Did that mean…?

Apparently, yes. Ian soaped her breasts, her stomach, her pussy. "I canna get enough of ye, lass. No sooner do I leave your body than I want to be inside ye again." He kissed her, deeply, then drew back to gaze into her eyes. "I've dreamt of ye, lass." His gaze shifted to her mouth. "I've dreamt of yer lips…"

Raye closed her eyes and let her head fall back, ready for the ravishing kiss that Kieran had given Tess under the waterfall. It didn't come. Instead, his big hands closed on her shoulders, urging her down. "Slide my cock between yer lips, lass."

Her knees hit the slippery tile. "You want a blowjob?" she asked, peering up at him through the spray of water.

"Aye, lass."

Well, it wasn't in the script, but she guessed a little improv was a good thing. Gripping his hips, she opened her mouth and took him in.

Or tried to, anyway. The head of his cock was so damn big, it was a tough job. She backed off a bit. "I don't know, Ian..."

He gripped the back of her head and guided her back. "Do it, lass."

She opened as wide as she could, trying to accommodate him. It was damn uncomfortable, though. The water kept getting into her eyes and nose, causing her to gag.

He didn't seem to notice. He kept his big cock sliding, his fingers threading through her hair, holding her head immobile. He fucked her mouth hard, driving deep. Raye did her best to deep throat him. It was tough work. But after the mind-shattering orgasms Kieran had given her, it was the least she could do.

After what seemed like forever, he pulled out. Hooking his hands under her arms, he lifted her. Pressing her spine against the wall of the shower, he impaled her pussy on his cock.

"Again?" Raye gasped. She was reaching the end of her strength, but Ian didn't show the slightest sign of letting up. Whatever he'd paid for that enhancement product, he was getting his money's worth. The trouble was, would she survive until it wore off?

He fucked her into insanity. She screamed as her third climax broke, hot, hard and endless. His cock pumped inside her, pounding the entrance to her womb. Her orgasm split and multiplied, shaking her battered body. There seemed to be no end to the pleasure—she was sure it would go on into infinity.

She must have blacked out, because the next thing she knew, she was lying on the bed, drops of water still clinging to her skin. Ian dried her with a soft towel, causing a twinge of pain now and then when the terrycloth brushed against her swollen pussy and tits. She was too spent to protest, however.

When he finally finished, she heaved herself off the bed, despite her screaming muscles. Fantasy time was over. The real world—a.k.a. Coffee and Scones—awaited them.

He rose as she limped across the room. "Where do ye think ye be going, lass?"

She turned and gave him a rueful smile. "I really loved the role-playing, Ian, but I think we can drop it now." She nodded toward the clock. "It's seven thirty-five. We've got to go."

"Yer not going anywhere."

She snorted. "Oh, come off it." She opened her closet.

He grabbed her wrist. "I mean it, lass. Ye'll not be leaving my bed. Not afore yer father signs the betrothal contract."

Raye blinked at him. He'd read that far into *Highland Passions*? A tremor of apprehension fluttered through her belly. In the chapter after the waterfall scene, Tess, beset with guilt, declares her intention to return to her father's house. Kieran, enraged, ties her to his bed.

But surely Ian wouldn't go that far.

"Yer mine," he growled. "I'll not let ye forget it." He snatched the belt from his bathrobe off the floor. Before Raye knew what had happened, her right wrist was secured to the brass headboard.

She gaped at him. "Let me go!"

He gave her a broad smile. "Nay."

"You jerk!" Raye yelled, tugging at the belt. It didn't give an inch.

He turned his back, striding toward the dresser.

She clawed at the knot, to no avail. "Ian! Get back here and untie me!"

He appeared at her side, three neckties dangling from his fingers.

Raye's eyes widened. "Oh, no, you don't."

His hand closed on her ankle, pulling it to the footboard. She gave a savage kick, trying to wrest her leg free, to no avail. Ian tied her ankle securely, then repeated the process with her other leg. He did the same to her free arm, chuckling as he dodged Raye's punches.

When he was done, she lay spread-eagle on the bed, panting from the effort of fighting him. He drew closer. His cock was—incredibly—hard again. The expression in his eyes was heated.

And oh, baby, it was turning her on.

"What are you going to do with me now?" she said breathlessly, repeating Tess' line from *Highland Passions*. Kieran had answered with yet another mind-shattering fuck. Then he'd untied Tess, held her tenderly in his arms and declared his eternal love.

But Ian's gaze shifted to the clock. "Ye'll have to wait to find that out, love."

"Wait a minute," Raye protested. "That's not how it's supposed to go."

His gaze returned to her, stroking down her body, lingering on her exposed pussy. A small smile played about his lips. "Wishes rarely turn out the way ye expect them to, lass."

"What the hell is that supposed to mean?"

He didn't answer. To Raye's surprise, he rummaged in the very back of his closet, withdrawing the kilt and tartan she'd bought him in Maggie's shop—the Highlander costume he'd so far refused to wear. Once dressed, he reached to a high shelf and took down his grandfather's bagpipes.

Raye watched, bemused, as Ian examined the instrument, making adjustments as if he actually knew what he was doing. He filled the bellows with air and blew an experimental note—an exquisitely plaintive tone. Then, tucking the instrument under his arm, he headed for the door.

She found her voice. "Ian, don't you dare leave me like this." She tugged on her bonds. "Untie me. Right now."

He turned and smiled. He wasn't wearing his glasses—they still lay on the nightstand where he'd left them the night before. His dark eyes flared, and for an instant Raye caught a glimpse of something behind them. Something cold and soulless. Instinctively, she shrank back.

"Lass," he said. "In case ye hadn't noticed, yer not in any position to be making demands."

# Chapter Four

It was a wonder Raye's anger didn't burn right through the ropes. How dare Ian leave her here, trussed up on the bed? This wasn't sexy at all. It was fucking uncomfortable.

Her leg itched, and she couldn't scratch it. She'd pulled so much on the ropes that her hands were going numb. She had to go to the bathroom, and pressing her legs together was definitely not an option. What if she wet the bed before Ian came back? That thought was too humiliating to contemplate.

Could she get loose on her own? The bathrobe belt securing her right wrist seemed a little less snug than the neckties binding her other limbs. Maybe she could work it loose.

She flexed her hand and caught her fingertips on the knot. Slowly, she worked them under the fuzzy fabric. An hour ticked by. She made a little progress, loosening the knot enough to slide one finger into it. Another hour, and she'd undone the knot's outside loop. By lunchtime, her stomach was growling and her bladder was ready to explode. Damn Ian. What the hell was he thinking, leaving her like this?

Another hour, and she finally tugged her wrist free.

The phone rang.

Ian? She hoped so. She was ready to blast him from here to Loch Ness. She stretched her arm as far as she could and managed to snag the receiver.

A woman's voice came over the line. "Raye? Is that you?"

"Angie?"

"Where the hell are you, chica? I would've thought you'd be here, right in the middle of it."

"In the middle of what?"

"The crowd, girl. It took me an hour just to get inside the door. I'm calling you from my cell."

"The door? What door?"

"The door to Coffee and Scones, you idiot. The place is mobbed."

"But I don't understand. Why are there so many people at the café?"

"It's your husband," Angie said, enunciating each word as if she were speaking to a five year old. "He's wearing a yummy kilt, and he's playing the bagpipes."

"That should run the customers off, not bring them in," Raye said darkly. "Ian sounds like an asthmatic cow on the pipes."

"How can you say that? He plays like a dream. Listen."

There was a rustle as Angie shifted her cell phone. Music swirled into Raye's ear. Bagpipes, yes, but not as Ian had ever played them. The tone was rich, full, enticing. Sensual. Erotic. Her pussy throbbed. She wanted to dive into the phone, be absorbed into the sound of it.

Angie's breathless voice came back on the line. "See what I mean? It's incredible. Ian's like the goddamn Pied

Piper, only he's not attracting children. Half the girls from the college are fighting for a chance to buy coffee." She lowered her voice. "The other half are propositioning him. One little slut even reached under his kilt. I think you should get over here, Raye. Right now."

"Um..." Raye eyed the remaining knots securing her to the bed. "I'm a little tied up right now. And besides, Ian's not like that. He'd never hit on a college girl."

"I wouldn't have thought so, either," Angie replied. "But watching him now... Look. My advice to you is get over here. It's one babe after another throwing herself at your husband. Even a good guy like Ian's only got so much willpower."

*Shit.*

Raye dropped the phone and went to work on the knots.

* * * * *

Angie hadn't been kidding.

Coffee and Scones was mobbed, and the crowd was mostly nubile young college women. Raye pushed through the press of bodies, shoving her way toward the door.

A young woman with multiple piercings blocked her path. "Hey, wait your turn,"

"For what?"

"For a chance at the hottie in the kilt."

A sick feeling stirred Raye's stomach. She went up on tiptoes, straining for a glimpse of the door. A girl emerged, holding a cup of coffee over her head like a trophy.

The crowd pressed in. "Did you see him? Did you touch him?"

The girl smirked. "He kissed me," she said. "Right on the lips. And he wants to see me later."

A collective squeal went up from the crowd.

Raye stood stock-still, stunned, as they surged around her, pressing for the door. Ian would never cheat on her. She knew that as certainly as she knew her own name. At least she'd known it yesterday. After this morning, she wasn't so sure. There'd been something different about Ian, and it went beyond the sexual role-playing they'd been doing. It was as if he'd become another person.

Frowning at the thought, Raye turned and elbowed her way through the estrogen-fueled sea. When she reached the end of the block, she turned and made her way to the alley running along the rear of the stores. A minute later, she fished the key to the shop's rear entry out of her purse and unlocked the back door.

Cautiously, she tiptoed through the storage room and peeked through the door to the shop.

Ian was so completely surrounded by women that he might as well have been a Highland castle under siege. Three girls she didn't recognize were frantically handing out coffee and pastries. The register was ringing like crazy. The cash drawer overflowed with bills.

Raye strode forward and snagged the closest barista. "What do you think you're doing?"

The girl's brows went up. "Working the counter." She nodded in Ian's direction. "Just like *he* asked me to."

"Well, you can stop now."

"And just who the hell are you?"

"*His* wife," Raye told her.

The girl eyed her, clearly not buying it. "He's not wearing a ring."

"That doesn't mean any—"

"You can't fool me," the girl said hotly. "You just want to weasel your way into some action. Well, forget it. I was here first." She tossed her head and went back to the register.

Raye gaped at her. "Why, you—"

She cut off as Ian suddenly lifted his head, searching the crowd, his eyes surprisingly sharp despite the fact he wasn't wearing his glasses. Was he looking for her? Following some instinct she didn't know she possessed, Raye ducked back into the storage room.

She pressed her spine against the door, heart pounding. What the hell was going on? Just yesterday, Ian was sitting right there, at his wobbly desk, absorbed in payables and receivables, sex the farthest thing from his mind. Now, after fucking the bejesus out of Raye, he was ready to start in on the rest of the women in town.

She eyed the candle she'd left on the box after their fight. Something wasn't right. Somehow, her easygoing, faithful, *nearsighted* husband had morphed into an insatiable, macho eagle-eyed sex fiend. Just like Kieran MacKenzie.

Had she really fantasized about a transformation like that? She must have been out of her mind.

A queer feeling crept into her stomach.

Maggie's soft brogue echoed in her mind. *Wishes hold power, lass. They shouldna be made lightly. Sometimes they bring things we dinna expect.*

And what had Ian said this morning? *Wishes rarely turn out the way ye expect them to, lass.*

More damning words came to mind, this time from the book she'd read at Maggie's shop. *Changeling: a faerie being who takes the place of a human…empowered by an ill wish.*

Raye frowned. No. It couldn't be.

*The switch comes at dawn, accompanied by the laughter of the fairy folk.*

She'd heard laughter. She'd thought it was the radio, but… She closed her eyes, picturing Ian as he'd been this morning. He'd been Ian—but *not*, somehow.

*The Changeling takes the appearance of their beloved. This is a false visage, however. The glamour of the faerie folk obscures the Changeling's true features.*

She drew in a sharp breath. Strains of bagpipe music wafted through the closed door. The melody was haunting, so beautiful it made her ache. Made her stomach quiver. Made her pussy wet.

*A Changeling plays magic on the pipes, ensorcelling all who hear it. It bewitches all it touches.*

Ian—*her Ian*—couldn't play the bagpipes, not even to save his soul.

*Its hunger is extreme, and can never be sated.*

A rush like a roaring waterfall sounded in Raye's ears. It wasn't possible—was it? Could the man out in the shop—the one who looked so like Ian, really be a Changeling? She crept to the door and cracked it open. There, surrounded by eager women, stood the man she'd thought was her husband. He was tall, broad-shouldered, and handsome. His rugged features provided a tantalizing counterpoint to his sensual lips. And under his kilt…Raye shuddered.

Maggie's soft words drifted through her mind. *Do ye truly wish to have this man for your lover?*

Raye had said yes. *Yes.*

*Oh, Ian, how could I have wished you away like that?*

A dark head lifted, eyes boring into hers. They weren't Ian's eyes. Looking into them now, Raye wondered how she ever could have thought that they were. The expression in them was flat, empty. Devoid of emotion or any other spark of humanity.

*A Changeling has no soul…*

She gripped the doorframe, fighting to keep her knees from buckling. Ian—no, not Ian!—lifted a hand, waving her closer. Raye felt the pull of his command in her belly, and lower, in the tingling that sprang up, unwanted, between her thighs.

She tore her gaze away, her breath coming in short gasps. It did nothing to weaken the spell binding her. Lust washed through her, drawing beads of sweat on her brow. Her nipples and clit tingled. Her pussy contracted, aching to be filled. She wanted to fuck him. Again.

She fought to get her body under control. She couldn't go to the creature that had taken Ian's place. She wouldn't.

Where was Ian now? Where had her ill wish sent him? Tears welled in her eyes. She'd give anything to see her husband's easy smile, hear his low, sexy laugh. It had been her fault as much as his that their sex life had stalled. She'd replaced him with a fantasy.

Light flared in the Changeling's eyes. A spike of intense arousal speared Raye, tearing a gasp from her lips.

Her hips gyrated, seeking more. Could he drive her to an orgasm with just a look? She couldn't control her response. Another few seconds and she would come her brains out.

A college girl rubbed her breasts against the Changeling's chest, linking her arms around his neck, going up on her tiptoes to kiss him. The Changeling's eyes broke away from Raye for an instant—it was all the opportunity she needed.

Stumbling backwards, she slammed the door, chest heaving. She was in deep shit. She had to get rid of that thing before it came at her again.

Maggie. She had something to do with this, Raye would bet money on it. She had to get to Maggie, ask her what to do.

She ran to the back door. It wouldn't budge. The lock was jammed, or broken, or—the thought froze the blood in her veins—bewitched.

Her knees buckled. She sank slowly to the floor, her spine sliding over the cold metal door.

She wasn't going anywhere.

* * * * *

The Changeling came for her when the last customer had gone and the shop was dark.

"Ah, lass, there ye be."

He stood in the doorway to the storage room, dark eyes glinting.

Raye fought to keep the panic out of her voice as a fire sprung to life in her pussy. "Don't touch me."

He took a step toward her, then another. "Och, lass, dinna turn me away. Ye are my hearth, my home. My life."

"A pretty speech," she said, inching backwards. "But I've heard it before. It's a line from *Highland Passions*."

"Nevertheless," he said, "'tis true. I canna live without ye."

He backed her up against the wall, caging her between his arms. He smelled faintly of smoke—not a pleasant, woodsy smell, but the odor of a rotted log that had somehow been persuaded to burn.

"What are you?" she gasped.

His cold gaze consumed her. "Yer dream, lass. Ye called me to the upper world, d'ye not remember?" He smiled. "Am I nay all ye wished for?"

Raye stood rigid, nerves thrumming with arousal, thighs slick with cream. She wanted him. God help her, but she wanted this creature. Another minute, and she would beg him to fuck her.

She couldn't let him do it.

Her hand, hidden behind her back, gripped the only weapon she'd been able to find in the storage room—the lighter she'd used the day before. When he lowered his mouth to hers, she struck. She jerked her arm forward, snapping the flame to life as she shoved the lighter into his gut.

The Changeling jumped back, breath hissing between his teeth. Too late. Flames darted across the wool of his kilt, licked the plaid of his tartan. Ignited the white linen of his shirt. Snapped at his face.

A high-pitched screech, more animal than human, issued from his throat.

Raye scrambled sideways, driven by heat and terror. The Changeling made no move to follow. He stood, arms spread, a grotesque burning cross. His eyes burned black, lit with tiny dancing flames.

His features transformed, Ian's handsome features morphing into a hideous visage. Skin darkened. Nose and ears elongated. Teeth grew pointed. The air grew putrid.

She gazed in horror at the true face of the Changeling for what seemed like an eternity. Then, with a deafening clap and a blast of fiery smoke, the creature vanished.

Raye stood, staring at the spot where it had been, her body frozen, her mind numb. Incredibly, the storage room was untouched. Nothing had burned—not a trace of smoke or a single sooty streak remained. Even the scent of decay was gone, replaced by the familiar aroma of coffee.

Had it worked? Was the Changeling truly gone?

"Raye? Are you in there?"

The door to the front room rattled. It swung open revealing the figure of a man dressed in Highland garb.

*Oh, God.* The nightmare wasn't over.

"Stay away from me," Raye screamed. She scrambled around Ian's desk, putting it between her and the Changeling. "Not one step closer."

"What the hell?" The Changeling rubbed the back of his neck, eyes frowning behind his glasses.

*Glasses?*

Raye loosened her grip on the desk. Could it be…?

"Ian? Is that you?"

"Last I checked." He glanced downward with a short laugh. "Though I probably should get my head examined for letting you talk me into wearing this getup."

"Oh, God. *Ian*!" Raye flung herself into his arms. "I'm so *glad* to see you!"

He caught her, stumbling backwards under the force of her weight, half-laughing. His hands ran up her back, steadying her as she showered kisses on his jaw, his neck, his chest. Dropping to her knees, she lifted his kilt.

A laugh of pure joy bubbled into her throat. Ian's cock, already half-hard, was just the size it was supposed to be.

She wrapped her fingers around it, stroking.

He chuckled. "I'm glad to see you, too, Raye, but you know, I wasn't gone *that* long. It only takes about five minutes to lock up."

She kissed the head of his penis. "It felt like forever. I'm so sorry we fought. Forgive me?"

Ian's dark eyes were inscrutable. "Nothing to forgive. You were right. I've been neglecting you. Neglecting us. I don't concentrate on you when we make love."

"It doesn't matter."

"Yes, it does." Bending, he lifted her into his arms, fingers questing under her skirt. "I'll show you how much it matters," he murmured as he slid her panties over her hips and down her thighs. Positioning her ass on the desk, he stepped between her legs and flipped up his kilt.

Raye caught his gaze. "You want to do it here? In the storage room? I thought—"

He entered her with one strong thrust.

"Don't think," he said. "Just feel."

# Epilogue

*To rid your home of a Changeling, drive it into a fire.*

Well. She'd gotten one thing right, at least. Raye closed the ancient tome and looked up—right into Maggie's eyes.

"Come on, Maggie," she wheedled. "Tell me. Did you do it? Did you send the Changeling?"

The old woman's brows went up. "Och, lass, how ye talk! That old book's naught but a fanciful collection of legends, written long ago. 'Tisn't any sense to it."

Raye shook her head. She had a hunch Maggie knew more than she was letting on about the Changeling, but after three months of asking, Raye figured she might as well let the subject die. Maggie wasn't going to admit to anything.

She left Highland Magick and headed back to Coffee and Scones. Nodding to the new girl at the counter, she made her way to the back room.

Ian looked up from his laptop, grinning broadly. "Come here," he said. "Check this out."

"What?" Raye asked, bending to peer at the screen.

He swiveled the computer to give her a better view. "Last quarter's reconciliation," he said.

She blinked. "We made *that* much money?"

"Numbers never lie," Ian said smugly. "We're back in the black with a vengeance." He rubbed his chin. "Though I'm not sure what caused the turnaround."

"It's you and that kilt," Raye said, a hint of annoyance creeping into her voice. "Ever since you started wearing it around the café, you've attracted a cult following. I swear the college girls spend more time in Coffee and Scones than they do in class. I bet they go back to their dorms and pretend their vibrators are you."

Ian grimaced. "What a thought. Yeah, well, as long as they keep buying coffee, I can deal." He glanced up at her, suddenly serious. "You don't think I'd cheat on you, do you?"

"No," Raye said. "I know you wouldn't."

He touched her cheek, his eyes soft. "I love you, Raye."

"I love you, too."

He tugged her down onto his lap. "So where do you want to go on vacation?"

She looked at him in surprise. "Vacation? You mean we can afford one of those?"

"Sure. Two weeks. Anywhere you want." He paused. "What about Scotland?"

*Scotland!* Raye had always wanted to visit the land of *Highland Passions*. Of course, she hadn't spent much time with her book lately. Every spare moment seemed to be taken up by Ian. Their sex life had revived big time. In just the past week they'd fucked on the bedroom floor, the kitchen table, in the backseat of their car, and in the café storage room—twice!

She hesitated. "I don't know. Is there anywhere *you* want to go?"

"Not Scotland," he said promptly. "The weather sucks this time of year. My vote goes to someplace hot and sunny. What do you think about the Caribbean? We could lie on the beach all day and screw like drunk rabbits at night."

Raye snorted. "That sounds *so* romantic."

He kissed her neck, just below her ear. "It will be," he said. Reaching down, he pulled something out of his briefcase and slid it into her hands. "Especially if we bring this along."

Raye's eyes widened. Ian had given her a book. And not just any book—a volume from the same publisher as *Highland Passions*. The cover featured a naked couple in a jungle setting. Her heartbeat kicked up a notch as she read the title.

*Tropical Passions.*

"Do you like it?" Ian asked.

She caught his gaze and smiled. "I love it."

His cheeks reddened a bit. "I read some of it. It's pretty hot." He swallowed. "I thought maybe…if you want, that is…we could act out a few of the scenes."

Hot lust exploded in Raye's pussy. "Really?"

"Yeah."

She started unbuttoning her blouse. "Well, then—what are we waiting for?"

## About the author

Callista Arman explores the dark side of the human psyche in tales of sweet love and hot possession. Her stories may take place on far-away worlds, or right next door. Either way, she hopes you enjoy the journey.

Callista welcomes mail from readers. You can write to her c/o Ellora's Cave Publishing at 1337 Commerce Drive, #13, Stow, OH 44224.

# BREAKING THE RULES

B.J. McCall

# Chapter One

Ri Anzer scanned the narrow ribbon of water winding through the heavily wooded valley, looking for Indar insurgents. South of her position, the river plunged down the valley in a stunning display. Mist from the falls blanketed her helmet and uniform as she moved along the footpath. At the falls, she had a panoramic view of the valley. Downriver, beyond the falls, the water changed from crystal clear to muddy brown. Ri understood why the Indar had protested the presence of Wath Mining. Although the Mitian Confederation had given permission to drill and had guaranteed compensation to the Indar, the damage to the river was appalling.

Beneath her feet, the ground shuddered. The heavy drills pounded into the hillside, boring through rock and tearing through earth, dumping the carnage into the pristine river. Ri swore beneath her breath. Sometimes the mission sucked.

Robots extracted valuable Mitian crystals and Ri's well-armed security unit provided protection for the machinery. Wath paid for Elite Security's best and Ri's team had earned that title. Thirty missions and she hadn't lost a man.

A small red flash in the right corner of her face shield indicated movement in the direction of the falls. Ri turned.

"Identify."

Her shield adjusted, honing in on the entity. Between the noise of the falls and the drills, an army could march up the valley and never be heard. She relied on her high-tech helmet and shield to warn her of impending threats.

*Human. Male. Non-threat.*

Ri sucked in a breath.

Below, Jac Dancer stripped off his boots and uniform revealing broad shoulders, lean hips, well-formed legs and a wonderfully taut ass. Dancer's muscles rippled as he padded across several rocks toward the spray. Bathing with water was a luxury and her team took advantage of the one pleasure this mission offered. Space Station VN2845, Elite's base headquarters for this sector, restricted all personnel to sonic showers.

Dancer hesitated and turned slowly to look in her direction. Although her uniform automatically camouflaged to match any terrain, Ri dropped to a squat. Peeking through the foliage, Ri released a tortured breath. She should have looked away and moved farther down the path, but Dancer's thick jutting erection mesmerized her.

Too many nights, she'd speculated, dreamed, imagined Dancer, naked and aroused, but no more. Now she knew. Naked, Jac was gorgeous. Erect, he was magnificent.

He stepped beneath the spray and fisted his erection. Shivers of need slid down Ri's spine, heat pooled between her legs as Dancer stroked his firm flesh.

With each stroke of his hand, desire burned through her middle.

From the moment she'd laid eyes on him two years ago, she'd wanted him. Mission after mission, her need grew. Now, her whole body burned as his hand performed the sensual function she ached to do. His strokes quickened. Her mouth watered. Flames of desire licked her pussy.

She should respect his privacy, let him ease the tension of the mission and find satisfaction, but need overwhelmed her. She caressed her breast, rubbing her palm over her erect nipple, stroking the soft, achy flesh.

His cock was long and thick, larger than she'd imagined. Heat poured from her body. Begging for relief, her pussy flexed.

She'd been celibate too damn long. She wanted Dancer. Working with him was an education. Having him on her team was an honor. Wanting him was pure hell.

Unable to resist her need, Ri switched off her audio and opened the seam of her uniform pants. She licked her fingers and slid her hand beneath the waistband of her underwear. If her team heard her moans, they might well believe she was dying. When her wet fingers touched her hot pussy, she gasped. Sensitive, her flesh sizzled beneath her fingers. Dipping into her wet flesh, Ri pumped with the same delicious fury Dancer gave his cock.

A shudder passed through her. Her palm paddled her aching clit. Her finger fucked her pussy. Moaning, she imagined his thick cock in her mouth, the heat of his rigid flesh upon her tongue and the feel of his body trembling as she suckled him. Her pussy heated, responding like a well-trained soldier to her fingers, imagination and Dancer's erotic manipulation.

Sucking in a ragged breath, Ri pounded her pussy, skating the edge, waiting for Dancer. When his thick cream spilled from his cock, Ri cried out. Release came in a sharp, sweet peak, followed by a numbing wave.

Her whole body vibrated from the orgasm. Dancer turned into the spray to wash the climax from his cock.

Ri fastened her pants. She welcomed the relief, but acknowledged something had to give. Despite her climax, she remained aching and unsatisfied. Afraid her feelings for Dancer had progressed beyond a physical desire, Ri shook her head and closed her eyes.

*Fool.*

Unit leaders didn't fall in love with team members. The mission was the focus, not a brief moment of physical pleasure. As one of the few female UL's and the only one in this sector, Ri refused to let her personal feelings interfere with the job.

*Get over him.*

Hauser Wath, the president of Wath Mining, wanted her. Rich and handsome, Hauser offered luxury and wealth but Ri would rather face a lifetime of dangerous missions with Dancer than becoming Hauser's woman.

A pulsing red light penetrated her closed lids. Ri opened her eyes and activated her audio.

"Identify."

Rising, Ri turned to her left.

*Enemy. Two. Armed.*

Two insurgents approached the falls from downriver. Standing beneath the spray, Dancer was exposed and unaware.

Running along the footpath to intercept the enemy, Ri pulled her laser rifle from sling resting across her back. She stopped, lowered her rifle and took out the insurgents in two clean shots. They fell within twenty yards of Dancer.

*Enemy terminated.*

Ri headed downhill toward the falls. By the time she reached Dancer, he was fastening his pants.

*Don't look.*

When he reached for his boots, Ri raised her face shield. After fastening his boots, he stood. Beads of water covered his broad chest and shoulders. Ri ached to lick each drop from his skin.

*Look him in the eye.*

His gaze fastened on hers. "I'm glad you happened to be passing by."

Did he know she'd watched him?

He pulled on his uniform shirt and slipped into his weapons vest. Picking up his helmet, he was armed and ready.

"Bring backup next time. That's an order."

"Understood." He stuck out his hand. The same one he'd used to pleasure himself. "Thanks, UL. I owe you my life."

Team members addressed each other by their last name, but to Dancer she was the UL. Which meant, despite all their missions, hours spent planning missions and relaxing in the base lounge, she was the Unit Leader. Not a woman, not a friend, but the boss.

His respect made her job easier, but his distance gave her many sleepless, aching nights with only a mechanical pleasure tool to satisfy her needs.

Her hand slid against his. The same hand she'd used to bring herself to climax. His fingers wrapped around hers for a moment. Smiling, he slipped on his helmet.

Turning, Ri scrambled across the rocks. Dancer followed her back to camp.

She should be thankful. Given Dancer's rep, her team might turn to him as the authority, but just once she'd like to hear him call her by name.

# Chapter Two

"Thank you again for dinner."

Ri held out her hand to Hauser Wath, the president of Wath Mining. His lips brushed her palm suggestively. His gaze moved over her slinky evening dress.

"You're sure you can't stay? I enjoy hearing about your work. Your missions are so much more interesting than balance sheets and dealing with investors."

Ri smiled. He didn't want to know about her job or what it took to lead one of the best intergalactic security teams. He wanted to fuck her. Like any member of her team, she could kill Wath within seconds and unless he'd tucked a blaster beneath his business suit and had it set to fire, he couldn't do a thing to stop her.

"Thank you, but I should meet with my team. I have a mission to plan. We'll be leaving within twelve hours."

He still held her hand. "You are unlike any other woman."

*A challenge.* Rich beyond comprehension, Wath could buy anything. He probably got off on the knowledge Ri led four of the toughest, well-trained men in the outer sector. Her team had earned their reputations the hard way. When other teams fucked up, Ri and her guys either saved their butts or retrieved their bodies. Some of the missions were gruesome.

His soft fingertips slid along her bare arm. His fingers were long, manicured and without a single callus. Hers were working hands.

"Lovely gown."

Her usual working attire of camouflage uniform and heavy boots masked the female curves complimented by the slinky material of her evening dress. The soft, clinging black fabric molded to her breasts and draped wickedly about her thighs. Other than the gown, Ri wore nothing but heels with beaded straps that matched the delicate straps of her gown.

She had after-dinner plans. Those plans had nothing to do with Wath, and underwear would only get in the way.

Ri planned missions well. Failure never entered her mind. Tonight's mission was pleasure and Jac Dancer would provide it.

"Thank you, Mr. Wath. Good night."

"Let me walk you to the elevator."

"No need, I'll be fine."

When Wath closed the door, Ri breathed a sign of relief. She strolled down the corridor. As she rounded the corner, Dancer stood before the elevator. Had he been waiting for her or did he want to know if Wath had renewed the contract with Elite guaranteeing future missions for the team?

As she stepped into the waiting elevator, his gaze slid over her, slowly. A smile teased the corners of his mouth. "Nice dress, UL."

Dancer looked good enough to eat. He wore black pants, a black shirt that molded to his muscled chest and sandals. He never wore socks unless he was in uniform. Ri's heart thumped.

"You clean up good, too."

The last time she'd laid eyes on him both of them had been covered in Olirium slime. Even drenched in stinky, brown goop, Dancer was sexy. Despite the scars, his body was one fine work of art. That day at the Indar falls had haunted her dreams.

He stepped inside and stood next to her. "Habitation Level Three," he said directing the elevator to the floor assigned to Elite Security's employees on VN2845 Space Station.

His gaze lingered on her feet. "Wath has retained us for another mission?"

"Two."

"That should make Payts happy."

Their boss, Silus Payts, ran the show the outer section of the galaxy. Ri and her team took the risks.

The elevator stopped and the doors slid opened. Dancer took her arm and guided her down the corridor. His fingers curled about her elbow. Dancer's hands were big and rough, his arms bulged with hard muscles, but Ri had watched him tend wounds, gently cradle victims and pray with the dying.

Given Elite's rules of conduct, relationships between team members were viewed as an infraction and those between leader and subordinate, a serious infraction. Although rules were broken, those caught were demoted, stripped of all earned credits and suspended from action. Security units were composed of two types, those who love the mission and those who love the money. Like her, Dancer was a lover of the mission. He thrived on the adventure. Losing credits wouldn't mean much to him, but suspension meant a desk job and that would never work for a man like Dancer.

After tonight, Ri understood she'd have to cut him from her team, but working with him had hit an impossible wall. Assured Payts intended to give Dancer a promotion to UL and total control of his missions, Ri planned her seduction.

She wanted Dancer, but what did he want?

She had to do something. She'd hit the wall hard that day at the falls. Her desire for Dancer had begun to interfere with her performance and concentration. Seriously interfere. She hadn't saved his life. She'd failed her duty.

The rules and her respect for Dancer had prevented Ri from giving in to her urges, but they couldn't stop her heart from hammering every time she looked at him. His eyes were blue, his hair dark and thick. He wore it short. His chin was strong and his smile devastating. Dancer was worth breaking the rules.

*It's sex, not love.*

Sexual desire, once acted upon, usually lost its edge, but love had a way of digging into you and holding on. *Get it done and move on.*

"When do we leave?"

"In twenty-four hours."

The lie came easily to her lips. Her team would be headed to Lak within hours. Payts would inform Dancer about his new assignment. Dancer would lead another team to Borliz.

Perhaps when they met again, on-station between missions, something might develop between them. Ri pushed aside the thought of how much she wanted that *something*.

When they reached her room, Ri placed her palm against the lock panel. The door slid open. Dancer released her arm. "Where are we headed, Borliz?"

Ri stepped into her room and turned. Dancer remained in the corridor.

"Yes." Dancer read everything published concerning the sector's private and public scientific explorations. Few assignments surprised him. "Borliz and Lak."

His eyes widened. "Lak?"

"Join me for a drink?"

Dancer gave her a brief nod and stepped into the room.

"Wath's exploratory drilling team hasn't been heard from in three days," Ri said. "One emergency blast message, then dead silence."

Frown lines furrowed Dancer's brow. "I'd hoped never to see that place again."

Ri spoke to his back. "You led the rescue mission?"

He shook his head. "The mission failed."

After two exploratory teams were attacked and murdered, the Federation had placed a restriction on the planet until a sky scan performed by Wath Mining provided evidence of the suspected deposits of racth deep beneath the surface.

Dancer turned and shoved his hands in his pants pockets. "Wath must have several politicians in his pocket to obtain permission to drill. But why bother with deep drilling on Lak? A large deposit was just discovered on

Tinyan. The surface climate on Tinyan is far more hospitable than Lak. I don't get it."

"If he can prove the deposits exist with a drilling sample, Wath will be awarded exclusive rights to mine Lak."

"That's because no other mining concern is interested. The daytime temperature makes drilling near impossible and the indigenes are hostile. The removal of the racth would cost far more than on Tinyan."

"Wath wants Lak drilled."

Dancer swore under his breath. "And he wants us?"

"He does." Ri crossed the room and picked up a bottle of Mitian spirits from the kitchen counter. Elite's employees shared small rooms with two bunks, one upper and one lower, shower and sink. ULs were rewarded with a compact private room with built-in kitchen instead of a lower bunk, a desk, computer, and communication access. "Wath made a mega-offer to home office. Payts couldn't refuse."

She poured two glasses of the rare but potent liquor and handed a glass to Dancer.

"If the deposits are as rich as reported, Wath said mining Lak would make a thousand percent profit. Tell me about Lak."

"It's mostly rock and sand. The air is breathable, but dry. Only a few plants and small animals that have adapted to the extreme heat survive on the surface. If the sun doesn't kill you, the Laks try at night. They look like humans, except for the raised ridge along their spine and the short tails at the base. Their eyes are large and multifaceted, and their night vision is akin to infrared, giving them an advantage over unprepared landing parties. Their skin is dark and provides excellent night camouflage. Their weapons are primitive, but the poison-tipped spears and darts cause instant paralysis."

"Light armored uniforms and our helmets should suffice. We'll have to arrive at sunset, secure an area for the drilling party, set up a defensive perimeter and be out before sunrise."

Shaking his head, Dancer took a long swallow. "Let another team take this one."

Ri bristled. "I can handle it."

"The Laks execute the males, but the women are raped."

"I've heard."

"You didn't see Dansi Larii. After a night of rape, they left her staked out in the blistering heat. She died in my arms."

Unable to save his lover, Dancer's team had taken out the Lakian band that had captured Dr. Larii and her geological survey group. Although Larii died seven years ago, Dancer's voice was cold as ice.

"I heard you quit after that mission?"

"I did for a while, but Payts tracked me down."

Ri hoped he would elaborate, but instead he stared at his drink. "No female should ever be assigned to Lak."

"Payts has accepted the mission."

Dancer downed the rest of the liquor and set the empty glass on the counter. "Let me take this one."

"Because of the success of the Mitian and Olirium missions, Wath gave my team the assignment. I can't refuse."

He reached out and touched her cheek. His fingertips were warm against her face. His gaze met hers. "I can't take the chance."

"I know you cared for Dr. Larii."

"Dansi has nothing to do with us."

He brushed his lips to hers. Ri's breath caught. "Us?"

His gaze bored into hers. "Us."

He caught her about the waist and pulled her tight against him, crushing their mouths together, thrusting his tongue between her parted lips. He stroked her hips, his big hands gently cupping her ass, his fingers suddenly digging into her flesh, holding her even closer.

The swell of his cock pressed her belly, inflaming her with heat and need that melted bone and muscle.

Heart hammering, Ri twined her arms about his neck and rubbed her aching breasts against his muscled chest. She kissed him hard, letting him know she wanted him.

When Dancer slid a hand beneath her dress and touched her bare ass, a tortured groan tore from his throat.

He grabbed a fistful of her hair and pulled her head back. Although he held her left buttock in an iron grip, Ri felt no pain. Intense and burning, his gaze held hers. "The dress, it wasn't for Wath?"

"No."

"Then who, why?"

"For you."

A grin teased the corners of his mouth. "Just me?"

"Just you."

"You're mine." He caressed her ass. "This belongs to me, understood?"

"Possessive, aren't we?"

"I am."

His hand slid between her thighs, the tip of his index finger skated her damp pussy, found her center and dipped. Ri gasped. He sucked in a deep breath. "This is mine?"

Ri smiled. Since Dancer had joined her team she'd been as celibate as a monk. She'd ached body and soul for this moment. "Yours."

His grip relaxed. When he touched his lips to her neck, Ri shivered. He kissed his way to the tender curve of her neck and pulled the strap of her dress off her shoulder with his teeth. The dress dipped, exposing her breast.

Cupping her ass with both hands, he lifted her up until her nipple met his mouth. He suckled lush and deep, nursing her aching flesh. Heat flowed and pooled in her pussy. Want and need burned through her veins and arteries.

"Please, Jac. Please."

Holding her tight, he guiding her to the narrow ladder leading to her bunk. He turned her around and lifted the hem of her dress to her waist. "Ohhhh. Fuck." He pushed her shoulders forward. "Grab the ladder, Ri."

He cupped her bare ass and kneeled behind her. Stroking her from hip to thigh, he nipped one cheek.

"For two years I've been thinking about your ass."

He licked the crease between her cheeks, teasing her with slow, wet strokes. The combination of tongue, lips and teeth on her flesh sent a shiver up her spine.

"You've driven me crazy, Ri."

His hand slid between her legs and his fingertips touched her wet pussy.

"Open for me. Let me taste your honey."

His tongue slid lower to replace his fingers.

Ri spread her feet slightly, giving him access, wanting his tongue deep inside her. He kneaded her ass and licked her pussy. With each lush lick, he made her wetter, and hotter. He flicked her clit with his tongue, back and forth, taking her to the sweet edge. Then he plunged inside, fucking her with his hot tongue. Ri screamed her pleasure.

He slapped her gently on the ass and rose. When she heard the rustle of his pants seam, Ri wriggled her ass in anticipation and arched her back.

"That's the prettiest thing I've ever seen."

Ri loved the huskiness in his voice. "What is?"

"Your heart-shaped ass inviting me. Your pussy, primed and ready, wanting me."

His thick cock slid between her spread cheeks. His bare thighs touched hers. Ri's fingers tightened on the ladder rung as the thick tip of his cock nudged her wet pussy.

The thick head probed, once, twice. Ri glanced over her shoulder. He was looking at her ass. "Fuck me, Dancer."

His cock plunged inside her. He anchored her hips with his big hands and thrust, again and again. With each hot thrust, he slid deeper into her wet pussy.

"Fuck me, hard."

Drenched with need, Ri welcomed his length. Long and hard, he filled her, answering her needs, satisfying her throbbing flesh.

Her moans mingled with his breathy grunts. Heat poured from their bodies as skin slapped skin. Hot cock slammed into her wet pussy making lush sucking sounds.

His fingers dug into her skin, holding her as his body stilled, shuddered. His cock pulsed filling her with cream and her pussy contracted in lush, warm waves. He withdrew, thrust, and pumped his hips until her body ceased its sensual flutter.

Releasing her hips, he gripped the ladder. After a long minute, he took a couple of deep audible breaths and withdrew. "I should have known."

Ri turned within his bracketed arms to face him. Perspiration dewed his forehead. "Known what?"

A salacious grin tugged at the corners of his mouth. "You'd ruin me for other women."

He stood before her naked from the waist down with his pants pooled around his feet. Ri dropped her gaze to his cock and licked her lips. Cum slid slowly down her thigh. "I'm just getting started."

After releasing the ladder, he removed his sandals. Stepping out of his pants, he kicked them aside. "Promise?"

When he pulled off his sweat-dampened shirt, Ri's breath caught. Up close and naked, Dancer appeared bigger, stronger than ever. His powerful shoulders and arms tapered down to a narrow waist and hips. His thighs were muscled, his legs long. The partially erect cock dangling between his legs made her shiver.

Ri slid to her knees. She touched the tip of her tongue to his cock. "Have you dreamed about this, Dancer?"

His blue eyes narrowed and his hand slid into her hair. "Oh, yeah."

Closing her eyes, Ri took him in her mouth. When she ran the tip of her tongue around the thick edge of his crown, he moaned. She grasped the root of his cock, tugging firmly on his growing length while she suckled him. She took him deep, licking slowly, lushly, teasing the underside of his cock, finding the sensitive spot at the base until his fingers dug into her scalp and his hips jerked.

Moving up and down his length, Ri made love to him. Now that she'd crossed the line from co-worker to lover, Ri never wanted to let him go.

He pulled her head back. She released his swollen cock. Leaning down, he snaked his free arm about her waist and lifted her to her feet. He eased her back against the ladder. Grasping her thigh, he positioned her leg about his waist and his cock at the entrance of her pussy.

"Make love to me, Ri."

She loved the sound of her name on his lips. "Love?"

His gaze penetrating hers, he stared at her for a long moment. "I've been waiting all this time and you just want a fuck?"

"I want more than a fuck. I want you, Jac."

He lifted the hem of her dress and drew it over her head. He dropped it gently onto a chair and reached for her. Cupping her breasts in his big hands, he rasped her nipples with his thumbs.

"I've dreamed about this."

With each sweet stroke, she ached for him. "Please, Jac."

Bending his head, he kissed one nipple then the other. Then he kissed her. His tongue slid between her lips. He explored her mouth, taking his time, firing her needs until a volcano burned in her core. She clutched his shoulders, loving the feel of his hot skin beneath her hands.

He lifted his head and slowly, he entered her. His gaze remained locked to hers as he slid deeper inside her. The change in his eyes to a dark, intense blue made their joining both erotic and tender.

Anchoring a hand on the ladder at the small of her back, he said, "Make love to me, Ri. Love me with your pussy."

Closing her eyes, she contracted her muscles around his thick length. Squeezing, releasing, grabbing, tugging him. He filled her, perfectly.

"Look at me."

Ri opened her eyes.

"I want you to know who's inside you."

Time slowed and reality condensed to this moment, this joining. Ri knew she'd met her mate, the man who'd hold her heart forever. Love filled her heart as she skated the edge of climax. Her pussy flooded, hot and wanting.

He moved then. His hips pushed into her, driving his cock deeper still. Her pussy fluttered, coming in tight contractions. She gasped and arched her back. He caressed her breast, kneading her aching flesh.

Groaning, he pistoned his hips. The cords of his neck strained, his chest heaved, but his gaze never wavered.

His cock rammed into her, giving Ri what she needed, wanted.

Gasping, she dug her fingers into his shoulder. Her climax came in a hot rush, surrounding his cock.

"That's it," he said, thrusting again. "Yes."

He stilled, holding her tight. Beneath her fingers, his muscles rippled. His grasp on her breast eased. His fingertips brushed her flesh. A smile curled his lips. "I may be able to run for hours, but you exhaust me in minutes."

Ri uncurled her leg, releasing the death grip she'd had on his hips. From head to toe, her muscles were hot and relaxed. She glanced up at her narrow bunk. "Right now, I'd pay a million credits for a big, soft bed."

"I'm staying the night?"

"You are."

He stepped back and looked up. "How about we drag your mattress and blankets onto the floor?"

She nodded. Reaching up, she caressed his smooth, shaved cheek. "Nice."

He brushed the underside of her breast with his fingertips. "I didn't want to scratch you."

Ri realized he'd planned to seduce her. "Water?"

"I could drink a gallon."

While Jac pulled her bedding from the bunk, Ri retrieved two containers of water from her cold unit.

Sitting cross-legged on her mattress, he drank the entire container and set it aside.

Ri joined him. "Why tonight?"

"Like I said, you were driving me crazy. Following you through that fissure on Oliri, I knew I'd hit the wall."

The fissure was so narrow they had removed their weapons vest. The walls were wet and so slick with slime they'd stripped out of their uniforms.

"I was covered in slime. I stank."

A grin tipped one corner of his mouth. "All I could think about was fucking you. That's when I knew it was a lost cause."

"I was getting close to crawling into your sleep bag."

"Why didn't you? It was damn cold the night before we found the raiders' camp."

"I thought about it," she admitted. "I didn't sleep for thinking about it."

He reached out and grasped her by the wrist. "If you're thinking about kicking me off the team, don't! You're not going to Lak without me."

"How can we work together?"

"We've been doing fine." He eased her down onto her back and leaned over her. "Just because we're together doesn't mean we can't do our jobs."

"I can't have my decisions questioned, nor can I display favoritism."

He kissed her on the forehead. "Have I ever refused an order? Shown any disrespect?"

"Never."

He kissed her on the tip of her nose and laid his head on her belly. "Then trust me."

She ruffled the short strands of his hair with her fingers. "I do trust you, Jac. I've trusted you with my life several times."

"You may be the UL, but I'm not going to let anything happened to you, ever."

His breathing evened out. Within minutes, he slept. Ri did trust him, but now that she'd put her plan in motion, she wasn't about to deny him the chance to lead his own team. She ordered the lights off, closed her eyes and drifted into a sweet, sated sleep.

Some time later, Ri awoke. Snuggled against her back, Jac stroked her breasts and belly. His thick cock was wedged between her thighs. His lips slid down her neck, leaving a hot, wet trail.

She whispered his name.

Rolling her onto her back, he positioned his big body between her legs. He cupped her pussy and slipped a finger into her warmth, tenderly stroking. Slowly pumping and stretching her flesh, he added a second finger. When she was slick and hot, and ready to accept him, he removed his fingers and probed her heat with his cock.

Ri gasped as the thick head pushed into her aching flesh. Lifting her legs, she wrapped her ankles around his torso.

Ri held him tightly as he drove into her, pushing deeper with each stroke. Heat emanated from his body. Beneath her fingers, his biceps bulged. He slid a hand beneath her ass, lifting her off the mattress. Still he drove into her, burying his cock deep with each long, lush stroke. He fucked her hard. *Her wet dream.*

He stilled and eased her back to the mattress. He pulled back, leaving the tip of his cock inside her. He shuddered. "If you move, I'm gonna come."

After a long moment and several deep breaths, he grasped her by the waist and slid his bent knees beneath her thighs. Kneeling, he lifted her until she straddled him. Holding her tight, he kissed her thoroughly. His tongue attacked her mouth.

"Ride me, Ri. Ride me hard."

Placing her feet flat onto the mattress, Ri lifted her hips and rode him. He let her control the pace and Ri let loose, pounding his cock with her pussy. The hot friction, the wet heat bringing her to an explosive point.

He held her tight, kissing her as she touched oblivion. His cock flexed, telling her he'd found his pleasure.

After a long moment, he eased her onto her back and stretched out between her legs. He wrapped his hands around her thighs and licked her pussy.

"I want to taste you, Ri. I want to taste your pussy when it's filled with my cum."

He thrust his tongue inside her heat. Her pussy still thrummed from her climax. Reaching up, he grasped her breast. Slowly, he rolled her nipple between his thumb and forefinger while he tenderly fucked her pussy with his tongue. Heat coiling in her middle, Ri lifted her hips. His hot mouth covered her pussy, his lips and tongue sucking and laving her eager flesh.

Covering her clit with his lips, he suckled. With his free hand, he probed her hot pussy with his fingers. Pumping her hips, Ri spiraled to climax.

When her pussy ceased shuddering, Jac lifted his lips and removed his fingers. He stretched out beside her. Using her breast as a pillow, he slept.

# Chapter Three

Jac rolled over. He reached for Ri. His hand met mattress. He opened his eyes and called to her. The room was dark and silent. Ordering the lights on, Jac rose and stepped into the sonic cleansing unit.

He dressed, finger-combed his hair, and went in search of Ri. He figured he'd find her in the command center drinking coffee before an Intel unit learning all she could about prior missions to Lak. She'd analyze the missions' failures and plan how to avoid them.

Ri.

He'd worked his ass off and kept his heart separate from the job until he'd been reassigned to her team. One look and he'd wanted her, badly. After a few missions, she'd gotten under his skin.

Jac checked the time. He had only few hours to work on Payts before the team was scheduled to leave for Lak. Determined to prevent Ri from leading that mission, Jac entered Elite's command center.

By this time, Ri and the team should be in the strategy office, but the place was empty. Several employees he didn't recognize sat before Intel units. One of them looked up and jumped to his feet. Jac acknowledged him and knocked on Payts' office door.

Payts gave him permission to enter.

Twelve years Jac's senior, Silus Payts remained fit and trim. He held up his hand and watched the telecommunication screen on the corner of his desk. A message scrolled up the screen. Payts hit a button blacking out the screen and looked up.

"Dancer. I expected you hours ago. Take a seat."

"Where's UL Anzer?"

Payts gave him a quizzical look. "Three hours out from Lak."

Jac pushed out of his chair, placed his hands on Payts' desk and leaned forward. "What?"

"The team left on schedule."

"Without me?"

"Your team's been waiting. I suggest you get your ass into that strategy room. Borliz isn't as hot as Lak, but it'll challenge those green recruits."

Jac fisted his hands. Ri had fucked him good in every way possible. "My team?"

"Anzer didn't tell you?"

Apparently, she hadn't told him a lot of things. "Tell me what?"

"Anzer recommended you for UL right after the Mitian mission. The board has been reviewing your performance records. You're ready, Jac. You've been promoted. Reinstated to your former position, but this time the bonus is bigger."

"I refuse."

"It's been seven years, Jac. A day doesn't pass that I don't think about her, but Dansi knew the risks."

Payts had loved Dansi Larii. She'd shared his bed until the night Jac had transferred into the sector. Unaware of her relationship with Payts, Jac had met Dansi and bedded her within hours of his arrival. The last time her name had passed in conversation between them was the day of her funeral.

"Her team went in without proper intel," Jac said. "They were told the planet was uninhabited."

"Thanks to Dansi and you, we know what to expect. Anzer's prepared. The team is wearing armor. Lak spears can't penetrate the Hevar suits."

"If they get caught in the direct sun in those suits, they'll fry."

"They're arriving at sunset. All they have to do is hold the perimeter while the drilling bots take a sample. The team will be out by sunrise."

"UL or not, Ri shouldn't be leading a landing party. If Wath needs the racth, then let the army blast the place at night. That will keep the Laks in check long enough to drill."

"Wath might have political clout, but not enough to use the army. Once he's proven that Lak is rich with racth, the Federation will give him anything he wants."

"Why is Wath so focused on Lak? The Tinyan discovery shows more promise."

"The Federation Commodity Alliance needs this resource. They've given permission to take whatever action is necessary."

"As long as Federation troops aren't involved."

Payts nodded.

"This doesn't add up. Unless the Federation gives permission to obliterate the Laks, the costs outweigh the profits. I'm not leaving for Borliz until Ri's team is clear."

"Ri?"

"Things happen, Silus."

Payts shook his head. "I should have known."

"I should have led the team."

"Damn right you should have, but Wath is calling the shots."

The image of Dansi dying in his arms filled Jac's mind, clutched at his heart. If he lost Ri, he couldn't bear it.

"Delay the Borliz mission. I have to know Ri's safe."

"Agreed."

"Thanks, Silus." At the door, Jac turned. "If anything happens to her, Wath's ass is mine."

A slight smile lifted the corners of Payts' mouth. "I didn't hear that."

# Chapter Four

Ri tried to move. Her hands and legs were bound, and pain laced through her head. Trying to clear her vision, she fought the thick fog holding her brain hostage.

*Where am I? What the fuck happened?*

She blinked several times, focused and recoiled. Large, iridescent eyes loomed before her. A Lakian native leaned over her. A long, dark finger tipped with a black nail scraped across her face. A thin stream of drool dripped from a wide mouth.

Ugly fucker.

The Lakian slid his nail down her throat to her chest, pausing over her breast to poke at her nipple. He made a grunting sound.

Voices rose, speaking rapidly in a language she didn't understand. Flickering torches lit the area. Ri counted more than twenty male natives and cringed. All were naked, with long cocks dangling between their legs.

How had she been captured? Her team had secured the perimeter. Their weapons were far superior. How had she ended up on a stone altar with legs spread wide at the mercy of a band of primitive Lakians?

*Cris. Balder. Yung.*

What had happened to her team? What of the bot drillers? Everything had been fine until they'd tapped into a vein of racth. A cloud had filled the air. Choking, gasping, she'd tried to give orders, sent a distress signal. Had the station received her emergency blast?

*Jac, help me.*

The Lakian moved around the altar to stand between her spread legs. He ran his fingers through the tight, dark curls of her pubic hair. He probed her pussy with his finger. She recoiled, tried to resist, but the bindings held her fast.

He thrust his finger deep into her pussy as if testing how far his finger could penetrate her. When he removed his finger, he lifted it to his broad nostrils. He turned to the others of his kind and spoke. Unable to understand, she searched their faces. Although several spoke, she couldn't glean the meaning of their words.

Larger than the average human male, the Lakians stood a good seven feet. When several stroked their penises, Ri understood her fate and their discussion. They were deciding on the order. Each would rape her, but who was first had become a topic of dispute. Ri shuddered and steeled herself for the inevitable. She'd survive until Jac arrived. He would not let her die on Lak.

*I love you, Jac. Help me.*

Instead of approaching her, the Lakians moved away and encircled an open fire pit. The dispute continued. Finally, two faced off. The group moved back and a fight ensued.

Fists connected and bodies thudded against one another, propelling the fight away from her. Ri tested her restraints. Unable to move, she swore.

"Ri, speak to me."

The familiar voice clutched at her heart. "Jac."

"Yes, love."

Ri kept her voice a bare whisper. "The guys?"

"Dead."

She closed her eyes against the pain as Jac cut her restraints.

"Don't move your arms or legs."

"Give me your word, Jac. You'll end it—"

"Hush," he ordered. "This whole place is going up—Damn, the fight's over. First flash you see, move to your left. I'll be waiting."

"I love you, Jac Dancer."

Her whispered declaration met silence.

The Lakians approached and gathered in a wide semicircle. When the winner strutted toward her, Ri mentally prepared to strike. Stepping between her spread legs, he stroked his cock. The knotted appendage was long, pinkish in color with a pointed tip.

Instead of entering her, the native turned and displayed his erection to the group. Grunting, the group began to jump up and down. A few beat on drums.

The Lakian turned his attention to her, positioning his penis for penetrating. Ri sucked in a breath and readied herself for the thunderous flash signaling the series of explosions Jac had set.

The sky lit up with a bang. The Lakian looked away, allowing Ri the advantage. She slammed the heel of her foot into the side of his head. Stunning him, she followed with another powerful kick straight into his broad nose. He dropped like a rock. Recalling Jac's orders, Ri jumped off the left side of the platform. Taking advantage of the confusion and carnage caused by the explosions, Ri ran for her life.

Powerful arms caught her and her breasts slammed into a weapons vest. A spear landed nearby.

"We've got to get out of here, now!"

Holding her hand in an iron grip, he moved. Despite the thorny ground cover digging into her bare feet, Ri ran. Another spear landed, barely missing her. Jac dodged to the left, forging a path around the boulders dotting the barren landscape.

"Run! Don't stop!"

The few plants that managed to survive Lak's furious sun cut into Ri's bare feet. The ground cover thinned out and gave way to rocks. Her instep slammed onto the edge of a rock. She stumbled, nearly going down. Jac grabbed her about the waist and propelled her forward. Her heart threatened to burst before Jac eased the pace. Despite the pain radiating up her leg, Ri forced herself to keeping moving. The pace Jac set was grueling.

They ran for at least another mile toward a stand of huge boulders. The harsh rhythm of her breathing and the fierce beating of her heart were the only sounds. No drums, no shouts, no spears.

*Had they outrun them?*

The rocky terrain gave way to sand. They were out in the open, exposed and vulnerable. The boulders loomed large. Two more explosions lit the sky.

Almost there. Keep moving.

Her muscles burned as Jac broke into a sprint. Finally, Jac slowed, guiding her into the narrow space between two large boulders.

She leaned against his chest and sucked in several deep breaths.

He cupped her head. "Are you okay?"

"I'll live. Transportation?"

"Two-man pod. See that stand of rocks?"

Pods were designed to handle extreme temperatures, but had limited fuel reserves. Ri looked out upon the open plain. Another group of massive boulders was silhouetted against the faint moonlight.

"How far?"

"Farther than it looks. Once we commit, we can't stop. We've got one shot to get off this place. I couldn't take the chance the Laks would discover it."

"Elite sent you, alone?"

"Since your monitor was the only one emitting a signal, we assumed the worse. I waited for a team last time and Dansi paid the price."

Each team member had an implanted monitor. As long as you were alive, no matter what your condition, a signal was emitted.

He removed his vest and uniform shirt. He draped the shirt over her shoulders. "I won't lose you, Ri. Together, we can make it."

She slipped her arms through the sleeves and rolled up the cuffs to free her hands. At least his shirt was long enough to cover her bare ass.

"I hate leaving them here."

After putting on his vest, he drew her into his arms and kissed her hair. "So do I. Maybe now Wath will put pressure on the army."

"I lost them." She pressed her thumbs hard against the bridge of her nose to hold back the tears. She couldn't lose it.

Nothing made sense. "We weren't attacked. I don't remember being captured."

Jac stroked her back. "What do you remember?"

"When the bot drillers removed the sample, a cloud of racth dust was released. I recall choking. We were all coughing and choking. Given the atmosphere, we felt no need to seal our helmets and use re-breathers. I remember asking the guys their status. Cris began to hum. Balder was laughing between bouts of coughing. Yung managed to say he felt high."

"High?"

"Actually, when I stopped coughing, I felt euphoric. Cris started singing. You remember that night we celebrated after the Crotis mission."

"Yeah. He was so drunk he couldn't walk. I had to carry him. He sang all the way to his quarters."

"The last thing I remember is his voice. When I awoke, I was strapped down on that altar with a major headache. Like I had the mother of all hangovers."

"I found their bodies. Their throats were slashed. Not one of them had activated their weapons."

"You think they just allowed the Lakians to walk up and slash their throats. Our guys?"

"That's how it looked."

Ri felt like a giant fist grabbed her heart. Rage welled inside her. She couldn't believe she'd lost all three. They were seasoned, the best. "I can't imagine how a cloud of racth could immobilize us."

"It can't. I've worked racth drilling before. Drilling dust doesn't make you high." Dancer swore. "I knew things didn't add up. Dansi wasn't—"

He swore again. "I'm going back for that sample."

Ri head's pounded. "The sample?"

"Dansi's last words were about the sample. I didn't pay attention at the time. I didn't care about the sample, but she knew racth wasn't the objective."

The facts fell into place. "Wath isn't drilling for racth."

"Not here. I've got to get that sample."

She clutched his arms. "I'm going with you."

"Not a chance. You'll only slow me down."

"Those are—were—my guys."

"And my friends. Think like a UL. If we don't want to lose another team, we'd better find out what Wath is really mining."

His mouth settled on hers. Although his lips were firm, the contact brief, his kiss communicated he cared. He released her, pulled off his wrist unit and placed it in her palm.

"Right now your job is to survive." His fingers curled around hers. "If I'm not back in twenty minutes, run for the pod. And don't look back."

Despite the warm temperature, Ri felt cold and vulnerable without Jac's arms around her. She wasn't going anywhere without him.

"Be careful, Jac. And hurry. In case you haven't noticed, I haven't any pants on."

"I noticed."

Despite the situation, his voice held a husky quality.

"You'll find a survival pack deeper in the crevice. Food and water."

"I'll be waiting."

"Half-naked and waiting. I like that."

He moved to the edge of the boulders. Ri's heart swelled. She tried to swallow, but her throat was dry. "Be careful, Jac."

After he had disappeared from view, Ri moved deeper into the rock crevice. She located the pack. She had water, nutrition bars, a blaster, and a first aid kit. Thirsty, she drank a packet of water.

Placing her weight on her left foot, she tested its strength. Already swelling, her foot would hinder her ability to run. She opened the first aid kit and searched by feel until she found several tiny packets. After opening one, she spread the enclosed gel around her ankle and instep. The gel heated, expanded and molded to her foot and ankle. After the gel cooled, Ri tested the temporary brace. She should be able to run.

Blaster in hand, she slipped down deep between the boulders, wrapped her arms about her knees and waited.

"Ri."

Jerking awake, Ri raised her head and shook off the lethargy. Her headache had eased.

"Jac," she whispered.

"Are you okay?" His voice remained hushed.

She rose. His thigh touched hers.

"I have the sample. They're searching for us, but as soon as dawn breaks they'll be forced underground. We can go now, or wait until dawn. We'll have a narrow window. If we're caught out in the open, we're toast."

She placed the blaster into the pack. "You're in the best position to make the call."

"If we make a run for it, they might believe they forced us into the open. If we're lucky, they won't follow us. They think we're trapped out here and we'll die when the sun rises."

"How long until dawn?"

"Less than an hour. If we're going to move, we have to go now. "

"And if we stay?"

"There's an open fissure deeper between the rocks. The space is small and low, but out of the direct sun. Outside the pod, it's our only chance for survival."

After a day in the extreme heat, her ability to maintain a fast pace was questionable and the Lakians would have had all day to rest and regroup.

"Let's run for it."

He cupped her head and lowered his mouth to hers. His swift, forceful kiss gave her courage and comfort.

"We'll make it, Jac."

Ri handed the survival pack to Jac. They slipped out of their hiding place between the boulders and started running.

The light on the horizon forced Ri to pick up her pace. Despite the pain shooting up her leg, the throbbing in her ankle, she kept moving. Soon the temperature would rise along with the sun. If they were caught out in the open, they wouldn't last long.

Her foot slid out from under her and Ri fell forward, landing on her hands and knees. Without a word, Jac pulled her to her feet and lifted her over his shoulder. He clamped an arm around the back of her thighs, slapped her on the bare rump and took off.

The sky turned red, glowing from the rising sun. Ri's heart pounded, keeping rhythm with the thudding of Jac's booted feet.

Fists clenched, Ri prayed they'd make it. Jac had jeopardized his life to save hers, and she damn well didn't want to lose him now. The red was changing to bright orange when Jac threw his weight and her ass against a solid object.

Sucking the hot air in large gulps, Jac released her thighs. Ri slid to her feet and leaned against the pod. Jac released the hatch and pushed her inside. As soon as she dropped into a seat, Jac tossed the pack toward her. Ri caught it.

He yanked off his weapons vest, shoved it aside and climbed in behind her. Once he'd secured the hatch, interior lights bathed them in a yellow-green glow.

Unable to stand inside the compact pod, he remained on his knees. He pulled the sample canister out of a deep, side pocket of his uniform pants and released a latch built into the pod's wall. After sliding the canister into a slot, he secured the latch.

Ri removed two water packets. After they drank, Ri dropped the empty packets into the pack and secured it for flight.

Instead of climbing into the unoccupied seat, Jac slumped forward and rested his head against her thighs.

His shoulders heaved. "I think my heart's going to explode."

She reached out and ran her fingers through the short strands of his sweat-dampened hair. For several minutes she couldn't speak. Finally, her heart and lungs calmed.

"That was close. Thank you, Jac."

Remaining on his knees, he lifted his head. His hands slid up her bare thighs. "Open your shirt and really thank me."

"You can barely breathe and you're thinking about sex."

He grinned. "Since I laid eyes on you, I've thought of little else. I've had a hard-on for two years."

"You poor thing." Wrapping her arms about his neck, she pulled him close. The tip of her nose touched his. "Sex in a two-man pod, is it possible?"

His lips brushed hers. "Shall we find out?"

"Tight fit."

"Yes, you are."

The compact pod left little room for movement. Designed for two, either could pilot the craft, but neither could stand.

He opened the seam of her shirt and pushed it off her shoulders, exposing her breasts. He kissed her hair, her forehead and both of her cheeks.

"I want to take away the hurt, make you forget the pain. If I could, I'd kiss you properly from head to toe."

Her heart lurched. She loved this man, his power and his gentleness. Despite her training and abilities, Jac made her feel protected. For years, Ri had felt compelled to conceal her femininity behind a uniform and a tough, no-nonsense attitude. She had to compete in a male-dominated business and prove herself capable of leading a seasoned team into dangerous situations.

With Jac, Ri felt truly, utterly female. If she wanted to cry, he'd kiss away her tears. If she needed a shoulder, he'd hold her.

His lips brushed hers. "You are the sweetest thing."

No man had ever called her sweet. *Bitch* she'd heard on more than one occasion. "I like the way you lie, Jac Dancer."

He pulled back. "I never lie."

"Sweet?"

Cupping her chin in his big hand, he leaned close. "There isn't a man on-station that would turn down a night in your bed."

"Now you are lying. Not one of them has made so much as a pass at me."

"Not if they wanted to live."

"You— You didn't…"

"I did. You belong to me. It just took a while for you to want me enough to come to terms with it."

"You knew?"

He dropped his hand to her shoulder. "I thought I put on a damn good show on Mitia."

Although the lighting made it impossible for him to see, Ri knew her cheeks went pink with embarrassment. "You knew I was watching."

"I was using my hand, but mentally I was loving you." He slid his hand down to cup her breast. His hand was big and warm. Her nipple peaked in anticipation.

"I would have climbed into your pants right then," he said, kneading her flesh with slow deliberation. "But you weren't ready to accept *us*. I intended to wait until you came to me."

She arched, pushing her breast into his palm. "What changed your mind?"

"That dress." His voice was a bare whisper. "You looked so good in that little black dress."

"I wore it to seduce you."

"It worked."

Leaning forward, he licked her nipple. The sensation of his wet tongue and heated breath sent fire racing through her middle. Flames of need licked her between her legs, making her wet. Despite her exhaustion, she arched, wanting, aching, needing him. Her skin burned for the feel of his hands and mouth. Her pussy contracted.

She cupped his head, urging him to suckle. She needed Jac to erase the memories of the Lakian's touch. Fastening on her nipple, Jac laved her with sweet, strong strokes of his lips and tongue. Pulling and tugging, he nursed, satisfying her needs and driving her mad with desire at the same time.

Releasing her breast, he slid his tongue up to her shoulder.

"Love me."

Grasping her by the hips, he pulled her forward and guided her thighs around his waist. Her nipples grazed his chest.

Ri pushed her hair off her dewed forehead. "I must look a mess."

He laced his fingers through her hair. "You look beautiful. I could look at you forever."

Her heart thumped against her rib cage. "Forever is a long time."

Slanting his head, he touched his lips to hers, brushing against them softly. "Not long enough."

His husky tone sent shivers down her spine and fire racing over her skin. The hard bulge of his erection pressed against her inner thigh. She reached down and stroked him.

"Touch me."

She opened the seam of his trousers. When she grasped his hot length, he groaned. His fingers tightened, gripping her hair.

"I love your hands on me, the way you make me feel."

She stroked his hard length, tugging gently on the broad head and running a fingertip along the thick ridge of its crown. His cock jerked. Her pussy throbbed for him.

"Do that again."

Again, she slid her fingertip along the ridge. "This?"

His cock jerked. "Yeah."

She stroked him, caressing the soft tip, the thick ridge, and the long length of his shaft. Hot and thick, his cock flexed.

"I want you, Ri."

His lips captured hers, rubbing over them slowly, letting her feel his need. His hands slid from her head, down her shoulders to her breasts. He cupped them, kneading her flesh, grazing her taut nipples with his thumbs.

Shifting her ass, she positioned his cock. Moving her hips, she urged him to enter her, to fill her, to love her. His fingers gripped her breasts, as if claiming them as his. His lips hardened, taking possession of her mouth, drawing her into his fire.

Given the tight quarters, he could barely move. She rocked her hips, taking him deeper into her heat, stretching her wet, aching flesh with slow, lush leisure. Fully embedded, he shuddered.

He slid his hand down to her ass and cupped one cheek. He wrapped an arm about her waist and held her firmly to him. Her breasts flattened against his muscled chest. He raised his head. "You feel so good."

Ri smiled and brushed her palm along his shadowed jaw. "Facing death sharpens the drive to procreate. Fear gives a delicious edge to sex."

"*You* give a delicious edge to sex."

She squeezed his cock, gently mimicking how she'd take him with her mouth. Concentrating, she tugged greedily on his hot, hard flesh. His response rippled along her walls. Her pussy fluttered, grasping him with intensity.

Pulsing waves moved along his length. His chest heaved and the muscles in his back quivered beneath her hands. His skin heated, grew slick with sweat, as the pulses grew stronger.

She clamped down on him, stroking and suckling his cock with her pussy. Wet silk gripping hot steel. The muscles in his arms jerked. Her breath came in burning pants from the needy heat building deep in her core. Her thighs held his hips in a death grip and her fingers dug into his back.

Clenching and releasing, fire washed over Ri, consuming her so utterly, so completely, she shook. Heart pounding, her climax fragmented and spread through her muscles and bones.

Jac's cock contracted, pumping against her wetness, filling her with his pleasure.

Exhausted, her muscles rubbery and limp, Ri slumped back into the seat. Gulping air, Jac sagged against her chest. She cradled him in her arms, his head pillowed against her breasts.

He remained in her arms until his breathing returned to normal. He placed a kiss on each breast and lifted his head.

Closing the seam of her shirt, he said, "Let's fire up this thing and get out of here."

After fastening his pants, he slid into the seat next to hers.

"Lock in."

Ri swiveled to her right and Jac to his left. Seated back to back, they readied for takeoff. Reaching up, Ri slid her helmet in place. Next, she pulled down the control screen.

With the ease of a pro, Jac guided them through the check-off list.

"Let's go home."

Although the pod was a fireball ripping free of Lak's gravitational force, Ri smiled. G-forces pressed her chest as they entered a high-speed orbit. They hurled around the planet once before Jac engaged the thrusters. Like a slingshot, Lak released the pod into space.

The roar of the thrusters ceased and silence settled over them. The pod tumbled slowly in space.

"Course set. Are you okay? How's your leg?"

It hurt, but she'd deal with it until they reached the station.

"I'm fine."

"When the authorities confront Wath, he'll try to discredit us and come after our jobs."

"If that sample is as strong a drug as we think, he might come after *us*."

"True. Are you ready to take him on?"

"He has to pay for the guys and Dr. Larii. We can't let him send another team to Lak. Jac, we're off course."

"The army's spaceport is closer. Once the sample is in the hands of the military, Wath's desire for exclusive mining rights on Lak will be exposed. Wath might have the politicians in his pocket, but he doesn't own Colonel Wotring. I served under Wotring and he'll listen."

"What about Payts? Can we count on his support?"

"We'll contact him from the spaceport. When he learns why Dansi died, he'll be Wath's worst nightmare. Don't worry, Ri. We're in this together. I'll never let anyone or anything harm you."

If Wath came after them, he was in for a fight.

"What do you think about a permanent assignment, with me on-planet?"

Ri's heart contracted. "Earth?" *Home*.

"I've been offered a partnership in a start-up security firm. It's a great offer. We could work together and raise our kids."

*Babies. His babies.* "You're ready to quit Elite?"

"After we expose Wath, Elite will place both of us on leave. Eventually, they'll release us. I want to marry you, Ri. Officially. Irrevocably."

The practice of an official marriage had virtually disappeared in the last century.

"Payts said you were a traditionalist."

"You know how I am about my weapons."

Jac had a rep for being anal about the condition of his weapons. No one dared to touch them.

"You mean more to me than anything. I want to mean the same to you."

"You do, Jac. You do."

"Is that a yes?"

She wished she could touch him, look into his eyes. She'd have to settle for the joy she'd heard in his voice.

"Absolutely, that's a yes."

## About the author

The youngest of seven sisters born in the hills of West Virginia, B.J. McCall lives beneath the redwoods of Northern California. Combining her love of romance and science fiction, she invites the reader to explore her universe.

B.J. is a multi-published author of contemporary and sci-fi romance. Visit her website at www.bjmccall.com.

B.J. McCall welcomes mail from readers. You can write to her c/o Ellora's Cave Publishing at 1337 Commerce Drive, #13, Stow, OH 44224.

## Also by B.J. McCall:

Deep Heat

Icy Hot

Short, Tight & Sexy

Slumber Party, Inc.

# Abduction

Lynn LaFleur

# Chapter One

Michaela Ware crossed her arms beneath her generous breasts and tapped her foot. Someday she'd learn to say no when Jax invited her to a party. He partied hearty while she sipped a plain Coke because she always volunteered to be the designated driver. That didn't bother her since alcohol held little appeal to her anyway. What *did* bother her was always having to wait until her friend decided it was time to go.

She wouldn't have anything to do with him if she didn't love him so much.

Sometimes the heart could be so stupid. Mike knew she had a better chance of being struck by lightning than developing a relationship with Jaxon Greene. Six-two, shoulder-length dark brown hair, a thick mustache, piercing silver eyes, an incredible body…they all combined to make him a gorgeous male specimen. Someone that handsome, that confident of himself, should be disgustingly conceited. Instead, he was a wonderful person as well as good-looking.

Life simply wasn't fair.

She watched Jax talking to a willowy blonde with a flat chest. He always went for tall, slim, women with no breasts, usually blondes. Mike fingered a curl of her long red hair. With her frizzy hair, plain looks, and full-figured body, she would never be more than Jax's friend. She'd accepted that months ago.

She wished it didn't hurt so much.

Jax took a slip of paper from the blonde and slipped it in his shirt pocket. Probably her phone number or e-mail address. The Great Stud scores again.

Unable to stand around and watch him flirt with other women any longer, Mike squared her shoulders and strode toward him. Ignoring the blonde standing next to Jax, she looked up into his face. "Jax, I'm leaving."

"Sure, Mike, no problem," he said, his gaze still on the blonde's face. "In a few minutes."

"No, not in a few minutes. *Now.*"

Jax turned his head and looked at Mike. A slight frown drew his eyebrows together. "What's wrong?"

"I'm ready to go. If you want me to take you home, you'd better get your jacket."

The blonde touched Jax's arm. "I can give you a ride."

*I'll bet you can.* "Fine. Whatever. See you around, Jax."

She didn't wait to see whether or not he took the blonde up on her offer. Digging her car keys from the front pocket of her jeans, Mike headed for the front door.

The wind hit her face and made her shiver. One week from Halloween usually meant mild, comfortable temperatures in North Texas. Not this year. A cold front had barreled down from Canada, dropping the temperatures to below-record levels. The heavy sweater she wore had been fine in the warm house, but sadly lacking outside. Mike hurried to her small sports car, slipped inside, and started the motor. Blessed heat poured from the vents in only moments.

Mike glanced at the house as she shifted into reverse. Jax came out the front door, stuffing his arms into his heavy denim jacket.

A tiny part of her rejoiced that he hadn't accepted the blonde's offer.

He slid into the passenger seat with a frown. "What's eating you?"

Mike maneuvered her car between two SUVs and backed into the street. "Nothing's eating me. I was ready to go, that's all."

Jax barely got his seat belt fastened before Mike shifted into drive. She hit the gas harder than necessary. The car shot forward with a squeal of tires, throwing Jax back in his seat.

"Jesus, Mike, take it easy! This isn't the Indy 500."

"You don't like the way I drive, let the blonde bimbo take you home."

"Is that why you're pissed, because I was talking to Tiffany?"

Mike rolled her eyes. Tiffany. A stereotypical name for a blonde bimbo. "Don't be stupid."

"Well, something's pissed you off. This isn't like you."

"Oh? And what am I usually like?"

"You're sweet and good-natured. You don't lose your temper."

"In other words, I'm boring."

"I didn't say that. Don't put words in my mouth."

"Hey, if you want to waste your time on another show pony, that's your business."

He chuckled. "Show pony?"

Mike glared at him for daring to laugh at her choice of words. "You think that's funny?"

Jax fingered his mustache. She figured he did that to hide his grin. "I've been in Texas less than a year, Mike. I haven't figured out all the native terms yet. You want to explain what you mean by 'show pony'?"

Mike pressed the accelerator when an upcoming signal light turned yellow. She made it through the intersection as the light turned red. "You get involved with a woman—usually a blonde—who is all beauty and no brains. You parade her around like a pony at a horse show. When you get tired of her because you can't carry on an intelligent conversation for more than thirty seconds, you find another one and repeat the cycle. It's pretty stupid, Jaxon."

"And I suppose you have the perfect solution for me?"

"You might try getting involved with a woman who's intelligent and easy to talk to, not just an easy lay. Date a woman who isn't blonde. Date one with *breasts*, for Pete's sake!"

"Like you, Michaela?"

His use of her full name in that low, husky voice made shivers dance down her spine. She whipped her head toward him. He leaned against the door, stroking his mustache, and studied her intently.

Tightening her hands around the steering wheel, Mike turned her attention back to the road. "You're being stupid again."

"Why?"

"Because we're *friends*."

"Friends can be lovers, too."

He pushed her hair behind her shoulder and cradled her nape. The slow caress of his thumb against her jaw made Mike's eyes cross. He'd never touched her, not like this…the way a man touches his lover.

She could become addicted to his touch in a heartbeat.

Mentally chastising herself for indulging in a silly fantasy, Mike opened her mouth to tell him to stop teasing her. A strange light in the sky made her stop before uttering a word. It looked like a bright star, except the sky was overcast tonight and no stars were visible. The light seemed to pulsate, going from yellow to red to green and back, repeating the cycle of colors. "Look at that."

Jax leaned forward and looked out the windshield. "Look at what?"

"That light. What is it?"

"I don't know, but it looks like it's coming right at us."

Mike gasped as the light brightened and seemed to engulf her car. A second later, the light disappeared.

Shaking her head, Mike silently continued toward Jax's house. She felt…different, but didn't know why.

"You okay, Michaela?" Jax asked softly.

"Yeah, I think so. That was weird, wasn't it?"

"Very weird." He tugged on a curl by her ear. "Maybe it was a UFO."

"Ha-ha."

Mike pulled into Jax's driveway. She left the motor running while he unfastened his seat belt.

"You wanna come in for coffee?" he asked.

It wasn't unusual for him to offer an invitation into his home, or for her to accept that invitation. For a reason she didn't understand, she felt uncomfortable at the thought of being alone with Jax tonight. She shook her head. "I'd better get home."

"Hey, it's still early. It's only..." He stopped as he looked at the clock on the dash. "What the... Is that time right?"

"Of course it is." Mike gazed at the clock. Her eyes widened in shock. It read 5:48.

"It can't be, Mike. We left Tim's house about eleven. It's only a twenty-minute drive from his place here." Jax shifted in his seat to face her. "Your clock must be wrong. I can't see my watch. Turn on the radio."

His serious expression made Mike shiver. Her hand shaking slightly, she twisted the volume dial.

"...high today of forty-four with winds out of the north at fifteen to twenty miles per hour. It's currently thirty-three degrees at 5:49."

The music of "Hotel California" began while Mike tried to grasp what she'd just heard. Seven hours had simply vanished. It wasn't possible. Her palms began to sweat. "I don't understand," she whispered.

"Michaela, come inside with me."

Mike shook her head. "I need to go home."

"You need to stay with me so we can figure out what happened," Jax said, his voice firm.

"No. I want to go home. Get out, Jax."

He hesitated for several moments before releasing a heavy breath and climbing out of the car. With his hand on top of the door, he leaned down and looked at her. "I'll call you later."

Not wanting to argue with him, Mike nodded. As soon as Jax shut his door, she shifted into reverse and peeled out of the driveway.

## Chapter Two

Jax stood in his driveway and watched Michaela's car until it disappeared from his sight. He wished she hadn't left. Something had happened to them, something he didn't understand. They needed to talk about it, despite her obvious fear.

Seven hours had disappeared.

Digging his keys out of his jacket pocket, Jax slowly made his way to the front door. It made no sense. A huge hunk of time couldn't simply vanish, yet it had. Fifteen years as a reporter, and he'd never seen anything like this.

Jax hung his jacket on the coat tree inside the front door and headed for the couch. Slouching into the soft leather, he pushed his long hair back from his face with both hands. He'd worked at large, nationally known newspapers in New York, Boston, Washington D.C., and Chicago. Although he'd covered many stories, including "paranormal happenings", he'd never met anyone who'd lost hours of time.

The hectic pace, crazy hours, and lack of any kind of social life working at the majors made him decide on the move to a small-town newspaper in North Texas almost a year ago. He liked the slower pace here, the personal interaction with the local people, several of whom he now knew by their first names. They'd shared many stories with him…stories of their lives, their families.

Still, nothing like what he and Mike had just experienced.

Releasing a heavy breath, Jax rested his head on the back of the couch. Thinking about Michaela always made him feel…warm inside. He liked her, truly liked her, the way he'd never liked another woman. She was different from anyone he'd ever met…sweet, funny, considerate. He'd never heard her say a bad word about anyone. Yet he sensed a fire inside her, a smoldering blaze waiting for the right man to make it flare to life.

He treasured her friendship, yet that's all they had together. He'd teased her tonight about friends also being lovers. He liked to tease her and watch her eyes widen, her cheeks turn pink. They were pals, buddies. He felt as if he could talk to her about anything. He'd never had that kind of relationship, that camaraderie, with a woman. Wanting to keep that special friendship with Michaela, he turned to other women for sex. And yeah, he had to admit his choices in women lately had been…lacking, other than for sex. There was never a short supply of that. So what if the women couldn't keep him involved in a conversation for more than a few minutes? Sex didn't require talking.

Sounds pretty lame, Greene.

He hated to admit that Michaela was right, that he'd been listening more to his cock lately than his brain.

Reaching into his shirt pocket, he withdrew the slip of paper that contained Tiffany's home and cell phone numbers. She'd made it abundantly clear she'd be happy to go out with him. Hell, she'd practically stuffed her hand down his briefs in Tim's kitchen. Easy? Oh, yeah, she'd be *really* easy.

He had absolutely no desire to call her.

Crumpling the piece of paper, he leaned forward to toss it on the coffee table. He winced when his jeans cut into his sore penis.

"Damn," he muttered.

Jax leaned back on the couch again and adjusted the tight denim over his groin. If he didn't know better, he'd swear he'd spent the evening fucking his brains out. Since he knew that was an impossibility, he had no idea why his cock would be sore.

Curiosity made him unfasten his jeans and pull his shaft from his briefs. The strong scent of sex hit his nostrils.

*What the hell?*

Continuing his investigation as any good reporter would, Jax raised his hands to his nose and sniffed. They smelled like pussy.

Some time in the last seven hours, he'd obviously had sex and couldn't remember it.

Shivers galloped down his spine. This simply wasn't possible. It had to be some kind of crazy dream, or a practical joke. Tim loved to pull jokes on his friends, especially at his parties. That must be it. Somehow, his friend had set up this whole thing to make Jax think he'd forgotten seven hours of his life—seven hours that included a wild fuck session.

Jax ran one hand through his hair. Not even Tim could come up with a joke like this, and he definitely didn't have the know-how to pull it off.

*What happened to us, Michaela?*

The reporter inside him screamed to investigate, find out what happened. He especially wanted to check on

Michaela. He should've insisted she come in his house, stay until he'd been certain she was all right.

A night without sleep should've left him wiped out, but he was too wired to sleep. He'd shower first, then grab a bite to eat before heading to Mike's house.

Jax dropped his clothes in the hamper and stepped beneath the warm spray. Tilting his head back, he let the water cascade over his body for several moments, enjoying the sensation of the water on his bare skin. Wiping the moisture from his eyes, he reached for the bottle of shampoo.

The feel of his fingers on his scalp made him pause. Someone had touched his head a short while ago. Someone had clutched his hair while kissing him. But that wasn't possible. He'd been with no one but Mike, and she hadn't kissed him.

Jax stood still as a picture formed in his mind…

*The light filtered through the glass, highlighting Mike's red hair. Jax ran his hands through it, over and over, enjoying the weight, the texture. So soft. Leaning forward, he buried his nose in the curly strands by her ear. Flowers. Her hair smelled like flowers.*

*The hitch in her breathing made Jax pull back and look into Mike's face. Her green eyes stared back at him, wide and filled with uncertainty.*

*"Are you afraid, Michaela?" he whispered.*

*"Yes," she whispered back.*

*"Why?"*

*"Because I don't… I'm afraid you'll be disappointed with me."*

*Jax chuckled. "I could never be disappointed with you, Michaela, don't you know that?"*

*"I'm not very…experienced."*

*"I'm not either, with you. I don't know what you like or dislike." Cradling her jaw, he tilted up her face so he could look deeper into those incredible eyes. "We'll learn together."*

*His lips covered hers in a tender kiss. Her mouth made him think of smooth, warm velvet. Her kiss was hesitant at first, her lips closed. Jax waited, giving her time to relax and respond to him. He nipped gently, then soothed the nips with a slow sweep of his tongue.*

*The groan from deep in her throat made his blood race.*

*Still not wanting to rush her, Jax slowly deepened the kiss. Tilting his head to one side, he slid his mouth over hers while dipping his tongue along the seam of her lips. His actions were rewarded by an increase in her breathing. She clutched at his waist, bunching his shirt in her fists, and parted those full, luscious lips. He took immediate advantage and thrust his tongue inside her mouth.*

*She relaxed in his arms, parting her lips even wider. Her tongue touched his, just a bit, before retreating. Jax would've grinned if he hadn't been so involved with devouring her mouth. He wanted to be inside her…in every way possible.*

*Stepping closer to her, Jax ran one hand up into her hair to hold her head the way he wanted it. He slowly slid his other hand down her back until it rested on the curve of her rounded buttock. Finally, he could touch her the way he wanted, the way he'd longed to for months.*

*One more step brought his groin in contact with her stomach. He shifted his hips from side to side, brushing his rapidly growing erection against her. She tensed a moment, but quickly relaxed again and clutched his waist even harder.*

*Jax released Mike's mouth long enough to whisper, "Wrap your arms around me." He didn't wait to be sure she obeyed his command before kissing her again. He couldn't get enough of that delicious mouth. Only the need for oxygen made him move his lips to her neck. A gentle nip of his teeth, a swipe of his tongue, and he heard her moan.*

*He loved that sound…the sound of her surrender to her feelings.*

*Jax felt her hands slide up his torso. Her fingers gripped his hair, as if to hold him in place so he wouldn't let her go.*

*Fat chance of* that *happening.*

*Her breathing became more choppy. Jax cupped both her buttocks in his hands and pulled her against his groin. Her sharp gasp of pleasure made his control snap. No longer able to wait, he fumbled for the snap on her jeans…*

"*God!*" Jax groaned loudly when the orgasm grabbed his balls.

He didn't realize he'd started pumping his cock until after he came. Unable to stand upright on his shaky legs, he leaned against the shower wall for support.

*Wow. Where did* that *come from?*

Closing his eyes, Jax took a deep breath and released it slowly. He didn't understand what had just happened to him. Daydreaming about Michaela wasn't something he did on a regular basis. And it hadn't seemed like a daydream, but a memory. That wasn't possible. He'd never been intimate with Mike, had never kissed her.

And yet, he would swear he could see sunlight reflected in Michaela's hair. He could hear her moan of pleasure. He could taste her kisses, feel her fingers clutching his hair, caressing his back…

Jax released his own moan of pleasure.

Letting the memory continue, he pictured her mane of red hair. She usually wore it pulled back in a ponytail, but sometimes—like tonight—she wore it down so it fell over her shoulders. That ivory complexion, that cute turned-up nose, those full lips…they all combined to make her lovely. Yet Mike didn't seem to realize the extent of her looks. She did little to draw a man's eye, to make him notice her as a woman. Her makeup was practically nonexistent, her clothes plain and unflattering to her figure.

Her sexy, voluptuous figure.

They might only be friends, but that didn't mean Jax hadn't noticed that incredible body, hadn't fantasized about touching those lush breasts. His cock stirred as he imagined taking off Mike's bra so her breasts could fall into his hands. He'd caress them, rub his thumbs over her nipples, while she arched her back and closed her eyes in pleasure.

He wouldn't stop with taking off her bra. He'd remove her clothing, bit by bit, until he could feel her skin against his. He'd drop to his knees before her, part her feminine lips with his fingers. Jax swallowed hard as he imagined swiping his tongue along her creamy pussy until he found her clit. He'd suckle it until he made her come.

When he was sure he could move without his legs giving out, Jax turned off the water and opened the glass door. Grabbing a towel, he quickly dried his body. As soon as he got dressed, he planned to drive to her house. He had a lot of questions and Mike was the only one with the answers.

# Chapter Three

Mike turned to her right side and punched her pillow, trying to maneuver the lump into something that actually resembled a pillow and not a rock. She didn't remember her pillow ever being this uncomfortable.

She couldn't remember her body ever being this uncomfortable either.

Mike winced as she shifted on the bed. Little aches tugged at her muscles. The area between her thighs felt swollen and sore, almost as if she'd spent several hours having sex. Since she was sure *that* hadn't happened, she didn't understand the tenderness.

This whole evening had been a mystery.

Seven hours had disappeared. It simply couldn't happen, yet it had. She and Jax had been together, and he'd experienced the same thing. They'd both looked at the clock on her car's dash. They'd both heard the disc jockey announce the time.

Mike didn't scare easily. This scared her.

Sleep wouldn't be possible, no matter how much she wanted to simply lose consciousness for a while. With a sigh, Mike rolled to her back. She gasped when the covers rasped across her tender nipples. Cradling her breasts in her hands, she gently rubbed her thumbs over the nubs. They were hard and very sensitive.

Her sexual experience included all of three men. Only one of them had been a good lover, and he'd been incredible. He'd taught her to enjoy her body...how to touch, *where* to touch, to give her the most pleasure. Her nipples were close to the top of the list. She'd always wanted them to have a lot of attention, so they'd often been tender after lovemaking.

Like now.

She whisked her thumbs across the hard tips again. She didn't understand why they would be so tender. It'd been months since she'd had sex with a man, and she hadn't touched her nipples for several days. An image formed in her mind as she continued to caress herself...an image of full lips wrapped around one hard tip...

*Mike leaned her head back, rested her palms on the desk behind her, and sighed from pleasure. She could feel Jax's gentle suckling of her nipple all the way down her body. Oh, he did that so well! He didn't simply latch onto her nipple and try to suck it off—he made love to it, using his entire mouth.*

*"Tell me if I do something you don't like," he whispered against her breast.*

*"I will. No problem so far."*

*She felt his lips curve. He raised his head and grinned at her. "I like a woman who knows what she wants."*

*"I know* exactly *what I want." Mike tunneled her fingers into his hair and tugged him back to her breast. "More."*

*He obeyed her instantly, cupping both breasts in his hands while licking her right nipple. Her left nipple received a long swipe of his tongue before he stood up straight again. "I've thought about you, wondered what you look like beneath the loose clothing you always wear." His hands kneaded her breasts while his thumbs circled the areolas over and over. "These are beautiful, Michaela."*

*His praise warmed her heart…and the rest of her body.*

*So far, she'd received all the attention from Jax. She hadn't complained at his passionate kisses, or when he'd slipped her sweater over her head. She definitely hadn't complained when he'd removed her bra and started touching her.*

*But now it was* his *turn to show some skin. "Take off your shirt."*

*Jax continued to caress her breasts. "Take it off for me."*

*The sexy, smoky look in his silver eyes made Mike swallow hard. She clenched her hands into fists a moment before reaching for the top button of his Henley pullover. She'd seen him without a shirt several times, but never this close, this…intimate.*

*Releasing the top button gave her a glimpse of dark chest hair. More hair was exposed as she slowly unfastened the remaining three buttons to the middle of his chest. She parted the edges and pressed a kiss on his warm skin.*

*"Michaela," he said thickly.*

*"Hmm?" She inhaled deeply. The scent of musk and man made her head spin.*

*"Take off my shirt."*

*"I'm busy." She licked him from the center of his chest up to his neck.*

*He squeezed both nipples between his thumbs and forefingers. "You shouldn't tease me when I have you literally in my hands."*

*Feeling impish, she grinned as she tugged his shirt from the waistband of his jeans. "If you want to hurt me, that isn't the way to do it. I like my nipples squeezed." She ran her hands under his shirt and up his stomach. The crisp hair tickled her palms.*

*Mike decided she'd teased too much when she heard Jax growl. She'd never heard a man growl. He jerked his shirt over his head and dropped it to the floor. She had only a moment to admire that glorious chest before he plastered it against her breasts.*

*She had no complaints about that.*

*Jax wrapped his arms around her and kissed her hungrily. His tongue darted past her lips to tangle with hers. Mike couldn't breathe, the sensations were so powerful. She'd never felt such overwhelming desire, such need to be joined with a man. Clasping his head, she feasted on his mouth.*

*She felt his hand between their bodies. He'd already unsnapped her jeans, but hadn't unzipped them. That fact quickly changed. The rasp of the zipper made Mike catch her breath.*

*Jax lifted his head and gave her a devilish grin. "Now it's* my *turn to tease."*

The pounding on her front door made Mike jump. Confused, she looked around her bedroom, expecting to see Jax.

*He isn't here. You were daydreaming.*

But it seemed so *real*. Her body still hummed with unfulfilled desire. Her breasts felt heavy, her labia wet and swollen. She would swear she'd been with Jax…kissing him, touching him…

The pounding came again, followed by three short rings of her doorbell. Throwing back the covers, Mike scampered from bed and grabbed her thick terrycloth robe from the floor. She wrapped it around her nude body while hurrying to the front door.

A peek through the peephole showed her a scowling Jax standing on her small porch. A bolt of desire zigzagged through her body, ending in her clit. She couldn't let him in, not after the intense daydream she'd just had. Maybe she could go back to her bedroom and hide under the bed.

"Open up, Mike," Jax said loudly. "I know you're home."

*So much for hiding*. Mike tightened the sash on her robe and opened the door.

Jax stood with his shoulders hunched against the brisk north wind. "It took you long enough," he said with a frown.

"I was in bed." Standing aside, Mike motioned for Jax to enter. "Come in. That wind is cold."

"You're telling me."

He crossed the threshold and Mike quickly shut the door. Taking a deep breath for courage, she turned and leaned against the door for support. "What are you doing here?"

Jax removed his denim jacket and tossed it on her couch. "We need to talk."

Mike was afraid he'd say that. "About what?"

"About what happened to us tonight." Hands on his hips, he faced her. "I have to figure this out, Mike. It's making me nuts. We lost *seven hours*!"

"That isn't possible."

"So explain to me where that time went."

Mike couldn't, so remained silent.

Jax pushed one hand through his hair as he started pacing her small living room. "I thought maybe Tim was pulling one of his practical jokes. Then I realized Tim isn't smart enough to think of something this huge."

Mike didn't think Tim was smart enough to figure out how to crack an egg, but she wouldn't say that to Jax.

He stopped pacing and looked at her. "Help me, Mike. We have to figure out what happened."

"*You're* the world-famous investigative reporter. I'm just a photographer."

Jax frowned again. "You're an incredibly talented photographer as well as an intelligent woman. Don't put yourself down."

His compliment tickled her ego, yet she didn't feel very intelligent right now. She couldn't explain those lost seven hours. The different possibilities terrified her. "I don't know what happened, Jax," she said softly, "and I'm afraid to think about it."

His frown faded. He crossed the floor to stand in front of her. Raising one hand, he brushed her cheek with his thumb. "Don't be afraid, Michaela."

Mike caught her breath. She'd heard him say those same words recently…

*"Don't be afraid, Michaela."*

*"I'm not."*

*"Then why are you trembling?"*

*"Because I want you so much."*

*Jax smiled. "The words a man loves to hear." He cradled her breasts again as he kissed her neck. "I want you, too."*

Mike shook her head to banish the daydream and bring the *real* Jax back into focus. His eyebrows were drawn together in a frown again.

"Are you all right?"

Annoyed by the sexy thoughts that kept popping into her head, Mike said the first thing she thought. "No, I'm *not* all right. I keep having..."

She stopped and bit her lip. She'd almost told him about her erotic daydreams. That was something she could never admit to him.

"You keep having what?"

"Nothing." Mike moved past him and headed for the kitchen. "I'll make some coffee."

"I don't want coffee, Mike." He grabbed her arm and jerked her back to him. "I want to talk."

Ready to reprimand him for manhandling her, she stopped before speaking when she noticed the direction of his gaze. She looked down to see her robe gaping open. Half of one creamy breast peeked out.

Jax slowly raised his gaze back to her face. "Are you naked beneath that robe, Michaela?"

# Chapter Four

The adorable blush that bloomed in her cheeks answered Jax's question. Mike had nothing on beneath that robe. She said she'd been in bed. That had to mean she slept in the nude.

Mike, who dressed in unflattering clothing and used little makeup, wore nothing to bed but her birthday suit.

A hint of a smile turned up the corners of his mouth. "Do you sleep naked, Mike?"

She jerked her robe's lapels closed and tightened the belt. "That's none of your business."

"It's been my experience, as a world-famous investigative reporter, that when someone avoids answering a question, that's usually because the answer is yes."

"You can be really annoying sometimes, do you know that?"

Jax grinned. "Yeah."

"I need coffee," Mike muttered.

Chuckling, Jax followed her into the kitchen. He sat at the counter between the kitchen and her dining room and watched her while she prepared the coffee. Teasing her almost made him forget the real reason for his visit.

Almost.

"We need to figure out what happened to us, Michaela."

She stared at the dark liquid dripping into the glass carafe as if it held the answers to obtaining world peace. Jax figured she did that to keep from looking at him. "Are you listening to me?"

"Yes."

"Then look at me."

He saw her chest rise and fall with a deep breath before she turned her head toward him. "That's better," he said softly. "I want to look into your eyes when I talk to you."

Her throat worked as she swallowed. Her tongue darted out to lick her lower lip. A mental picture hit him, a memory of that tongue on his body…

*Mike pushed on his chest until Jax was forced to take a step back. "What are you doing?"*

*"I want to trade places." She jumped down from the desk. Jax enjoyed that move since it made her breasts bounce. "Sit."*

*"I was perfectly happy standing between your legs."*

*"Humor me."*

*Wanting to please her—and also intensely curious about what she planned to do—Jax obeyed. He hoisted himself up on the desk, legs spread wide, palms flat on the wood that still held the heat from her body. Mike moved between his legs. She touched his thighs, watching her hands as she moved them up and down his legs. Jax's breathing quickened when those soft hands came close to his groin, but he didn't move. He switched his attention back and forth between her hands and that enticing strip of skin exposed by her open jeans.*

*He wanted to fuck that cute belly button with his tongue.*

*Her gaze shifted from her hands to between his legs. One lone fingertip traced the length of his erection.*

*"You must be uncomfortable in those tight jeans."*

*"Nude would be better."*

*Those incredible green eyes snapped up to his face. "Do you like being nude?"*

*"I* love *being nude. Don't you?"*

*She didn't answer his question. Instead, she leaned forward and kissed the center of his chest again. Jax inhaled sharply and closed his eyes. Her lips were so soft and warm against his skin. Her tongue flicked out and caressed his left nipple.*

*"Michaela," he said gruffly.*

*Slowly, her tongue traveled across his chest to his right nipple. She circled the hard nub, then made the return journey back to his left nipple. Jax ran one hand underneath her hair and gently massaged her scalp while her mouth loved him.*

*His hand tightened in her hair when he felt her fingers at the waistband of his jeans. He waited, breath held, for her to release his cock from the strangling denim.*

*Mike kept moving her mouth down his body as she unfastened the snap of his jeans. Jax leaned back, resting his free hand on the desk behind him. He watched that pink tongue swirl through the hair on his stomach. It darted into his navel. Jax forgot how to breathe when it licked his skin between the open snap of his jeans.*

*The sound of his zipper made him take a breath. He leaned back a bit farther and lifted his hips. If she didn't touch his cock soon…*

*Mike's hand slipped inside his briefs and palmed his hard flesh. Jax groaned and fisted her hair, trying to draw her mouth closer to his shaft. She pulled his briefs away from his body. His cock popped free, hard and throbbing against his abdomen.*

*"Lick it, Michaela."*

*She looked into his eyes as she ran her tongue from the base of his shaft to the head…*

"Jaxon!"

Jax jumped when Mike said his name sharply. "*What?*"

"I asked you if you want coffee."

"Uh, yeah. Sure."

Jax shifted on the stool and tugged on the fly of his jeans. He was glad to be behind the counter so Mike couldn't see his hard-on. He didn't understand why he kept having erotic memories about Mike when they had never made love.

He followed her movements as she filled two mugs with coffee and took liquid creamer from the refrigerator for him. Her robe gaped a bit, exposing her chest and a hint of cleavage. He knew her nipples were dark pink, the areolas much paler and the size of a silver dollar. She had a small brown mole beneath her right breast, and one on the curve of her left buttock.

He couldn't know those things unless he'd seen her body.

She placed his mug in front of him before sipping from her own. Instead of drinking his coffee, he wrapped his hands around the warm mug. "Are you ready to talk about what happened to us?"

"We don't *know* what happened to us."

"And that scares you."

She nodded.

"So let's figure it out."

"How?" She set her mug on the counter so sharply, coffee sloshed over the side. "How do we figure it out? We have no idea where those seven hours went. All I know is I've had…" She stopped. Eyes wide, she bit her lower lip.

Her slip intrigued him. "You've had what?"

"Nothing."

"Uh-uh. That's not good enough." Jax rose from the stool and rounded the counter. He stood before her, no more than six inches away. "Finish your sentence."

She stepped back, until her bottom hit the counter and she could retreat no farther. "It isn't important."

"It is to me."

Her gaze skittered away. Jax touched her chin. "Whatever it is, you can tell me. You know that."

Mike kept her eyes lowered for a moment before looking at him. "It's nothing. Really."

He didn't believe her, but wouldn't push if she wasn't ready to talk. Instead, he tweaked the end of her nose. "Okay. You'll tell me when you're ready, right?"

She gave him a weak smile. "Right."

Maybe they needed to get their minds off their mystery, at least for a while. "I have an idea. Get dressed and I'll take you out to breakfast."

"I can cook something—"

"Why cook when you don't have to? Go get dressed."

"I need to shower first."

"Want me to wash your back?" Jax teased, hoping to bring back her smile.

Her chin went up a notch. "I don't think so."

Jax grinned as Mike sashayed from the room. He did love teasing her.

His grin faded. He and Mike would have a relaxing, leisurely breakfast, then they had to talk about those lost seven hours. Somehow, they'd figure out what happened.

Jax wouldn't be able to rest until he solved the mystery.

# Chapter Five

Mike stood beneath the warm spray and let it beat on her head. She couldn't believe she'd almost told Jax about her sexual fantasies. She'd be absolutely mortified if he found out she'd had such a vivid daydream about him this morning.

Or a memory.

She pushed her wet hair back from her face. No, not a memory. A person couldn't have a memory of something that had never happened.

The water seemed a bit cool to Mike. She picked up the bar of soap and held it between her breasts as she leaned over to adjust the temperature. A glance at the soap made an image come to mind…an image of something else between her breasts…

*She looked into his eyes as she ran her tongue from the base of his shaft to the head. She almost grinned when she saw his eyes go unfocused.*

*"Do you like that?" she asked before circling the head with the tip of her tongue.*

*"Oh, yeah," he said huskily. "Very much."*

*"Lift your hips."*

*He obeyed her instantly. Mike tugged his jeans and briefs to mid-thigh. Now both her hands were free to caress him. Wrapping her fingers around his shaft, she slowly moved them up and down his length.*

"You're thick."

"Yeah." His voice sounded strangled.

She continued to caress him while he pumped his hips. "Can you come with me touching you like this?"

"Oh, yeah."

Wanting him naked, Mike pulled off his clothes and dropped them on the floor. On impulse, she leaned forward and cradled his cock between her breasts. "How about like this?"

He sucked in a sharp breath. "Jesus, Mike!"

"You don't like this?"

"I can't…" He stopped and leaned his head back. "God, that feels good."

Mike couldn't believe these brave, daring moves came from her. She wasn't a virgin, but she'd never been so bold with a man.

This new freedom felt good.

Mike pushed her breasts closer together. She caressed the length of Jax's cock for several seconds, then released him to take him in her mouth. Her tongue wet his shaft thoroughly before she placed it back between her breasts. She repeated the sequence over and over, until Jax grabbed her head and pulled her mouth away from him.

"Stop!"

Mike frowned. She was enjoying herself too much to stop. "Why?"

Jax cradled her face in his hands and kissed her thoroughly. "Because I was about to come."

"I want you to," she said softly.

"What about you, Michaela?"

*She looked around the small room. The only piece of furniture it contained was the desk where Jax sat. "Well, it isn't like you're going to roll over and go to sleep."*

*Jax chuckled. "No, I won't do that." He ran his hands into her hair. "I want to come. Believe me, I want to come. But I want* you *to come first." He kissed her again before whispering in her ear, "I want my tongue inside your pussy."*

*His words made heat fill her face. So much for her newfound freedom. Twenty-nine years old and the word "pussy" could still make her blush.*

*"Will you let me do that?" Jax asked after kissing her once more.*

*Her clit pulsed and warm cream dampened her panties at the thought of his mouth on her. Mike nodded her head.*

*Jax gave her another blistering kiss that left her legs weak before he slid to the floor. Dropping to his knees, he gripped her jeans and slowly pulled them down her legs. When they reached her calves, he went back for her panties. They, too, made the slow journey down her legs. Mike toed off her shoes and held onto Jax's shoulders as he removed her clothing. She assumed he would stand once she was nude. Instead, he stayed on his knees before her, his hands sliding up and down the outside of her legs, while his gaze traveled over her.*

*"You have a beautiful body, Michaela."*

*He tilted his head back and looked at her face before focusing his attention between her thighs. A single fingertip ruffled her red pubic curls. The corners of his mouth twitched.*

*"I guess there's no doubt you're a natural redhead."*

*His teasing made her smile. "Nope. No doubt about it."*

*"I think redheads are very sexy." He leaned forward and nuzzled her mound. "*You're *very sexy."*

*Mike couldn't believe this was Jax—the man she adored, the man she'd loved since the moment she saw him—saying these beautiful words to her. She couldn't believe it was Jax touching her, parting her labia with his thumbs, swiping his tongue across her clit.*

*She groaned.*

*He licked her slowly, his tongue delving through the folds to find all the spots that gave her pleasure. Mike closed her eyes and simply* absorbed. *Spreading her legs farther apart, she tilted her hips forward to bring her clit closer to that incredible tongue…*

Mike stopped rubbing her clit and shoved two fingers inside her pussy when the orgasm raced down her spine. Her body shook, her legs grew shaky. She had to bite her bottom lip to keep from crying out. She didn't want Jax to know she was masturbating in the shower.

She had no idea how long she'd stood beneath the water, fantasizing about the man in her kitchen. It had to be several minutes. If she didn't hurry and get dressed, Jax would be pounding on the door.

The thought of Jax coming in her bathroom, seeing her wet, nude body, made her clit throb despite her recent orgasm.

Mike soaped her skin and rinsed off in the cooling water. Drying quickly, she wrapped her robe around her and opened the door.

Jax stood in the hallway, leaning against the wall.

"Need some help getting dressed?" he drawled.

Steam billowed out of the bathroom around them. The sight of him so soon after her erotic fantasy sent heat through her body that had nothing to do with the steam.

He teased her often. Mike always teased right back. She loved their friendly banter, the laughter they shared. This didn't feel like his usual teasing. This felt…real.

*You're wishing for things that aren't there. He doesn't care about you the same way you care about him.*

Mike pushed her wet hair behind her ears. "I've been getting dressed by myself for a long time, thank you."

"I'll bet it isn't nearly as much fun as if I helped you."

"I thought guys liked to *undress* a woman, not *dress* her."

His gaze dipped to her breasts for a moment. "Undressing is fun, too."

She wondered, for one insane moment, what he'd do if she accepted his offer. What if she reached out and touched his chest, let her hand glide down his stomach to the hem of his Chicago Bears sweatshirt? What if she slipped her hand beneath that sweatshirt and touched bare skin?

Curling her hands into fists to keep from doing exactly that, Mike took a step back. "I'll get dressed so we can go to breakfast. Give me fifteen minutes."

She hurried into her bedroom before he could comment, closing the door behind her.

# Chapter Six

Jax rested his hand lightly on the small of Mike's back as the waitress led them to a booth in the back of the restaurant. He'd asked for privacy, or as much privacy as they could get in the large family-style establishment that Mike liked.

He waited until she slid into the booth, then took the seat opposite her. Smiling brightly, the waitress handed Mike a menu first, then Jax. He ordered coffee for both of them, figuring that would get the waitress to leave. She hovered instead, as if she had all day to wait for their order before they'd even looked at the menus.

"How about that coffee?" Mike asked.

The smile disappeared from the waitress' mouth as she looked at Mike. "Oh, sure. I'll be right back." Her smile returned when she gazed at Jax again before leaving their area.

Mike shook her head. "It doesn't matter where we go. Women flock to you like vultures to a dead possum."

Jax couldn't help chuckling at her analogy. Her Texas accent always became a bit more pronounced when she spouted what he called Southernisms. "Well, I'm not sure if I like being compared to a dead possum."

"You know what I mean. You're just so gorgeous, women can't help it."

She'd never called him "gorgeous". While Jax's reflection didn't break any mirrors, he'd never given his looks much thought. They came from his parents. He simply tried to make the best of them.

Hearing Mike's praise made his heart swell. "You think I'm gorgeous?"

A hint of pink touched her cheeks before she lifted that stubborn chin. "Don't be modest, Jaxon. You know how handsome you are."

He shrugged. "I don't think about it. I'm not the one who has to look at me."

"Trust me, it's no hardship for anyone to look at you."

"It matters to me what *you* think, Michaela. I don't care what anyone else thinks."

That was true. Jax hadn't realized it until this moment how much Mike's opinion meant to him.

Propping his elbow on the table, he rested his head on his fist. He studied her while she studied her menu. Her hair fell in curls to her shoulders. She wore little makeup, but he could tell she'd applied mascara to her lashes. They were long anyway, the dark brown mascara made them look even longer, thicker.

His gaze drifted to her mouth. Full, soft lips, the lower one wet because she'd just licked it. A long ivory neck. Nice shoulders—not broad, but not narrow either. Lush breasts with those big pink nipples…

He still didn't understand how he knew the exact color of her nipples.

Mike shut her menu and laid it on the edge of the table. "I'll have a waffle with a side of ham."

"You *always* have a waffle with a side of ham."

She grinned. "I like waffles."

He knew that. He knew so many things about her. What he *didn't* know was why they lost seven hours of their lives last night.

"We have to talk about what happened to us, Mike."

Her grin quickly faded. "I know we do."

"Do you have a theory?"

The waitress returned before Mike could answer his question. Jax ordered waffles and ham for both of them, not wanting to waste any time looking at his menu so the waitress would leave again. He appreciated her obvious interest, but had more important things on his mind now than a conquest.

Once she left, Jax repeated his question. "Do you have a theory?"

Mike shook her head. "I wish I did, but it's a complete mystery to me. Those seven hours simply vanished."

"Shit." Jax pushed one hand through his hair. "Maybe it *was* a UFO and we were abducted. That makes as much sense as anything else I can think of."

When Mike didn't laugh at his joke, Jax frowned. "Hey, I was teasing."

Mike pushed her hair behind her ears. She looked around their area, as if checking to be sure she couldn't be heard. Leaning forward, she rested her forearms on the table. "What if that *is* what happened? What if we *were* abducted?"

Jax slowly leaned back in the booth, his mouth slack. He couldn't believe what Mike had just said. "You can't be serious."

A blush tinted her cheeks. "I know it sounds crazy. I feel crazy saying it. But what other explanation is there?"

"There has to be one."

"You told me you've covered stories about alien abductions."

"Well, yeah, but I never believed them."

Mike tilted her head. "Why not? Who's to say there isn't life out there somewhere? Do you really believe Earth is the only planet in this huge universe with inhabitants? Wouldn't that be…conceited?"

Put that way, Jax didn't know how to answer her questions. He'd always thought the people he'd interviewed about their "abductions" were simply looking for attention. He'd never believed someone—or some *thing*—had whisked them off in a spaceship.

"Do you agree there could be other life out there?" Mike asked.

"I agree it's possible. It's a big universe." He leaned forward and laid his hands on her forearms. "That doesn't mean we were abducted. Why choose us? We aren't special."

"I don't know. I just know I keep having…"

She stopped and her eyes widened. Pulling her arms away from him, she leaned back in the booth.

For the third time this morning, she hadn't finished her sentence. Jax's eyes narrowed. He had to know what she was hiding. "You keep having what?"

"Nothing," she said quickly, not looking at him.

"Michaela, answer me. You keep having what?"

The waitress arrived with their breakfasts before Mike said anything else. Jax silently cursed the interruption. Mike dug right into her food, obviously in no hurry to confide in him.

Fine. He'd eat his breakfast, too, before he grilled her again.

Mike could feel Jax watching her while she ate. She tried to act normally, pretend his eyes weren't boring a hole through her skull as if he were trying to read her mind.

Halfway through her breakfast, Mike stopped eating. Her waffle had begun to expand in her stomach, leaving no room for even a crumb. A glance at Jax's plate showed he had no such problem. He swirled his last bite of waffle through the maple syrup on his plate and popped it in his mouth.

Jax pushed his empty plate aside and picked up his coffee mug. "Why do you think we were abducted?"

"I didn't say we *were*, I said it's a possibility."

His eyebrows drew together in a frown. "Okay, okay. Why do you think it's a *possibility* we were abducted?"

"Because I *do* believe there's other life beyond Earth. And I believe it's a *possibility* that other life is more advanced than we are, that they can travel through space when we haven't developed the technology to do that yet. Maybe they're curious about us, so they…borrow us for a while to see how we…tick. Or maybe some even live right here with us."

Jax said nothing. Mike squirmed in her seat. She wasn't ashamed of her beliefs, but perhaps this wasn't the right time to share them with Jax.

He set his mug on the table with a loud *clunk*. "Let's go."

Her mouth dropped open as she watched him gather up his jacket from the seat beside him. "Go?"

"Yeah." He stood and pulled his wallet from his back pocket. "That waitress is heading this way again." Removing a twenty from his wallet, he tossed it on the table and reached for Mike's hand. A gentle tug had her on her feet. "I want to talk about this in private."

# Chapter Seven

Jax remained silent on the drive back to Mike's house. She glanced at him often, wondering if she should try to strike up a conversation. A slight frown marred his forehead as if he were deep in thought. Deciding not to bother him, she settled back in her seat and looked out her window at the passing scenery.

Mike noticed a couple standing near a parked car when Jax slowed for a stop sign. The man held the woman's face in his hands as he kissed her. The sight before her faded. Another image flashed through Mike's head…

*Jax's tongue lapped at her clit over and over, until the orgasm galloped through her body. Her legs grew weak and her knees buckled. Only Jax's strong arms around her kept her from falling.*

*Standing, Jax gripped her waist, turned, and set her on the desk. He cradled her face in his hands and kissed her deeply. His mustache was damp with her juices. Mike could taste herself on his lips, his tongue.*

*It was so erotic, tasting herself and him at the same time.*

*She felt his fingers between her thighs. Mike spread her legs farther apart, giving him room to touch her however he wanted.*

*"I love how wet you are," he whispered against her lips.*

*"Your tongue made me that way."*

*"My tongue helped, but this is mostly you." Lifting his head, he looked into her eyes as he pushed two fingers inside her pussy.*

*Mike hissed in her breath and arched her back. His touch felt so good.*

*"Am I hurting you?"*

*"No, no. It's wonderful."*

*"In that case..." A devilish grin crossed his lips. "Let's see how many times I can make you come."*

*He pushed his fingers farther inside her and moved them around a bit before pressing upward. Mike gasped from pleasure.*

*"Found your G-spot, huh?" he asked, a hint of smugness in his voice.*

*"Oh, yeah." Mike leaned back and rested her weight on her hands, leaving her body completely open for him. "Rub it harder."*

*He obeyed her instantly, applying pressure in a circular motion. "How's this?"*

*Mike sighed. "Perfect."*

*"Put your feet up on the desk."*

*She did, letting her legs fall wide open. Jax caressed her right nipple with his free hand while he continued to move his fingers inside her. Mike closed her eyes and bit her lower lip to keep from crying out. Another orgasm hovered, just out of reach...*

*It crested when Jax pulled her left nipple between his lips and suckled hard.*

*"Jaxon!" She couldn't help crying out when pleasure rushed through her body. Bucking her hips, she rode the waves until the final ripple faded. Only then could she open her eyes again.*

*Jax stood before her, his cock hard, his eyes fierce with desire. He looked as if he wanted to completely devour her.*

*Mike lay back on the desk. "Take me," she whispered.*

*Jax pulled his fingers from her body. Slipping his arms beneath her thighs, he lifted her hips and drove his shaft inside her with a single thrust.*

The lack of the pickup's movement brought Mike out of her daydream. She shook her head and blinked to bring her eyes back into focus. She wished she could bring her body under control as easily. Her skin felt hot, clammy. Her heart thudded. Her pussy wept. Her nipples ached. Mike knew one swipe across her clit would make her come.

Since she couldn't bring herself any relief now, she took a breath and let it out slowly. When she was sure she could speak without her words slurring, she turned her head and looked at Jax.

He sat with his left arm draped over the steering wheel, his right arm on the seat back, staring at her.

Mike swallowed. He couldn't know how she felt right now…how she longed to make her fantasies come true. She wished she could take him in her house and lead him to her bedroom. She'd push him on her bed and not let him up for the rest of the day.

He opened his door and climbed out of his pickup before Mike could say anything. She watched him round the hood to her side. Always the gentleman whenever she rode with him, he opened her door and held out his hand to help her.

Instead of releasing her hand once she'd exited the pickup, he continued to hold it as they walked to her back door. Mike's heart began to thud again. Such a simple thing, having his fingers entwined with hers, to make her feel so lightheaded.

Mike unlocked the door and led Jax into her kitchen. She slipped out of her jacket and draped it over one of the chairs in her small breakfast nook, watching Jax as he did the same. Her body still hummed with arousal. Standing near him didn't help.

Deciding she needed to do something ordinary to settle down her hormones, she turned and headed for the coffeemaker. She made it no more than two steps. Jax pushed her against the counter and penned her in with his arms.

"What happened to you in my truck, Michaela?" he asked softly.

Mike stared into his stormy eyes. Since she couldn't possibly tell him the truth, she frantically searched her brain for a convincing lie. "Nothing happened to me."

"Don't bullshit me, Mike. I saw you watching that couple kissing. I saw you rubbing your arms, shifting on the seat." His gaze dipped to her breasts. "I saw your nipples get hard."

He looked back into her eyes. The emotion in his own eyes had changed. Still stormy, they also reflected heat…and desire.

"Did watching that couple make you remember anything?"

"I don't know what you're talking about." Tearing her gaze away from his all-too-knowing one, she pushed on his left arm, trying to get free. "Let me go."

"No way. Not until we have this out."

She might as well be pushing on a steel rod. His arm didn't budge. She kept trying, determined to get away from him before she blurted out something she'd regret saying.

"We were in a white room," Jax said softly.

His words made her freeze. Slowly, she looked into his face. "What?" she said weakly.

"Everything was white—the floor, the walls, the ceiling. No door. No windows. There was a large skylight in the ceiling. The only furniture in the room was a big desk. I think it was mahogany."

Mike's heart began to pound. He was describing her fantasy. That wasn't possible. "How—"

"We stood in the middle of the room," he continued before she could finish her question. "I wasn't sure what to do. I don't think you knew either. You stood still, your arms wrapped across your stomach, frantically looking at every corner of the room."

"Looking for a way out," she whispered.

Jax nodded. "That's what I figured. After a few minutes, we knew there was no way out. We started talking..."

"About our jobs..."

"And our friendship. I teased you about your frizzy hair." He touched her hair, wrapping a thick curl around his finger. "Your hair is beautiful, Michaela, not frizzy."

Her eyelids grew heavy when he ran his hand beneath her hair and began to caress her neck.

"I touched you like this..."

"You kissed me..."

"You kissed me back." He stepped closer to her. "Sunshine came through the skylight. It highlighted your hair, made it shiny. I kept running my hands through it. I couldn't get enough of touching it."

"You asked me if I was afraid."

Jax nodded. "You said you were, that you were afraid I'd be disappointed in you. I told you I could never be disappointed in you."

A thousand butterflies had somehow taken up residence in Mike's stomach and were fighting for their own space. It was *real*. It hadn't been a fantasy or a daydream. She'd actually been with Jax in that room. They'd actually…

"We made love," she said, her voice shaky.

He tightened his hold on her neck. "Yes, we did."

"Well, of *course* you did," a loud male voice said. "That's exactly what I planned."

# Chapter Eight

Jax whirled around, automatically pushing Mike behind him to shelter her with his body. A man stood six feet from them. He had dark hair combed straight back from his full face. A white suit covered his generous frame. A glance down his body showed Jax that even the man's shoes were white.

Something about him looked familiar…

Mike touched Jax's arm as she leaned around him. "Claud?" she asked, disbelief in her voice.

The man grinned. "Hi, Michaela."

"What are you doing here? How did you get in?"

Jax looked at Mike over his shoulder. "You know him?"

"He's one of the janitors at the paper. Don't *you* know him?"

Jax shrugged. "He looks kinda familiar."

"Don't feel badly about not recognizing me, Jaxon. My appearance is a bit different today than it is at the paper. Plus I don't see you as often as I see Michaela."

The fact that he knew both their names didn't make Jax feel any more comfortable. He pulled Mike closer to his body.

"I can tell you're still unsure of me," Claud said. "Let me formally introduce myself." He tapped his heels together and dipped his head. "Claudius Ulysses Pervis Ichabod Derryberry, at your service."

"Claudius Ulysses Per… *C U P I D*? You're *Cupid*?"

This time, Claud gave a courtly bow. "I am."

Jax snorted with laughter. "Yeah, right."

A slight frown touched Claud's lips. "You doubt me?"

"Well, excuse me, *Cupid*," Jax said as he waved a hand in Claud's direction, "but you don't look anything like a cherub who carries a bow and arrow."

"Hogwash. An image created to sell cards on Valentine's Day. I assure you, I am Cupid. And I'm responsible for the two of you being together in that room."

Mike stepped out from behind Jax before he had the chance to stop her. "*You're* responsible? We weren't abducted by aliens?"

Claud smiled tenderly. "You were abducted, Michaela, but not by aliens. I've watched you ever since Jaxon came to work at the paper. I know how much you love him."

Jax whipped his head toward Mike. Her entire face turned pink. "You love me, Michaela?" he asked softly.

She crossed her arms beneath her breasts, but didn't look at him.

"Yes, she loves you," Claud said, "as much as you love her. Since you two weren't in any hurry to further your relationship to where it should be, I decided it was time to…nudge things along a bit."

Jax's mouth dropped open. Sure, he cared about Mike. He cared about her a lot and treasured her friendship. But *love*? "Now, wait a minute—"

"Oh, don't look so shocked, Jaxon. Think about it. She's the first one you go to when you've written an article you're proud of. She's the only woman you've ever been able to share your true feelings with. She's the one you call when you simply need to talk. Wouldn't you call that love?"

Jax looked at Mike. She stood still, watching him with apprehension in her eyes. He gazed at that glorious red hair that he loved to touch, her beautiful green eyes, her cute turned-up nose. He looked at her full lips and remembered how many times he'd wondered how they'd taste.

He thought about what Claud said—about how it was always Mike he talked to first, Mike he turned to when he needed cheering. It was always Mike who listened to him without judgment, without criticism…even times when he probably needed criticism.

He stepped closer and cradled her face in his hands. His heart thudded at the look of adoration in her eyes.

"Yeah," he whispered. "I'd call that love."

He kissed her gently, a bare mingling of breaths. When he ended it, he wrapped his arms around her. He rested his chin on her head and absorbed the feel of her body against his.

*Oh, yeah, definitely love.*

Claud beamed. "I love a happy ending. I knew when you two spent almost seven hours making love, everything would work out just fine." He grinned widely. "Good job, Jaxon."

An unfamiliar warmth seeped into Jax's cheeks. Mike buried her face against his neck. She had to be as embarrassed as he at the thought of Claud knowing everything about their lovemaking.

"Don't be embarrassed," Claud said. "I didn't *watch* you. And sex is a beautiful thing. Especially between two people who love each other." He rocked back and forth on his heels. "Well, my job here is done. And just in time, since I'm meeting Betsy for lunch."

"Betsy?" Jax asked.

"You know her as the Tooth Fairy."

"Of course," Jax said, struggling not to laugh.

"Be happy with each other. No problem is so large that love can't solve it."

With that remark, he disappeared.

Jax hugged Mike before pulling back to see her face. "Was I dreaming, or was there a guy here in a white suit who claimed he's Cupid?"

Mike smiled. "You weren't dreaming. Claud was really here."

"And you're in love with me?"

She slipped her arms around his neck, her fingers burrowing into his hair. "I'm in love with you."

"Ah, Michaela." He ran his hands up and down her spine. "Why did it take me so long to realize I love you?" Lowering his head, he pressed a kiss beneath her ear. "We could've been making love all these months."

Her warm breath caressed his neck as she sighed. "Yes, we could have."

Jax circled her earlobe with his tongue. "So, do you think we need to start making up for lost time?"

"Definitely."

Jax raised his head and grinned at her. "I like the way you think." He slid his hands underneath her sweater so he could touch bare skin. "Shall we start here and work our way through your house?"

Mike shook her head. "I want you in my bed first."

Taking his hand, Mike led Jax toward her bedroom. No man had ever made love to her in her own bed. She'd had sex, but had never *made love*. In her heart, there was a huge difference.

She stopped at the side of her bed. Facing Jax, she grasped the hem of his sweatshirt and pulled it over his head, letting it fall to the floor. To be able to touch him, freely touch him, made her hands tremble.

She didn't think it was possible to *need* this much.

Mike touched his chest. She didn't move her hands at first, but simply enjoyed the warmth of his hair-dusted skin. Soon, the longing for more took over. She slid her fingertips over his chest and down his stomach, stopping at the waistband of his jeans.

"Don't stop now," Jax said huskily.

Looking into his eyes, she laid one hand over his erection and pressed.

Jax hissed in a breath through his teeth. "Ah, babe, that's nice."

Yes, it was, but Mike had to have more. She had to be able to touch all of him.

He must have read her mind for he unfastened his jeans. Mike watched him toe off his shoes, then peel off his jeans, briefs, and socks at the same time. He stood before her nude and very aroused.

Every female part of her yearned for him.

"You're wearing way too many clothes, Michaela." He gathered the hem of her sweater in his hands, but released it before removing the garment. Instead, he sat on the edge of her bed. "I took off your clothes last night. Undress for me now."

A wicked thrill sped through her body. Mike had never undressed before a lover while he watched her every move.

She'd never loved a man the way she loved Jax. It gave her the courage to do as he requested with no hesitation.

Mike pulled her sweater over her head and dropped it on top of Jax's pile of clothing. His gaze dipped to her breasts.

"Pretty bra," he rasped.

Mike ran her hands over the pale blue cups covering her breasts. "I have a weakness for pretty lingerie."

"I thought you might, since you wore a pink bra and matching panties last night." He cleared his throat. "Do your panties match your bra again?"

"Shall I show you?"

"Oh, yeah."

A slow striptease would be fun…next time. Right now, she wanted Jax too much to do anything slow. Staring at that magnificent hard cock, she quickly shed the rest of her clothes. When she was as naked as he, she stepped closer to Jax. Wrapping her arms around his neck, she kissed him hungrily. She felt his hands grip her buttocks as he returned her kiss.

Mike lifted her lips from his. "Lie down," she whispered.

Jax shifted on the bed until he lay full length, his head resting on Mike's pillow. She crawled over his body and straddled his hips. Taking his cock in her hand, she impaled herself with one downward stroke of her pelvis.

Jax released a long moan. "My God, Michaela."

She lifted her hips until his shaft almost slipped free of her body, then impaled herself again. "You don't like this?"

"Hell, yes, I like it! But I thought you'd want some foreplay."

"I've had foreplay all morning. Now I want this."

She established a rhythm with him…a rhythm that soon had both of them covered in sweat and breathing heavily. She wanted it to last as long as possible, but she also wanted desperately to come.

Jax took the choice away from her. Slipping his thumb between her legs, he rubbed her clit in a circular motion. Three circles were all it took. Mike threw back her head and groaned when the orgasm gripped her body.

Jax shuddered beneath her.

Slowly, Mike stretched out on top of him. She folded her arms across his chest and rested her chin on her hands. A contented sigh escaped her lips.

"Happy?" he asked.

"Intensely."

Jax smiled. "Me, too." He ran his hands up and down her back in a slow caress. "You're a wonderful lover, Michaela."

"So are you." She moved one hand from beneath her chin so she could touch his chest. "You realize there will be no more blonde bimbos in your life. Or brunette ones, either."

"The only woman I want in my life is a beautiful redhead with a cute turned-up nose."

"Good answer, Jaxon."

He grinned. "I thought so." His hands wandered down to her buttocks. "Speaking of answers, you owe me one."

"I do?"

"Yeah. I asked you earlier if you sleep naked. You never told me."

Mike allowed a slow smile to turn up the corners of her mouth. "I guess you'll just have to stick around and find out."

*The End*

## About the author

Lynn LaFleur was born and raised in a small town in Texas close to the Dallas/Fort Worth area. Writing has been in her blood since she was eight years old and wrote her first "story" for an English assignment.

Besides writing at every possible moment, Lynn loves reading, sewing, gardening, and learning new things on the computer. (She is determined to master Paint Shop Pro and Photoshop!) After living in various places on the West Coast for 21 years, she is back in Texas, 17 miles from her hometown.

Lynn would love to hear from her readers about her writing, her books, the look of her website...whatever! Comments, praise, and criticism all equally welcome.

Lynn welcomes mail from readers. You can write to her c/o Ellora's Cave Publishing at 1337 Commerce Drive, #13, Stow, OH 44224.

## Also by Lynn LaFleur:

Enchanted Rogues anthology
Happy Birthday, Baby
Holiday Heat anthology
Two Men and a Lady anthology

# Dark-Pilot's Bride

Cricket Starr

# Chapter One

*Nightfall.* With the sun setting to her right, Josia had to twist her head painfully to watch the greenish-red disk sink behind the brown forest edge. Since her hands were tied to the tree limb over her head, there wasn't much else she could do.

One small flash and it was gone. A pang of dismay shook her as the remaining light faded from the sky, making way for the deep purple of evening. Her last sunset, the final time she'd see the sun of the misbegotten world she'd been born on. By tomorrow this time she'd be dead…or gone.

Or worse.

Josia sighed. Her life up to now hadn't been thrilling, but she was sorry to see it end—hence the bindings. The colony elders were taking no chances with the latest "bride" to be handed over in exchange for supplies from the inner colonies. War in another part of the sector had disrupted several expected visits, turning what should have been a short interval into over fifteen years now. Failure of this transfer could mean no further support from outside.

Long ago a bargain had been made with the Dark-pilot League that controlled space traffic in this quadrant. A ship would come every few years with mail from the home planets, plus much-needed medical and technical supplies, items that could only be manufactured off-planet. It would take away the homespun goods the colony produced—hand-carved figures and cloth spun from native materials. Some of Josia's best weaving was piled in the baskets on the edge of the clearing.

In exchange, the League asked for one other item in payment—a human blood donor for the Dark-pilot who controlled the ship, someone to snack on during his long trip through the stars. Josia couldn't resist her shudder—the Dark-pilots were vampires. Since the donors were usually female and the pilots male, the term bride had been coined for the sacrifice, but everyone assumed a darker fate awaited them.

No bride had ever returned and Josia could only assume the worse.

Even so, she remembered the pilot's voice through the colony comm-unit after he'd entered the Demma solar system two weeks ago. Deep, rich and masculine, the sound had made her shiver with need rather than terror as he'd given the final instructions for the handover. He hadn't sounded like a demon at all.

An evening breeze flitted through the clearing she'd been left in, stirring the edges of the open robe she wore. She shivered, only partly from the cold. As soon as they'd secured her hands to the tree, the bastards had untied the skimpy garment, baring her breasts, making her a fitting "sacrifice" to the Dark-pilot coming to claim her.

Never mind that she was far too heavy and old for the seductive garment. Well, maybe not old…after all she was only thirty-two in standard years. But tradition held the Dark-pilot's bride should be an attractive young woman, preferably a virgin.

The latter was the only reason she'd been able to convince the committee to allow her to substitute for

Kissa when her younger sister had drawn the tile with the Dark-pilot emblem. Josia hadn't any other choice. She'd argued with them, pointing out that her beautiful sister was more an asset to the colony than she was. While the cloth Josia wove was considered the best, other weavers existed to replace her, and unlike the other colony women she'd never found a husband. With her parents long dead, no one would miss Josia other than her sister.

The open robe had been designed for someone with a slender figure. It barely fit around her when she'd been allowed to tie it, and now it gaped, revealing every physical fault she had.

*It would have fit Kissa,* Josia thought. But she couldn't let them take her younger sister, not even twenty yet. The tile Kissa had chosen was now tied around her neck like a tag on a piece of meat in a butcher shop.

That's what she was—meat for a monster. Josia shuddered at what the pilot would do when he saw his sorry excuse for a bride. Perhaps he'd be too angry to do more than simply drink all her blood and kill her right away.

A cold comfort that was.

Josia tried to stretch her back against the tree trunk behind her to relieve the strain on her wrists. She longed to be free of her bonds. In fact, she almost wished the demon would show up and put her out of her misery…

A flash of light lit the corner of her eye and Josia heard the steady drone of an approaching spacecraft. A slender needle lowered from the sky and settled onto the grass at the opposite edge of the clearing, far enough away that the collected goods and Josia were safe from the engine's backwash. Moments later, a door in the side opened, revealing a slender male figure.

Josia groaned aloud. She really should be more careful of what she wished for.

* * * * *

Dimitri stepped out of the ship and breathed deeply the fresh air of Deema 7. Through the open doorway over his shoulder came his fussy computer's last instructions.

"Now remember, these folks haven't seen a Dark-pilot in years. No doubt all sorts of strange ideas have sprung up. You represent their first contact with the outside in over a decade." The computer's clipped tones droned on about League protocol and Dimitri had to bite back the urge to tell him where to stuff his advice. This wasn't the first time he'd done one of these landings.

"Oh and one more thing." The computer's voice turned plaintive. "If you don't like the female, try and let her down easy this time. We don't want another incident like the one on Londas 4."

Dimitri winced. "I'll remember, Arthur. But I didn't have much choice."

Londas 4 had been a mistake, but mostly the fault of the people there, not his. Lovely to look at, if a bit too slender to arouse him, the Londas woman had taken to the ritual feeding with exceptional good grace until he'd explained what her role in the Dark-pilot world would be. After failing to seduce him, she'd been shocked to discover all he wanted was her blood…and he hadn't even wanted that once he'd read her mind.

Somehow she'd gotten the idea that his bite would cause her to become a vampire and she'd planned a whole campaign of revenge on the members of her colony once she'd become like him. Just what the Dark-pilot League needed, a lunatic offering.

He'd returned her kicking and screaming to her people, and had stuck to artiheme for the trip to Demma. Dimitri shuddered. The manufactured blood was supposed to be just as healthy as the real thing, but he was tired of its taste.

Truth be told, he was tired of more than that. Being a captain in the Dark-pilot League allowed him to see the universe, but he spent most of the time in space alone. Sure, he had Arthur for company, but he needed more than the occasional game of astrochess to keep him satisfied. He needed someone to touch, to hug. Someone to kiss and cuddle with in the long dark of space.

Someone with hot, sweet blood and a tight pussy…

Dimitri's cock jumped and he nearly groaned aloud. Good company Arthur might be, but a man couldn't fuck a computer.

With the war it had been close to twenty years since his last woman! Even if the female the Deemans promised turned out to be a nasty-minded bitch who was ugly as sin and skinny as a rail, he intended to take her with him. She'd provide him with blood and companionship until he could leave her on the next planet in his route. Sex too, if he could put up with being that close to her. If necessary he'd keep his eyes closed and his mind shuttered.

The breeze in the clearing picked up and wafted past him, giving him a nose full of fresh vegetation and other exotic scents. He breathed deeply, then again as one smell caught his attention.

*Woman.* A woman's scent was in the air, unique, warm, rich, and inviting. Eyes glowing, Dimitri's stomach growled while his cock hardened under his uniform pants. There was a promise in that smell, and he couldn't wait to test it.

He tried for nonchalance. "I'll be gentle with her, Arthur. You get the colony's goods ready for unloading."

The computer's chuckle said he'd failed to conceal his eagerness, but he ignored it as he moved down the narrow trail to where his senses told him the woman waited.

Dimitri stopped in shock when he got close enough to see her. *They'd tied her to a tree!* In horror he eyed the barely clad woman's arms stretched above her, leaving her helpless against anything that could have come out of the woods to attack her.

*Helpless against him, too.* The insidious whispering of his subconscious did not improve his mood, especially as his cock got even harder at the suggestion. He tapped into his outrage. It wasn't right that her elders had bound her.

*Bound for him,* came the whisper again.

Yeah, well, that didn't mean he was going to play their game. Dimitri strode forward, intending to free her. They'd no doubt tied her up well before nightfall so she probably was in real pain.

Her head went up as he approached and again he stopped in his tracks. Her face turned toward him, round like the moon, with pale smooth skin that looked like porcelain. His fingers curled as he stared at her flesh, already anticipating stroking that loveliness. It would feel like satin.

Dark hair fell in silken waves down the sides of her face, across her shoulders and down to almost cover her full, heavy breasts. Dimitri almost stopped breathing. Full, heavy, *bare* breasts. With her robe untied and open, only a scrap of lace across her woman's mound provided modesty from his eyes. The white robe framed her full body, soft belly and rounded hips. Her tits were enormous. A man could get lost in the woman's cleavage. In the dim light he could make out dark areolas and pointed nipples tipping them. There would be veins on those breasts, rich veins.

Dimitri's mouth grew dry as he stared at the heaving orbs, imagining how tender their flesh would be, how rich the blood from them would taste. Entranced, he stepped closer to her.

Her eyes widened at his approach and a voice sounded in his head. *What a beautiful man. I've never seen him before. Did he come with the demon?*

All this woman, and mental powers too? Attention caught, Dimitri gazed into her eyes. Dark eyes, frightened, but also curious. Curious about him. She didn't believe him to be the "demon" she waited for.

She'd chosen to bespeak him—he would answer in kind. He tried a smile, careful to hide his fangs. *You think me beautiful? I was just thinking the same about you.*

*You can hear my thoughts?* Excitement tinged her mental voice. *No one else can, only my sister sometimes. But beautiful?* her mental voice admonished. *I'm not beautiful.*

*But you are most beautiful.* He stepped closer. *Why did they tie you here?*

She shook her wrists, indicating the rope above her. *I'm the Dark-pilot's bride. I volunteered but they thought I'd change my mind.*

A volunteer. Dimitri felt a pang of misgiving. Perhaps this voluptuous beauty was like the last woman, seeking power from his bite. *Why would you choose to give yourself to a demon?*

*It was me or my sister. She's so young.*

That was better. She thought she was saving her sister a terrible fate. Hmm, which meant she thought being a Dark-pilot "bride" a terrible fate. Dimitri didn't much care for that although he did like the thought of her as his bride. His cock liked the idea even more, jerking greedily as it anticipated its wedding night.

Their wedding night, he told it firmly, his and hers as well. He would have her blood and sex, but not until there was agreement to both from the woman.

His subconscious joined the argument. *But she is agreeable...she waits for you and can't fight you.*

*Enough!* He argued with himself. *I won't take her when she's helpless like this!*

The woman's mental voice intruded on his internal debate. *Could you do me a favor?*

*For you, anything. What do you want?*

She shook her bound hands. *You should leave here before the Dark-pilot comes, but could you untie me first? I don't want him to see me like this—he'll be so angry anyway.*

*Why would he be angry? There is something very appealing about you tied like that.*

*There is nothing appealing about a fat sow tied to a tree!*

He couldn't help it, she looked so appetizing and so exasperated…he laughed, revealing the fangs he'd carefully kept hidden. Her eyes widened in shock.

"You're the Dark-pilot!"

It was the first time he'd heard her voice and he liked it immediately. Rich and sweet, like the rest of her. Melodic. She could sing with him on their journey.

He swept her a courtly bow. "Guilty, I'm afraid."

The red in her cheeks heightened. "Do you always tease your dinner this way?"

"Do I look like someone who teases?"

"No…" He read confusion from her at that admission. "You look hungry."

Dimitri stepped into touching distance, all thoughts of releasing her gone. His gaze raked her up and down, and the blush on her cheeks spread to the rest of her face and down to her neck. She had a long neck, a perfect neck. Not a blemish to it, or to any other portion of her skin. He reached to stroke her face, run his hand along the edge of her chin, then down her neck to her shoulder. Held firmly by her wrists, the woman couldn't move away and he found her helplessness more interesting all the time.

She had perfect skin. It felt like silk under his fingers and he longed to taste it. A red haze filled the corners of his eyes as a long-denied blood lust claimed him. It had been too long since he'd fed from a living being. He would have to be careful not to hurt her.

The woman raised her eyes to his. Defiance was in her pose, and it made him smile. "What do you want?"

She had a lovely voice and he could listen to it all night—except that he had other things on his mind.

"You were right, I am hungry," he told her. "Hungry for you."

# Chapter Two

Fear blossomed in her eyes and he quickly spoke in his mental voice. *You will feel no hurt. I will touch your mind and take the pain and fear away.*

She still trembled as he moved closer and slid his hands across her back, tilting her toward him. In spite of his reassurances he could feel her terror grow as he sent a mental caress to soothe and chase her fears away. Some of her tension eased even as he pulled back her hair and tenderly licked the skin over the vein in her neck.

She was delicious. The flavor of her skin almost undid him and it took all his control to be gentle, to soothe the skin with his tongue so that the pinpricks of his teeth wouldn't hurt. As their mind link deepened he could read as her arousal built, his slow licks sending sensual shockwaves through her body. A delicious confusion rose in her over her excitement. Whatever else she was, she wasn't very experienced.

She closed her eyes and leaned away from him, unconsciously baring her neck even more, ready for him. He bit down once, hard, piercing the vein, and even through the haze in her mind he felt her wince at the momentary pain. But then he flooded her mind with what he was experiencing, the glorious taste of her blood, the sweet sensation of drawing it from her neck. He swallowed and she moaned in the way he would've if his mouth hadn't been otherwise occupied.

Dimitri drew her closer into his arms, pressing against her full, soft body. All he'd intended was to take her blood, but his cock turned rock-hard, eager for more. His hands sought her breasts, reveling in their glorious fullness. As he kneaded them, she wriggled against him, her body experiencing the lust he now sent through their link.

He let one hand leave her breast to explore the thin fabric covering the opening to her sex. He found her tender clit and massaged it through her undergarment, feeling her gasp. His fingers slipped into the soft folds and found the dampness there. He didn't think further…he wanted her, she wanted him…what more was needed? He had to have her, take her body as well as her blood. Twenty years was a long time for anyone, even a Dark-pilot, to be celibate.

It only took a single jerk to rip the crotch from her underpants. Another tug opened the fly of his pants, freeing his cock to spring out between them. Through the link, he felt some faintness in her from the blood he'd taken, so he stopped feeding, sealing the holes in her neck. Sealing but not removing them…not now, not yet. Maybe not ever.

Dimitri grasped her buttocks and lifted her. His strength made it easy to push her against the tree behind her, raising her legs to open her pussy to him.

She caught his intention just before his cock speared home, her eyes widening in her beautiful moon-shaped face. "But I'm…"

He didn't wait for the rest, just drove deep inside her, her voice crying at his invasion. The maidenhead he tore through surprised him…she wasn't that young…but it was too late now. He sent soothing images into her mind, calming her and taking the pain of his first assault away. Her core's near-painful grip on him eased somewhat as her body grew used to, then began to appreciate, his presence within her.

Her pussy became a warm tightness, enveloping his cock, inviting his stroke. He pulled out and she cried out in protest at his leaving, then happily as he filled her once more. Soon all she was making were happy cries as he took her against the tree.

Her full breasts thrust up at him, and again he sank his fangs into her flesh, catching the vein and sucking her blood from the tiny holes. She shuddered against him, climaxing as much from his feeding as the presence of his cock in her. The heat of her blood set fire to the inside of his mouth.

Could he ever get enough of this woman? Possibly not—could she be the one? The questions formed in his mind, then passed, too fast for him to do more than acknowledge them. They were old questions, with him from the time he was a young Dark-pilot, and he first realized how alone his new world would be.

Darkmate. Even as he took her blood and her body, Dimitri named her that. The only woman he would ever need, his lover for all time, the end of a search he hadn't even realized he was on.

His new mate threw back her head and cried out as she climaxed again, her pussy pulsing around him, milking his cock. Her orgasm fed his, and he took one last swallow before taking his own pleasure. Releasing her breast, he breathed heavily, watching the astonishment in her eyes as he jerked once, twice, then cried out as he finished, his cum pumping into her.

Spent, Dimitri leaned heavily against her softness, still supporting her against the tree. Slowly he released her to stand on shaky legs. She was breathing heavily, her heart racing, but not so much as to alarm him. He'd had other women faint on him after lovemaking…this one didn't seem in any danger of that.

He smiled at her strength. "That was pretty astonishing."

Glassy-eyed, she nodded her agreement then indicated the bonds holding her hands. "Now that…that's done, would you mind untying me?"

Laughing, Dimitri pulled on the rope, breaking it easily. He helped as she struggled to free her hands, clucking softly over the damage to the soft skin around her wrists. "Those look bad…let me help—"

The sharp blow into his nose took him by surprise, but he managed to catch her second fist before it landed. "What are you hitting me for? I'm not the one who tied you up."

Fury radiated off her. "You took full advantage of it, though. How dare you do that?"

Dimitri rubbed his injured nose. "Advantage of you how, when? When I brought you to orgasm? Twice? Was that taking advantage of you?"

She tore the rest of the rope from her arms and threw it onto the ground. "You know what I mean. I couldn't have stopped you…"

"You could have at any time. Just said 'stop'. 'Don't'. Anything like that. I heard no protest."

"You weren't listening for one, either."

"I heard none because there wasn't any. Really, is that any way to treat your husband?"

She startled. "You aren't my husband."

Ordinarily Dimitri only gave token acknowledgement to local customs, but he wanted to keep this woman. If claiming her as his wife would do that, so be it. "But sweetness, I am. You were left here for me…you agreed to be my bride. My cock is still stained with your maiden's blood, something you did not object to, I might add."

An uncomfortable silence met his words. "I meant to. I was…distracted."

His grin broadened. "I meant to untie you, too, before feeding. We share the same distraction, I think. Perhaps we should introduce ourselves. I am Dimitri Devana, captain of the *Moonrise*, representative of the Dark-pilot League. I have other titles, but for now your husband is what I'll claim."

"You aren't my husband…" she broke off as he shook his head in amusement.

"All right, your bridegroom then. I want your name, sweetness."

"Josia Ashen."

"A lovely name for a lovely lady." He grabbed her hand, intending to kiss it, then saw again the raw bloody wounds on her wrist. Clucking softly, he applied his tongue to the open scrapes, using his healing saliva to remove them, and ease the pain. The taste of her blood assailed his senses, stirring his cock, and he had to fight the urge to couple with her again. It was too soon for that, he should wait for at least an hour before making love with her. After all, her blood on his shaft wasn't even dry yet. She was probably very sore…

*Oh, but he could fix that, couldn't he.* A small smile teased around his mouth with that wicked thought as he turned his attention to her other wrist.

# Chapter Three

Josia watched the Dark-pilot remove the signs of her struggle with the ropes from her wrists, the pain easing away immediately. "How do you do that?"

He paused to smile at her, his teeth white in the darkness. He had a great smile, she realized, warm and inviting. He was clearly a man with a sense of humor, a rarity in her world. It was hard not to smile back at him. But he wasn't a man—he was a vampire. He'd taken her blood and her body, but now he was so solicitous. It was also hard to keep her composure, especially after he'd claimed her the way he had. Of all the things she'd expected from her Dark-pilot, being ravished was the least likely. She'd expected him to turn away in disgust when he'd seen her, not exhibit lust.

On the other hand, she mused, maybe he'd just been in space a really long time.

"There is a healing agent in my saliva," he said. "It's good for sealing wounds and removing marks. It comes in handy when I'm feeding."

"You can take pain away, too. By touching your victim's mind?"

Dimitri flinched. "Victim is a little harsh. I've rarely taken blood from anyone who wasn't willing. I take pain away and provide a pleasant experience whenever I can." He held her hand up to examine the healed wrist. "That's finished. It doesn't hurt anymore, does it?"

She shook her head. He dropped her hand then opened her robe to touch the marks he'd left on her breast, narrow pinpoints that still dripped blood.

Josia intercepted his hand and pulled it away. "You can leave those alone."

His grin was infuriating. "Oh, no. I always clean up after myself. I can't let you run around leaking like that."

"They will heal…"

She didn't finish because he pushed her against the tree, grabbing her hands with his as she struggled fruitlessly against him. While he wasn't a big man, he was stronger than anyone she'd ever known. She remembered how he'd lifted her so effortlessly as he took her virginity against that same tree and she blushed furiously.

Her blush grew worse as he leaned down to tenderly run his tongue along the narrow driblets of blood, cleansing her flesh with obvious relish, then sealing and removing the marks completely. When he was done, there was no sign of his bite or any pain.

He dropped his hold on her and stepped back, exuding self-satisfaction. She wanted to slap the smug smile off his face, but as soon as she thought it, he frowned.

"Don't hit me again, Josia. I don't like it."

Flushed, she dropped her hands and tied the robe tight around her. "I don't like being touched without permission, either."

Dimitri folded his arms and stared at her. "You are mine to touch, my bride. Even so, I wasn't trying to do more than make you feel better. I didn't want to leave scars on your breast."

She fingered the sealed marks on her neck. "What about these, aren't you going to remove them?"

In the darkness his pale green eyes seemed to glow, a sensual radiance she felt right down to her still aching pussy. "No, not yet. Not unless I have to." Stepping back he turned away, leaving her wishing he still handled her.

He wandered over to inspect the goods piled up in the clearing. "Nice," he said, picking up a length of woven fabric. In the darkness the colors were muted, but the fabric shimmered enticingly. "Very nice indeed. This alone would pay for my trip."

Pleased, Josia smiled at him. "I wove that."

His eyebrows arched in surprise. "You made this? You're very talented. I'm surprised they would let you go."

Josia shrugged, hiding the old hurt. "My sister is nearly as good as I am, and she's pretty, too. Desirable, not like me."

Dimitri dropped the fabric and crossed the clearing in a heartbeat. Seizing her arms he pulled her close. "Not like you?" he hissed, eyes blazing. "Hear this, my bride, you are a very desirable woman as I can easily prove anytime you wish."

He bent his head to hers, capturing her lips in a kiss, the first she could remember in years. It was a kiss of possession, intense and passionate, and she melted under his assault. Her mouth opened and he swept inside, his tongue taking residence. His taste was heady, male, with a hint of copper, the taste of her blood, she realized. It went on for long moments and when she broke way from him her breath was ragged.

"Why don't you believe me when I say I desire you?"

She turned from his intense stare. "Because I'm a fat old maid, not the bride you deserve."

His grip grew tighter and he shook her, once. "To someone over five hundred years in age, you are scarcely old, and your maidenhood has been successfully dealt with. As for the rest, I like a woman who doesn't fall over in a stiff wind. There is so much of you to hold onto, sweetness."

He released her so unexpectedly that she did almost fall, catching herself at the last moment. His fingers captured her chin and forced her face up to meet his gaze.

"I'm not the least bit insulted by my gift from your people, Josia. You are lovely to look at, and fun to talk to." He grinned at her. "You're even more fun to make love with. I look forward to our long trip together."

"Long trip?"

"To the next star system. About four years, I think."

Her heart pounded. "I'm going with you?"

"Of course. You're my bride, remember?"

This beautiful passionate man really wanted her company? "But I thought it was only for a couple of days. In fact, I thought..."

He released her face, a look of hurt on his. "I can see your thoughts, Josia. You thought I was going to kill you."

All she could do was mutely nod.

His sigh was so deep it could have been building for the five hundred years he claimed. When he spoke his voice was so quiet she had to strain to hear his words.

"That's not what Dark-pilots do, Josia. We need blood to survive and stay healthy but we don't kill. We aren't that different from anyone else. We have reflections and souls. I've been alone a very long time, long enough to consider walking in the sun to end that loneliness. It was one reason I chose League service, to keep me from doing just that. Long periods in space where solar light is weak help to cure the depression all Dark-pilots face and I've always hoped to find someone I could bind with."

He placed two fingers over the marks on her neck, the ones he hadn't removed. "I want to leave these marks on you, Josia, because I want you to be my darkmate."

"What's a darkmate?"

"A companion who is both blood and body to a Dark-pilot, who supplies all his or her needs. Someone to feed from, someone to live with. Someone to love, forever."

She gave a short laugh. "Forever must mean something different to you. Humans grow old and die."

His smile was tender. "Not darkmates. Aging is slowed down, the result of the mark. It holds Dark-pilot DNA. You will age slower, ten to a hundred times slower, and be healthier than you've ever been. You'll produce more blood, enough that I can take some every day without draining you. Your blood will help heal me, too."

She couldn't believe what she was hearing. "If I come with you, I'll live longer, be healthier, and produce more blood? Are there any downsides to this?"

"A couple..." He hesitated. "I can't give you children and would not be happy to see you seek another man so you could have them. Besides, what you call your monthly flow would most likely cease."

"No problem." She'd never thought to have children anyway and she couldn't imagine missing her period. "What's the other problem?"

"Well..." Now he really looked reluctant.

It must be something very bad. Josia grabbed his arm. "Please tell me, Dimitri. What else is wrong?"

She should have known from the mischievous twinkle in his eye. He grabbed her waist and swung her high into the air as if she weighed little more than a doll. She yelped at the sudden change in altitude. Her robe parted, leaving her crotch exposed in front of his face.

Dimitri grinned impudently at her. "The other problem is that you will have to put up with me making love to you several times a day!" With that he swung her legs across his shoulders and buried his head between her thighs.

Josia groaned under his tender assault. At first he seemed to be concentrating on cleaning the semen and blood from her thighs, but as soon as that was done, he found the tiny nub of her clit and began to suck it mercilessly. From that tiny spot sensation sped outwards, until she could feel the tingles from his mouth in her fingertips and the ends of her toes. Each lick of his tongue caused another frisson to run through her until she was near senseless. Balanced on his shoulders, Josia feared she would fall, but a tree branch beckoned two inches over her head, so she grabbed it for stability.

He left off to smile up at her. "Hold on if it makes you feel better, but know that I'd never let you fall. I'd rather walk into the sun than see you hurt, my Josia."

Then he redoubled his efforts and she clung to the branch anyway, if only to have one solid thing to cling to. In moments she shuddered as wave after wave of delight ran through her. She threw back her head and screamed her joy.

Aftershocks from her climax made her limbs weak when he slid her off his shoulders and down his body until she stood shakily on the ground. His erection felt hard and stiff inside his pants, a hard rod waiting to impale her. Supporting her, he rubbed it against her.

He was whispering in her ear. "Let me make love to you, Josia. Say you want me to."

She nodded, but he growled in response. "I want the words, Josia. Tell me you want me."

"I want you," she said, her voice nearly as shaky as her legs. "I want you to make love to me."

He lifted her face to stare into her eyes. "Very well, come with me." He began to pull her along the path.

Confused, Josia followed. "Why? Where are we going?"

He cast a happy grin over his shoulder. "To my ship, sweetness. To my cabin where there is a bed so we may more comfortably enjoy this coupling. I would not take you on the cold hard ground and once against a tree is enough. You are new to love and I would show you properly how it should be."

Hard to argue with that logic, not to mention the firm grip he had. Josia followed.

# Chapter Four

The ship was taller than she'd expected, at least ten times the height of the largest building on Deema 7. Not that the largest building the colony boasted could be considered very large. But even so, Dimitri's ship topped the highest tree by at least fifty meters. The base was wide, with large fins that must stabilize it when flying through atmosphere. Everything about it was sleek and elegant.

"It's beautiful," Josia said.

Dimitri stared at it with obvious pride. "The *Moonrise* has been my home for a long time. I'm glad you like it."

When they reached the narrow opening that was the hatch to the ship, Dimitri swept Josia up in his arms. Again she was struck by how strong he was as he carried her into the ship.

"An old Earth custom. To carry the bride across the threshold."

A custom they had here as well, but not one she'd ever expected to be part of. Josia stared into his face, wondering at this handsome stranger who had claimed her.

He smiled, revealing the narrow fangs. Somehow this time they didn't frighten her. She barely felt them when he bent his head to claim her lips in another of his soul-stealing kisses and a pink haze of passion stole across her vision.

In her mind she heard his mental voice. *Mine, mine.* He started down the hall, but came to a sudden halt near an open doorway. After a moment's hesitation, he ducked through.

Josia glanced around at the crowded space. "This is your cabin?"

"This is the cargo bay." He headed for a soft-looking pile in the corner. He laid her gently on top and Josia found the pile was some sort of heavy hand-woven carpets. Immediately he tore off his clothes and lay on top of her. "I want to make love to you too much to wait."

The excuse sounded feeble but he followed it up with kisses so drugging that Josia didn't have the mental capacity to complain. Instead she gave in to his insistent hands and mouth and moaned as he latched onto her nipples with his lips, sucking and licking and giving her little nips with his fangs. Maybe he drew blood, but if he did he licked up the evidence too quickly for her to notice.

Moments later he rose over her, spreading her thighs to open her for his cock's possession of her pussy. He surged forward, joining them, and again Josia experienced that intimate connection with a man. Even more this time as his mind joined with hers, his thoughts sliding around hers until she wasn't quite sure who was thinking what.

*Bless the fucking stars you feel so good, so good…*

Was that her thought, or his? Probably his, but she shared the sentiment. Josia opened herself wider to him, both her mind and body. Dimitri responded by pushing harder, deeper, and faster, until Josia was sure she was going to scream.

*I need your sweetness.* She felt his fangs sink painlessly into her neck and then there was a scream cutting through her sensual haze, a scream that came from her throat. Josia came hard, just as Dimitri stopped his feeding, grunted and his mind seemed to explode within hers. Thoughts, images, and fragments of sensations from his hundreds of years filled her mind, and she was left reeling in the aftermath.

When she returned to some semblance of herself, the first thing she saw was Dimitri's very male smile of satisfaction. "Now that was pretty spectacular," he said.

She was about to agree when another voice broke in. "Spectacular indeed. Are you through making a mess of the Goeron rugs?" The acerbic voice shattered her remaining sensual haze, bringing her back to the present with a jerk. Someone else lived on the Dark-pilot's ship? *What would they think of her?*

Dimitri's low chuckle told her he'd heard her unvoiced concern. *Arthur is not someone to judge others…outside of me,* he finished wryly. *For some reason he's very fond of finding fault with me.* "The rugs are fine, Arthur. We were careful."

The reply was a disembodied snort. "Obviously you've found a woman to suit you for once. Are you going to introduce me, Dimitri, or have you lost your manners as well as your heart?"

*Now you know why we didn't go directly to the cabin.* With a sigh, Dimitri rose and helped Josia close her robe, only afterwards dressing himself. He led her to what must be the ship's control room and she swung around, trying vainly to locate the source of the voice amongst the blinking panels of lights.

"Of course I'm going to introduce you. Arthur, this is Josia, the lady awarded me as my bride."

He waved a hand around the inside of the room. "Josia, this is Arthur…my ship."

"Your ship?"

"Well," he amended. "Not the entire ship, I suppose. Arthur is the computer that runs the ship."

A computer? They had computers on Deema but none that could talk. Amazed, Josia stepped further into the room. "Will it talk to me?"

"Sweetness, once you get him started, you'll have trouble getting him to shut up."

"Now that's hardly a polite thing to say," the computer interjected.

Dimitri drew Josia to where a large chair sat before one of the blinking panels, pulling her into his lap as he collapsed into it. "I apologize, Arthur. You only speak when you have something to say—which is pretty much all the time. But now you have someone new to nag…that is, converse with. Say hello to Josia, Arthur."

"Hello, Josia," the ship said primly. "I'm glad to make your acquaintance."

"I'm glad to meet you, too." She glanced around, trying to ignore how Dimitri's hand was massaging her breast through her thin robe. "But I don't know where to look when I'm speaking to you."

"Ah, perhaps a visual aid would be helpful." In the corner a hologram leapt to life, the figure that of a tall, spare, moderately balding man with a thin nose, thinner lips, and dark, knowing eyes. He was dressed in an unusual costume—black pants with a blacker stripe down the sides and a matching coat much longer in back than the front, worn over an immaculate white shirt topped by a narrow black tie tied in a bow. After arching one thin eyebrow at Dimitri, he turned his piercing gaze on her and a smile curved his lips as he bowed. "I am Arthur, dear lady and I'm delighted you've decided to join us."

"Arthur? That's an unusual name."

Dimitri snickered. "I named him after one of my favorite twentieth-century films, sweetness. You know, a two-dimensional vid entertainment. He reminds me of the butler in the movie."

The hologram rolled his eyes. "It has been of no use reminding him that Arthur was the main character and not the name of the butler."

Unperturbed, Dimitri nibbled the back of her neck and she felt the tips of his fangs scratch lightly at her skin. "It's a great name, though. He looks like an Arthur, don't you agree, Josia? Well, you will eventually. Arthur can be a bit intimidating at first, but you'll get used to him. Soon you'll be following his orders just like I do."

A snort of disgust came from the computer. "*You* follow *my* orders? That will be the day. Pray, don't listen to him, dear lady. My only concern will be to make your stay as enjoyable as possible."

Dimitri found her nipple under her robe and tweaked it gently. "Her stay will be permanent, Arthur, and I'll make certain she finds it enjoyable."

Josia could not do this with anyone looking on, even someone as inhuman as a computer. Besides, there was something about the way Arthur stared at her that made her think he was something other than a mere program. She caught Dimitri's wayward hand and pulled it away from the breast he was fondling, much as she enjoyed what it was doing. "This is not the time, Dimitri."

He looked at her in dismay. "Why ever not?"

Before she could answer, Josia's stomach growled and she could have melted in embarrassment. While a grand "send-off" feast had been given her that afternoon, fear of her impending doom had left her unable to eat a bite and it had been a long time since her nervous breakfast that morning. She'd been too frightened of her future to eat. It was a testament to how comfortable she was with Dimitri that her appetite had returned.

Arthur's holographic eyebrows flew up. "I believe our guest is hungry, Dimitri! Why don't you take her to the lounge and I'll whip something together." With a look of immense satisfaction, he rubbed his virtual hands together and disappeared from view.

Dimitri chuckled. "Oh, now you have made him happy. He fancies himself a gourmet chef, but with only me to prepare food for he's had no one to practice on."

Lifting her in his arms, he stood up and started out the door. Josia put one hand on his face. "Please put me down, Dimitri. I must be getting heavy."

He stared at her with a perplexed expression. "You aren't at all heavy to me, sweetness. To me you weigh nothing and I enjoy holding you."

"Yes, but..." her voice trailed off as he squeezed her ass gently.

"Yes, your butt is really nice, too." He turned her face-forward against the inner corridor wall and rubbed his cock against the cleft in her ass. "I could really enjoy taking you here..." he leaned forward to whisper in her ear. "I don't suppose anyone has ever fucked you in the ass before?"

Not likely given that she'd been a virgin up to an hour ago. Even so, she got hot just thinking about it. Being with Dimitri was going to give her any number of interesting experiences, she could tell.

Down the corridor came the AI's disembodied voice, "If you please, Dimitri, could you bring the young woman here before she wastes away before our eyes. She'll need every bit of strength she can get to keep up with you."

Dimitri chuckled ruefully in her ear and leaned back, releasing her. "Arthur is right on that one. Let's see what he's cooked up for you."

Josia wasn't sure if what she was eating was gourmet, but it was certainly tasty, and she had a second helping under Arthur's reappeared holographic approval. Dimitri helped himself to a glass of something thick and oddly crimson in color.

She blanched. "It looks like blood."

With a sigh Dimitri swirled it around in his glass. "Not really. Doesn't really taste like it either, but it has the ability to keep a Dark-pilot alive. It's called Artiheme—an artificial blood product." He took another sip and grimaced. "You can live off it but many of my kind would rather die instead."

"If you don't like it, why are you drinking it?"

"Because my sweet, as delicious as your blood is, I can't really take as much of it as I need at the moment." He finished off the glass. "This is necessary for now."

"Will it be necessary later?"

He smiled and touched the small wounds on the side of her neck. "Not most of the time. Having you here will be a delight."

Arthur cleared his virtual throat. "Dimitri, this might be a good time to finish with the cargo."

Reluctantly Dimitri nodded. "If I do it now," he told her regretfully, "We'll be able to spend the rest of the night making love."

Josia watched him go, all at once fearful to have him out of her sight.

"Not to worry, Dimitri, I'll take good care of her," Arthur called after him before returning his attention to her. "Perhaps after you finish dinner you would like to bathe and dress in something more comfortable?"

A bath sounded heavenly and anything would be better than the too-small robe she still wore. "Would you have anything in my size?"

The image wavered a little and Josia could almost swear the AI was laughing. "Oh I'm sure I can come up with something." He pursed his lips as if deep in thought. "Perhaps a gown in an emerald green? And a silken fabric, I think, something clingy." He snapped his fingers. "Yes, I know just the thing."

Arthur disappeared in a burst of static and Josia dug into her delicious meal with renewed interest. Being a Dark-pilot bride was getting better all the time!

## Chapter Five

Josia lay back into the deep warm water and let the heat soothe her tired and aching body. She'd been surprised to see how big the tub was—big enough to easily accommodate two people. For a moment Josia thought about sharing the tub with Dimitri. Making love in the water, what fun that would be!

Even without him she enjoyed it. She was still a little tender from where Dimitri had taken her virginity. He'd shown her so much care afterward, particularly when he'd held her over his head and used his mouth on her. He'd promised the next time they made love would be in a bed…she was looking forward to it.

In fact, in spite of her soreness, her body reacted to the thought of his firm hard cock exploring her intimate spaces. She wondered what that long, firm organ of his tasted like…probably wonderful, if the taste of his lips was any indication.

Arthur's clipped tones interrupted her reverie. She'd told him she was growing used to his disembodied voice, so he didn't bother to materialize in the bathroom. It gave her a feeling of privacy to not have him physically here, even though being built into the ship, he was here, sort of… It was confusing when she thought about it, so she tried not to.

"Would Lady Josia like to try the tub's jets? They are excellent for relaxing."

"Sure, Arthur." Immediately, gently pulsating jets of warm water hit her back and front simultaneously. They felt heavenly on her aches, particularly her back, strained by being left tied up much of the afternoon, plus being held against a tree when Dimitri had taken her for the first time.

Not that she was complaining. But the jets really felt good.

*Particularly that one.* There was one jet on the floor of the tub that was positioned right between her legs. Josia slid forward enough to let the jet hit her sensitive clit. *Oh that felt good!* She let out a little moan.

Over the sounds of the tub's jets she could have sworn she heard Arthur chuckling. Immediately the jet between her legs became more animated, hitting her in pulsating waves that she found even more interesting.

The truth hit her immediately. *Stars above, Arthur was controlling the jets!* Self-conscious that the ship's computer knew just what she was up to, and even worse, was helping things along, Josia tried to slide back from the seductive jet in the middle of the tub, only to have another one fire up, directly aimed at her anus. The combination of the two nearly drove her out of the tub.

"Is something amiss, my lady?" The AI's solicitous tone belied his earlier chuckle.

"Are you controlling the jets in the tub?"

"Of course." Immediately they stopped and the water around her grew still. "Did you want them to do something else? They have many functions. Just tell me what you want and I'll be pleased to accommodate you." His enthusiasm took her by surprise.

"The jets…have many functions?"

"Certainly," Arthur continued in his clipped tones. "They are good for easing aching muscles, for relaxing tired bodies, and for stimulating the sex organs. They are particularly good for that I've been told. Not having sex organs, I have to take Dimitri's word on it."

"*Dimitri* uses the tub jets that way?" She couldn't believe the Dark-pilot sought pleasure at the hands…well, through the programming of a computer.

"Well after all, my lady, he *has* been in space a very long time. That can be very hard on anyone, even a Dark-pilot. He has to find some release."

Josia considered that. Of course Arthur was right. Why shouldn't Dimitri program special jets into his bathtub?

"You don't think he'd mind if I do the same thing?"

"My dear, Dimitri would never deny you any pleasure. He'd be more concerned if you denied yourself."

Put that way there didn't seem to be any harm in it. "Then turn them back on, Arthur, particularly the ones in the bottom.

"As you wish." The AI's voice sounded smug, but Josia didn't care as the jets resumed and waves of warm stimulating water hit her sensitive spots, sending wave after wave of sensation through her. She leaned back and let out a heartfelt groan as the water did its work.

"That feels so good, Arthur."

"Of course, Lady Josia. It's supposed to."

*****

Five exceedingly pleasant orgasms later, Josia tried on the new gown Arthur had found for her, emerald green as he'd promised and made of the silkiest fabric she'd ever felt against her skin. It fit her lovingly and as she turned in front of the reflective surface Arthur had turned the wall into, she was pleased with her appearance.

She looked…*beautiful*! Well, maybe not quite that, but she was at least pretty, and that was far better than she'd ever looked before. In addition, she felt different. She felt pretty, and that was pretty terrific.

*Dimitri thought she was beautiful.*

Warming at just the thought of him, Josia stepped back from the mirror and the wall returned to plain metal. She wondered how long it would be until Dimitri returned to her. She wanted to show him her new outfit, and tell him how wonderful she felt.

She also wanted to try making love to him in that bed he'd promised her. Her experiences in the tub had only whetted her appetite for more loving. Enough water sports. She wanted a man. Or a Dark-pilot with a hard-on.

She sank onto a comfortably soft cushion in the lounge. "Arthur, how soon until Dimitri returns?"

"Very soon I would think." The AI didn't sound concerned, but there was a hesitancy to his speech. "He should have been finished by now."

"Maybe some of the goods require special handling and he needs help."

"Perhaps you are right. I'll send a spy probe out to look for him. In the meantime, we should be preparing for your departure with us. Is there anything you might want to bring with you?"

She really was going to leave her home planet, and never see her sister again. Josia ignored the pang that thought caused. "Most of my personal items were with the trade goods. There was a small case with them."

"Hmm. I think I see it. A small blue one? I'll move it to the main cabin."

"Thank you, Arthur. I was thinking, since we will have so much time in space, I might want to bring my loom with me. And some thread to weave with."

"A capital idea." The AI sounded honestly enthusiastic. "I took a peek at some of the fabric Dimitri told me was your handiwork and I must say I was impressed."

The AI's praise made her beam with pride. "Thank you, Arthur!"

"Not at all, Lady Josia. Now, you'll want to say your goodbyes tomorrow evening before we take off. Perhaps we could have your family onto the ship and some friends for a going away party. How many should I prepare refreshments for?"

"There is only my sister. No need for a real party."

"No party?" Josia thought he sounded disappointed but then abruptly Arthur's voice seemed far away, as if she held only a fraction of his attention. "Your sister—what would you say she looks like?"

"Like me. Dark hair and brown eyes."

"Long hair, perhaps? But she is younger and her face and body are a good deal thinner, correct?"

Suddenly concerned, Josia sat up. "That sounds like her. Why do you ask?"

"Because my spy probe has located Dimitri, and a woman fitting that description is aiming some sort of weapon on him as we speak!"

# Chapter Six

In spite of Arthur's protests over what Dimitri would do to him if something happened to her, Josia found her slippers and dashed out of the ship, heading for her sister and Dimitri. She couldn't imagine what kind of weapon Kissa could have found that would keep a Dark-pilot prisoner, but her sister was pretty imaginative. It wasn't outside the realm of possibility that she'd come up with something that would be a threat.

She arrived to see that Arthur hadn't exaggerated. Sitting perfectly still on a case of supplies meant for the colony, Dimitri's gaze was fixed on the beam of purple-blue light hitting the ground just in front of his feet…and with good reason. The light emanated from a narrow cylinder in Kissa's hand and Josia recognized it as one of the colony's few ultraviolet torches. The light was used to cure minor skin ailments but it could give someone with Dimitri's sensitivity a nasty burn.

From behind a tree, she watched Kissa raise her makeshift weapon higher, the beam now hitting the case between Dimitri's open legs. Josia winced as it inched toward his crotch, wondering what damage it would do if it hit his cock and balls.

"I asked you where Josia was. I won't ask it again."

Dimitri frowned. "I told you that my lady is safe and where no one will harm her."

"No one but you, you mean."

"I intend only good things for her. I intend to make her my mate."

Kissa shook her head. "You expect me to believe that? No one wants Josia. No one cares for her but me."

The truth hurt more than a little, although she knew her sister honestly loved her.

Dimitri shook his head. "If you care for her then you know what a wonderful person she is. I love her too, little one. That's why I want her to go with me."

Dimitri actually loved her? It was all Josia could do not to run to him.

From the look on her face Kissa wasn't convinced. She glared at the Dark-pilot. "You only want to feed from her. You'll take all her blood and she'll die!"

"Not at my hand." Dimitri rose to his feet and raised one hand as if to swear by it. "She will never come to harm through me."

The beam jerked as the torch shook in her hand. "Don't come any closer. You're just trying to trick me. I want you to release her, now!"

"I won't do that. She is mine."

"Because they tied her up and gave her to you as payment? They had no right to do that. You would keep her enslaved for that?"

"I told you. She is no slave. She has given herself to me."

"She was given no choice."

The Dark-pilot's green eyes glowed. "She has now. I'll give her the choice."

"So if she wanted to stay here, you'd let her? You wouldn't make her go with you if she didn't want to?"

"I—" For a moment Dimitri looked uncertain then he faced her sister squarely. "That's right. If she wants to stay, then I won't force her to go with me."

Josia held her breath. She could stay? He cared for her that much, to let her free if she wished it? She stepped out from behind the tree. "Don't hurt him, Kissa."

Kissa jerked around, bathing Josia in a deep purplish glow. Horrified, Kissa dropped the torch and ran to her. "No! I didn't mean to burn you." Bursting into tears, she threw her arms around Josia. "You're okay? He didn't make you like him?"

Josia couldn't help laughing as she stroked her sister's back soothingly. "A UV lamp isn't going to hurt me unless I spend a few hours under it. I'm still human, Kissa."

"Oh thank the stars!" Tears flowed down her sister's face. "Did you hear him, Josia? He said he'd let you go."

Looking at Dimitri, Josia saw him watch her holding her sister close. "I heard him."

He hesitated, then his shoulders slumped. Even without touching his mind she could feel his despair.

"I promised no harm to you, Josia, and that includes sorrow of the heart. I could never separate you from someone you love."

"I know, Dimitri." She hesitated then turned her sister to her and kissed her on the forehead. "Go home, Kissa."

Her sister still had tears in her eyes. "Aren't you coming with me?"

"Not now. I was given to Dimitri for his time here at least."

"But Josia…you mean you want to stay with him?" Kissa's face clouded it had when she was little and being denied a sweet, and Josia was reminded of how young she was.

"I intend to fulfill my obligations to him for now. As for later…" Her voice trailed off. "There is much I need to think about."

"Oh. Okay. I guess that's fair." Kissa didn't look like she meant it, but she started for the edge of the glade. "I'll see you tomorrow, right?"

"My ship won't leave until tomorrow evening." Dimitri said. "Return then."

With a last bewildered look at Josia, Kissa nodded and left.

After a moment's hesitation, Dimitri crossed the space between them, took her into his arms and kissed her and again Josia fell under his spell. "Thank you for staying, for this night at least."

She pulled away and smiled up at him. "I'm too distracted to say no to you, remember?"

His grip tightened. "And I share your distraction. If you believe nothing else, believe that."

"I do." She needed a way to distract him. "Now, didn't you promise me a bed for next time we made love?"

His laughter sounded forced but he kissed her again and lifted her into his arms, clutching her as if she might disappear from his grasp. "I did indeed."

# Chapter Seven

*And an amazing bed it was.* Soft, warm, and with just the right amount of bounce to it, plus it filled the entire corner of Dimitri's cabin, giving them plenty of room for all kinds of sexual activities. Making love was going to be good in this bed. Making love with Dimitri was going to be fabulous.

Once again stripped of her clothing by an impatient Dark-pilot, Josia lay against the pillows, watching him pull his own garments off, nearly ripping the seams in the need to be free of them. A complaint came from Arthur over the damage, reminding Dimitri that *someone* would have to repair his clothing, but that was short-lived as the pilot told the computer to turn off all monitoring in the bedroom. At Josia's relieved sigh, Arthur muttered something about lack of respect, then the only sounds were those of her and Dimitri's harsh breathing.

He stood before her, unclothed and unconcerned, the most beautiful man she'd ever seen. His body was all hard muscle, toned from hours of exercise meant to reduce the symptoms of gravity loss. Her body tingled all over at his strength and his desire for her, obvious from the way his cock pointed at her, long and heavy. She couldn't believe how lucky she was to be with him. The lottery that had selected Kissa, forcing her to take her sister's place, had given her to a man who desired her. More than that, he actually loved her.

She felt like the luckiest woman in the universe. "Are you going to stand there looking at me all night?"

"Much as I'd like to, I can't. It will be dawn in a couple of hours and I sleep while the sun is up." He knelt on the bed next to her and crawled forward to lie between her legs. "I look forward to spending that rest with you in my arms. You will stay with me through tomorrow evening?" A melancholy note crept into his voice.

"I'll stay with you during your rest, Dimitri." She stroked his face. "Please, make love to me now."

This time when he kissed her there was something else in it, less possessive and more tender. She no longer heard his mental *mine, mine*. Perhaps the thought that he might lose her made him treasure her more—whatever it was, Josia felt the depths of his need for her and fell right into them. She reached out to him with her mind, letting him see just how much she wanted him.

He leaned over her, brushing his lips against her neck. She could just feel the tips of his fangs. "My pleasure, Josia."

"No…our pleasure," she said smiling up at him.

They'd had sex before. But this was different. Dimitri had been enthusiastic and nearly feral in his interest the first time, the second time he'd made love with the joy of possession.

He hesitated now before he claimed her body. This was less sex, the joining of two bodies, and more a joining of two minds, two hearts, and two souls. This was love, not sex.

"You told my sister you loved me. Do you think it possible to love someone the first time you see them?" Josia said quietly.

"I didn't used to believe in love at first sight. But that was before I met you." His lips twitched into a smile. "I must admit though that love wasn't the first thing on my mind. You just looked so appetizing tied to that tree." His hand ran down to lift her breast, bringing the nipple close, and his tongue leapt out to caress it. The tip pebbled and he leaned forward to suck carefully on it. Josia could barely feel the points of his fangs on the tender skin.

"You taste so good, sweet lady. Like..." his voice trailed off and he laughed. "Funny, I can't think of anything that tastes as good as you do."

She sat up and pushed him onto his back. "I want to taste you this time."

Dimitri's face showed deep appreciation as Josia wrapped her hand around his shaft and took her first tentative lick of his cock. *Oh, it was as lovely as she'd expected.* Using her free hand to fondle the soft sac beneath, she explored his man's parts with as much curiosity as passion. His satisfied groans told her she was touching him right, but when she took the tip of him into her mouth he nearly exploded.

*Hold it right there, Josia! I want to wait and come inside you.*

Sitting up, he knelt behind her, spreading wide her butt cheeks to give his mouth access to her pussy and clit. As he took his first lick, he opened his mind to her, letting her see how much he enjoyed her taste. In response, Josia shared the flavors she'd taken from him, the salt of his precum still on her tongue. Sharing their experiences, as much as Dimitri's mouth on her pussy, set Josia on fire until she was all but begging him to come inside her.

Dimitri entered her slowly from behind, his long, thick cock filling her and making her quiver. She whimpered, first from the size of him then at the way he moved, each stroke firm and strong. Glancing back, Josia saw his face, the near painful intensity on it. He draped himself over her, licking the skin of her shoulder before biting down, taking only a few sips before sealing the holes.

Uncertainty and doubt blossomed in her. He needed her for blood and sex, that's what she was to him.

But he'd heard her thoughts. *I need you for my life, Josia. You give me love and laughter and a future worth living.*

As before in the storage hold, as their passion grew and they came close to climaxing, their minds blended together. Josia saw his thoughts again, this time of how much he wanted her, how much it meant to have her…and how alone he would be when she was gone.

It was enough to break her heart, especially as she realized that like him, she too had been alone most her life. Her weaving had been her work, and her sister had needed her, but soon Kissa would choose one of the many young men who sought her favor. No one had or ever would seek Josia's hand and she too had long empty years ahead of her.

Dimitri sped up and her mind emptied of all thoughts but how wonderful it felt to have him behind her. Before her the wall became shiny, probably Arthur's work, and she saw their reflection. Dimitri's handsome face over her shoulder, his eyes closed in passion, his hands lovingly kneading her breasts, his hips pounding his cock into her backside. He opened his eyes and they lit up with love at the sight of them together.

Their combined images joined with all other sensations and pushed her into climax. Josia poured the resulting passion into their link, drowning it before it drowned her. Caught in the maelstrom, Dimitri lost control and climaxed with her, their minds blended even as their bodies peaked in simultaneous orgasms. With matching groans, they collapsed on the bed. In the aftermath their minds gradually separated, although the link still existed.

Josia lay replete in his arms, listening to the idle thoughts in her Dark-pilot's head. Sexual satisfaction gave them a warm glow, but there was still the sense of foreboding, his fear she would leave him. She herself felt drowsy, from the easing of her own sexual tensions and the lack of sleep.

"How much longer until dawn?"

He gave a short laugh. "Even after all these years spent in space, I can still feel the sunrise coming. We have maybe five minutes, then I'll fall asleep until the day ends." Lying on his side, he turned her to face him. "If you wanted to slip away during that time, you could. I wouldn't be able to stop you."

"I'm too tired. Besides, you could always tell Arthur to take off with me aboard as we slept if you wanted to."

"I could…but that would be wrong. I said I would leave it your choice to stay, Josia."

In that moment Josia knew just how much love he had for her. She'd seen what kind of life he led…the man had special jets in his bathtub to satisfy his passion, and drank artificial blood that he didn't like. She also knew how lonely he was, the long years he'd spent with only the company of his computer. For a long time he'd searched for someone like her. She'd felt his joy in being with her.

And yet, if she wished it he would set her free. That's how much he loved her.

"Dimitri, you promised you could never separate me from someone I love."

His eyes lost their sleepiness and grew watchful. "I said that, yes."

She couldn't resist teasing him a little. Josia allowed herself a heartfelt sigh and felt Dimitri tense as if expecting bad news.

"Well, I guess that means you'll have to keep me. I love you too much be separated from you. But on one condition only." She opened her mind to him for a moment so he would know what that condition was.

Dimitri sat up and knelt next to her. His hand seemed to sweat as he took hers. "Josia, would you be my bride?"

After a lifetime without choices, finally someone had given her the one she wanted most. "Yes, Dimitri, I will."

He whooped and swept her up in his arms, kissing her soundly. "I'm the luckiest Dark-pilot alive!"

"Of course you are," Arthur interrupted, a touch of smugness in his tone. "I've said that all along—after all, you've had me for decades. Now, shall I make plans for the wedding this evening?"

"There is just my sister…"

"Nonsense," Arthur said, his tone forbidding any argument. "It's not every day a Dark-pilot takes a bride—the entire colony must be invited." A deep hum erupted from the cabin walls as the computer spun into high gear. "There is food, drinks, decorations…we must have a cake with an artiheme slice for Dimitri. Oh, and a wedding gown, something gloriously sexy! So much to do... I'll take care of all the preparations...you two rest well!" There was an abrupt squawk and then silence.

Laughing, Dimitri collapsed back onto his pillow and drew a suddenly exhausted Josia into his arms. "I don't think I've ever heard Arthur so happy. He'll spend the whole day setting up for the wedding and the next year complaining about how hard he worked. Rest well, Josia...you're going to need it."

She yawned. "You rest well, too, Dimitri. I love you."

One last thought slipped through their link as the sunrise swept his body into sleep. *I love you too, Dark-pilot's bride.*

*The End*

## About the author

Cricket Starr lives in the San Francisco Bay area with her husband of more years than she chooses to count. She loves fantasies, particularly sexual fantasies, and sees her writing as an opportunity to test boundaries. Her driving ambition is to have more fun than anyone should or could have. While published in other venues under her own name, she's found a home for her erotica writing here at Ellora's Cave.

Cricket welcomes mail from readers. You can write to her c/o Ellora's Cave Publishing at 1337 Commerce Drive, #13, Stow, OH 44224.

## Also by Cricket Starr:

Divine Interventions 1: Violet Among the Roses
Divine Interventions 2: Echo In the Hall
Divine Interventions 3: Nemesis of the Garden
Memories To Come
The Doll
Two Men and a Lady anthology

# The Windsday Club

Charlotte Boyett-Compo

## Chapter One

They were extraordinarily handsome men and as they walked down the narrow lane that led to the room where they held their semimonthly meetings, women turned to stare and sigh and daydream of what it would be like to be held in the warriors' brawny arms.

"Those men have quite the reputation," a middle-aged woman commented. "It's a dirty little secret about what they do of a Windsday."

"They can do whatever they like with no one to gainsay them," her companion remarked.

"Corydon is the most beautiful, don't you think?" a shopkeeper asked her customers.

"Aye," the older of the two customers agreed with a wistful smile on her wrinkled face. "He can put his boots under my cot any time he likes."

"I'd take any one of the six of them," the customer's daughter stated, "but Brion makes my mouth water."

"Kaia, for shame!" her mother chastised. She fanned herself briskly. "Such talk is unseemly for a maiden."

Brion glanced around and when his eyes met Kaia's he cocked a wicked blond brow. A slight smile tugged at his lips.

"Don't encourage her, Brion," Keltyn snapped, elbowing his companion. "You want her to come up to the room? This is the first Windsday, not the third!"

Brion sighed. "Aye, I forgot." He rubbed at his unshaven jaw. "It's just as well, I guess."

Corydon had started the club three years earlier to give them something to occupy their time when not about military duties. They met twice a month to commit in private some of the sins they had been warned against as children—gluttony, gambling, and lust. The women they brought to their club were for pleasure only with no misunderstandings about commitment and the like. It was strictly for the men's entertainment without there being any chance of getting snared by the wedding bug. What happened at the club, stayed at the club.

"I intend to win back the money you cheated from me last month," Jubil grumbled. "So keep your mind on what this meeting is about."

The twin brothers—Owun and Timun—exchanged glances. Their purses were filled to overflowing and according to the seer, this was their lucky day. Timun winked at his twin.

"What was that look about, Timun?" Corydon asked as he reached up to tighten the queue of hair bound at the nape of his neck.

Timun turned to their leader. "Loxias said we would win big today," the young man said and yelped as his twin reached out to pinch him.

"There is," Owun snarled, "such a thing as being too honest, Brother! Don't tell everything you know!"

"Wouldn't take him long to do so," Jubil commented with a chuckle.

"Loxias is a crook, young one," Corydon remarked. "Best play your cards close to your chest."

Timun nodded. "I will keep that in mind, Captain."

"Corydon!" Owun hissed. "On Windsdays, he prefers we call him by his given name!"

Corydon was about to agree but his attention was caught—and held—by the shimmer of golden threads running through a length of fabric being held up to the sun at one of the open-air market stalls. The threads caught the sunlight, reflecting it and making the fabric seem to come to life. Behind the cloth was the silhouette of a woman.

"Who is catering the meal today?" Keltyn inquired.

"Our fabulous caterers, the Sisters from Hell," Brion answered with a wince.

"It's a good thing those women can cook because they sure as Hades have nothing else going for them," Jubil stated.

"Oh, I don't know about that," Keltyn said as he flicked a piece of lint from the shoulder of his tunic. "I fucked Helia once."

The other five men stopped in mid-stride at the same time and turned to stare at their friend.

Jubil snagged Keltyn's upper arm in a tight grip. "The older one? Keltyn, please tell me you're joking," he demanded.

Keltyn shrugged. "She wasn't half bad, actually. She's a little on the plump side but then again, I like my women with a bit of padding to hold onto."

"A little on the plump side?" Brion asked in a disbelieving tone. "The bitch is as big as a small hut!"

"Comes from taking too many samples of her own cooking," Jubil said. He was staring hard at his cousin. "Have you lost your mind, Keltyn?"

Sniffing, Keltyn jerked his arm from Jubil's grip. "She's got a very talented tongue," he said.

"The bitch is a sow!" Brion asserted. "Smells like one, too!"

"Gentlemen," Corydon said quietly.

The other five men glanced at their leader then followed where the tall man's gaze was directed.

"By Altascia!" Owun whispered. "Who *is* that?"

Had the goddess Herself stepped down from Mount Laoch to walk among her subjects, Corydon suspected Altascia's legendary beauty would pale beside the exquisite creature whose smile outshone the golden-shot fabric she was purchasing from the cloth merchant. The tinkle of her laughter rang like the sweetest little silver bell and the sound drove deep into the warrior's groin.

"She must be a woman of pleasure," Jubil suggested. "She's too beautiful to be some man's wife." He nodded toward two burly men who were standing near the beauty, their arms folded over thickly muscled chests. "They look to be her guards."

"I'd give a month's wages to get under that gown," Keltyn said with a sigh.

"If she's a prostitute, you'd have to pay more than that," Brion said. "That is quality flesh, my friend."

Corydon tuned out the discussion being carried on between his friends. His gaze was locked on the gorgeous woman whose slender arms were adorned with spirals of hammered gold and whose dainty feet were clad in very expensive sandals.

Her hair was a deep brown with reddish highlights that sparkled in the sun as though fireflies were winging through the elegantly styled tresses. Several strands of pearls had been woven through that lustrous mane piled high atop her head and spiraled down through one long braid that swung enticingly over her bare right shoulder. The gown she wore fit her shapely frame as sweetly as a lover's embrace—sweeping beneath her right arm to flow gracefully over her left shoulder in delicate folds. The fine silk fabric clung to her curving hips and molded her lush breasts so tightly the peaks of her nipples stood out in bold relief.

"She is breathtaking," Jubil declared.

"My cock throbs just looking at her," Timun—the youngest of the twins told them.

Another musical laugh escaped the lovely woman's throat and she looked away from whatever the merchant had said to scan the passersby. Her scrutiny passed over the men then snapped back. Pale violet eyes framed in long, thick lashes locked with Corydon's and the smile slowly slid from her beautiful face as she stood there with her lips parted and stared back at him. As she put the tip of her tongue to her bottom lip to wet that sultry surface, every male watching her felt a deep stirring of lust envelop him.

"You've made a conquest, Cory," Jubil said.

Corydon had met many a beautiful woman in his thirty-nine years. He had lain with more of them than he cared to admit except when drunk and in a typical manly state of boasting. He had known the pleasures of women whose flesh was as pale as freshly drawn milk and those whose skin was among the dusky shades. He had gazed into green eyes, blue eyes, brown and black and all the shades in between, but never had he seen eyes the color of this woman's. Even from a distance of twenty feet away those lovely eyes shone like the rarest Tranoliun amethysts.

"Timun," Brion whispered. "Go ask her price."

Corydon put out a stiff arm as the boy started forward. With a slight shake of his head the warrior lowered his arm. "I'll go," he told them.

Like a man in a trance, Corydon approached the exquisite beauty, his eyes never leaving hers. When he was but six feet away, the burly men standing off to one side strolled casually forward to block him. They glared at him—faces stony, lips pressed tightly together, arms folded over massive chests, and gazes as hard as flint.

Accustomed to having men step aside for him rather than get in his way, Corydon frowned. He was a man respected and admired and not one to be ignored or thwarted.

"I am Corydon Lesartes," Corydon announced. "I am..."

"Perhaps the handsomest man I've ever seen," the lovely woman said in a soft, melodic voice. She touched the heavily muscled arm of the shorter of her two guards and the man stepped away immediately, bowing his head as he did. "I am honored you singled me out, milord." She held out her hand.

Corydon stepped up to her, took her hand and brought it gallantly to his lips. He gazed at her through the sweep of his long lashes. "The honor is mine, Lady...?"

"I am Rosalyn," she told him and gently withdrew her hand from his. She cast a slow look to his companions. "You gentlemen are seeking companionship for the day?"

A part of Corydon's soul withered, for he was hoping against hope this beautiful female was not a woman of pleasure. He nodded, not trusting himself to speak for he realized he was grinding his teeth.

"All six of you?" she pressed.

Once more he nodded. Disillusionment settled along his shoulders and he tried to shrug it away. "How much?" he asked more sharply than he should have.

Rosalyn put the fingernail of her perfectly manicured index finger to her very white and even teeth and appeared to be considering. She looked from him to the men standing together watching them then returned her attention to Corydon, cocking her head as she studied him

"Well, I didn't bring all that much money with me today," she said. "How much do you normally charge?"

Corydon blinked, his eyebrows shooting up. "I beg your pardon?" he asked.

"Most likely I have enough for four of you—depending on your going rate, of course—but not for all of you." Her lips formed a cute little pout. "Although I would certainly have enjoyed the experience of all six of you, I'm afraid I can't afford it." She brightened. "Well, at least not today. Perhaps later in the week?"

The mouth of the Captain of the Imperial Guard of Dorschia dropped open. He was acutely aware that he wasn't breathing and that a portion of his anatomy was rock-hard as he stared at the beautiful creature standing before him. Her lovely eyes held a heat from which he found he could not look away and the smell of her was intoxicating.

"You think we are men of pleasure?" he managed to ask, wincing at the whine he heard in his voice.

She frowned. "Are you not?"

Corydon opened his mouth to say indeed they weren't but his gaze dropped to her lush bosom and he felt a tingle all over. He wanted so badly to mold his palms around those delightful globes, to stroke the nipples that were standing out against the soft fabric. He ached to have this lovely woman beneath him, her legs wrapped around his waist, and had to force his attention from her luscious chest.

"Have I made a dreadful mistake?" Rosalyn asked, a pretty shade of pink flushing her cheeks. "If I have, I apologize. Because you are all so handsome…"

"How much do you have?" he cut her off.

She shrugged daintily and looked to the shorter of her two guards—obviously the one she trusted most. "Davon, how much do I have left?"

The guard's eyes narrowed dangerously. "A little over nine hundred quesons, milady," he replied in a gravelly voice.

"Then you're in luck," Corydon said. "It's Windsday and we're having a two for the price of one sale."

Corydon heard the guard growl and looked at the man. There was murder in a set of gray eyes that were glowering at him as though he were vermin. The man's upper lip was cocked in a manner that suggested he not only thought Corydon was vermin but smelled like it, as well.

"Three hundred quesons for a pair of us, milady. Nine hundred for all six to give you the pleasure of your life," Corydon said, his gaze straying to the guard for he thought the man might well attack. "Windsday is..." Corydon threw out a negligent hand, for he didn't know how to finish.

"Hump day," the guard answered for him.

Corydon cast the guard a brutal look but the man was not withered by a stare many had called lethal.

"Delightful!" Rosalyn said. "Davon, pay him."

Davon thrust a hand into his leather jerkin and pulled out a hefty bag of coins. With a withering look, he tossed them at Corydon, who caught them against his chest.

She looked around. "Where do we go?"

Corydon could only point to the second floor of the building in front of which his friends were standing. He offered her his arm. "May I?" he asked.

"Thank you, milord." Rosalyn laid her arm gracefully atop his, threading her fingers downward through his. Sweeping aside the hem of her gown she walked with him toward the group of five men.

The men were grinning from ear to ear, jostling one another as Corydon and Rosalyn drew near. Their eyes were hot with lust.

"Lady Rosalyn," Corydon said, "may I present my fellow men of pleasure—Keltyn, Jubil, Brion, and the twins, Timun and Owun."

"Men of pleasure?" Jubil echoed.

Confusion wrinkled across the faces of the men and they looked to Corydon. He smiled tightly back at them, a muscle working in his lean cheek.

"Twins!" Rosalyn said with a deep sigh. "I've never had twins pleasure me before."

"One for each lustrous breast, milady," Corydon said as he shifted his gaze from man to man. "We guarantee to give you pleasure or we will refund your money."

Jubil's mouth dropped open. "She's paying us?"

"Not our usual rate," Corydon said, staring into Jubil's surprised face. "Since she is the most delightful woman we have ever encountered, I offered her two men for the price of one for today."

Keltyn put a hand over his mouth to suppress the laughter that had turned his face a most unbecoming shade of red.

Brion's eyebrows had become lost in the sweep of his pale blond hair.

Timun was shifting from foot to foot in anticipation, his attention glued to Rosalyn's chest.

Owun looked as though he would pass out and his hands were actually trembling.

"Shall we?" Corydon asked and swept a hand toward the stairs that led to the men's clubroom.

Rosalyn inclined her head and preceded him up the stairs, her gown lifted in both hands so that her shapely ankles were revealed.

Jubil shot out a hand and grabbed Corydon's arm. "She thinks we are men of pleasure?"

"Aren't we?" Corydon asked quietly. He shook off Jubil's arm and started up the stairs.

"She's paying us," Brion said, the words dropping like stones. The look on his handsome face suggested he didn't know whether to be insulted or to laugh.

"Aye, but not at our going rate," Keltyn quipped as he shoved Brion aside and took the stairs two at a time.

The room was cast in deep shade for the windows faced the west. It was cool inside the stone walls with a light breeze wafting in from the balcony.

"Welcome to the Windsday Club, milady," Corydon said. "You are in for a grand good time."

"How quaint," Rosalyn said as she surveyed the room.

There was a long, low table around which ten thick cushions had been placed. Along the walls were five cots big enough to accommodate two sleepers each. In each of the four corners, a brace of tall copper candleholders held fat white unlit candles and two brass three-arm candelabras sat atop the table, flanking a large bowl piled high with fruit. On one wall was an immense sideboard that held crystal goblets and tall decanters filled with varying shades of liquor.

"Would you like some brandy, milady?" Corydon asked.

Rosalyn shook her head. "The sun is not yet set, is it, milord?"

"In some part of the world it is," Keltyn answered for his Captain.

The lovely woman smiled sweetly. "I have no need of spirits, gentlemen. I am drunk of life already."

Corydon heard the door shut downstairs and glanced about him. His men were in the room with him and he frowned.

"Davon will see to our privacy," Rosalyn explained. "He takes his job very seriously."

Corydon had a momentary vision of the two muscular guards standing before the door, forbidding entry. He tugged at his chin. "We have two women who will be bringing our meal. They..."

"Davon will let them pass," Rosalyn assured him. She walked to one of the thick cushions, swept the skirt of her gown aside and before any of the men could step forward to assist her, sank elegantly to the floor with her legs crooked to one side. She bestowed a gentle smile on each of the men. "Who will be the first?" she asked.

"First?" Brion repeated.

"Shall we start with the youngest and work our way up?" Rosalyn asked, settling back so that she reclined on one slender elbow. "And please, gentlemen, take your time."

Jubil spoke to Corydon out of the side of his mouth. "Take our time doing what?"

Corydon had slaked his desires in the willing bodies of many women of pleasure and he knew what was expected of them. "Timun," he said, "you go first and take off your clothes very slowly."

Timun flinched and his head swiveled quickly to his twin. They stared at one another for the space of a few heartbeats but—being as game as the next boy in their class when it came to screwing—the young man put his hands to his shirt and began unbuttoning it.

"Slowly and shouldn't you take off your boots first, milord?" Rosalyn instructed. "I liken this pleasure to opening presents on my feast day. It is the anticipation that sets the juices to flowing, don't you agree?"

Every man there felt his cock leap at her words and it was all each of them could do not to groan. Carefully avoiding looking at one another, the men drifted to different parts of the room, blending into the deeper shadows as Timun took center stage, hopping about as he dragged on his boots and removed them. The boots hit the floor with resounding thumps and were soon covered by the young man's socks.

"Why don't you all remove your boots?" Rosalyn suggested. "It would speed things up."

All but Corydon dropped to the floor and yanked off their boots and socks before jumping back to their feet, their breathing loud in the still room. Corydon leaned against the wall and removed his boots, his gaze never leaving Rosalyn.

"Now," Rosalyn said, looking away from Corydon. "Where were we?" She smiled at Timun. "Go on, milord."

Timun's lips were slightly parted as he worked his way as slowly as he could down the buttons of his fine lawn shirt. He flicked the buttons aside with a jauntiness that was belied by the slight tremor in his long fingers. When the shirt hung free on his finely chiseled chest, he put his hands to the collar and shrugged the garment over his shoulders.

"You have a nice chest, young Timun," Rosalyn complimented the boy who had just turned twenty a few months before.

Beaming with pride, Timun ran the palm of his hand down the sparse hair that grew between his developing pectorals then slid his fingers to the waistband of his britches. He flipped the button of his fly aside and worked the drawstring loose in tiny increments to a rhythm only he could hear. All the while, his lips were puckered and his hips were sashaying from side to side.

"Showoff," Jubil mumbled.

The buttons undone, Timun slowly shoved the britches down his hips, wriggling out of them while he bent his knees. A large erection poked at the thin fabric of his underwear. Kicking out of his britches, the young man turned his back to Rosalyn then glancing back over his shoulder, reached down to lower his underwear over the high ride of his rump.

"Oh, yes," Rosalyn commented.

Pushing his underwear to his ankles, Timun stepped out of them and while the garment was still hooked to his left ankle, lifted his leg and propelled the underwear upward, snaking out a hand to snag it in midair.

"Bravo!" Rosalyn called and clapped her hands.

When he moved to face her, Timun covered his privates with his hands, his face stained a bright crimson.

"Let me see," she coaxed.

Shyly, Timun slowly removed his hands and stood there with his arms at his side and his erection at full mast.

"Very impressive," Rosalyn complimented then her gaze slid to Timun's twin and a delicate brow crooked upward.

Always the more cautious of the two, Omun was very slow in unbuttoning his shirt. His gaze was centered somewhere just above the lovely woman's face as he worked his way to the tail of his shirt. First flashing one side of his naked chest as he yanked upon the fabric, he then flashed the other side before dragging the shirt off and letting it drop to the floor. He—like his twin—had no belt to remove so he made slow work of his drawstring. Going down a ways, he then tugged the drawstring up again. The next time, the drawstring lowered a little more before closing almost to the top. The last time, it went down completely before Omun squatted and shoved the waistband of his britches all the way to his knees. With acrobatic skill, he stepped out of one trouser leg then the other before flipping the garment up as his brother had done and catching it just before it hit the floor.

Although Omun was not as well-built as his twin, his chest was solidly proportioned and muscular. There was no hair between his breastbones but just above the waistband of his underwear, his belly was thickly matted with crisp, light brown curls. He flexed his pectorals in a sweet little dance that made Rosalyn throw back her head and laugh.

"Delightful!" she pronounced.

Omun hooked a thumb in the waistband of the underwear and tugged it down with some difficulty for his large erection hindered the downward movement of the fabric. When he freed his staff—the underwear hung on his lean hips to underline the stiff muscle—he swept his hands downward to showcase his package.

"My, my," Rosalyn said. "You men are certainly very well-endowed."

Omun chuckled and finished removing his underwear. He stepped aside, lifting his chin to challenge Brion.

With a slight smile tugging at his lips, Brion stepped forward. The tunic he wore closed down the left side of his chest and he slowly flicked the buttons open, pushing aside the material to reveal thick pectorals with hard little nubs. Allowing the tunic to hang loosely open, he then turned his attention to his drawstring, slowly loosening it. When his britches hung precariously low on his hips, he removed his shirt and threw it aside. With an impish grin, he strolled to one of the cots, sat down, lifted his legs and jerked off his britches. Standing, he reached inside the fly of his underwear to free his cock. With that massive weapon in hand, he jiggled the stiff muscle, laughing as Rosalyn gasped then broke once more into applause.

"I love it!" the pretty woman giggled.

Jubil would not be outdone as he pushed Brion aside. He rubbed at his erection through the fabric of his britches—first quickly then while licking his lips, slowly. With his free hand, he thumbed the buttons of his shirt loose and when it was opened, ran his palm from side to side over his hairless pecs. He had large nipples for a man and they stood out against the darkness of his tan. Putting his hands to his belt, he made quick work of the accessory then tossed it aside, drawing down his drawstring before reaching inside to pull his cock out.

Rosalyn whistled softly for the muscle framed in the V of Jubil's britches was the largest penis she had ever seen. The bulbous head was huge, red, and a tiny drop of juice clung to its tip. She barely noticed the man removing his britches and underwear for her scrutiny was fixed on that mass of tubular steel. He was brandishing it as though it were paintbrush and she the waiting canvas.

"Step aside, squirt, and let me show her what a real man looks like," Keltyn grunted.

Reluctantly, Rosalyn dragged her eyes from Jubil's impressive staff and gave Keltyn her attention. If she thought Jubil's cock large, she had to gape at Keltyn's for when he lowered his britches in one deft move and pulled out his staff, she could not stop herself from gasping. The penis jutting from Keltyn's hips dwarfed Jubil's and had to be a good foot in length. Not only longer than Jubil's, this prick was thicker in circumference. Looking at the formidable pecker made Rosalyn's mouth water and her womb stir. Only dimly aware of Keltyn stripping to reveal a well-honed upper body and strong, well-formed legs, she ran her hands down her skirt, her palms itching to touch that jutting missile.

Standing in a loose line, the five men resembled a coat rack with their cocks jutting outward. Of varying sizes and colors, the cocks had one thing in common—they were fully erect and throbbing. Each man stood with a grin on his handsome face, his arms akimbo so Rosalyn could get a good look at what he had to offer.

Rosalyn demurely lowered her head in homage to the men's superior endowments but when she lifted her chin, it was to Corydon she looked. For a long moment they stared at one another—something intangible and dangerous passing between them.

Corydon walked slowly over to Rosalyn and stood above her, his eyes fused with hers. His shirt had no buttons and the dark pullover clung tightly to his broad chest and his heavily muscled arms. Black britches molded his tall frame to accentuate the length of his long legs and the neatly turned expanse of his high-riding ass that looked chiseled in stone. His breathing was slow, measured, and his demeanor calm but he gave off a vibrating, raw sensuality that everyone there—male and female—could not help but recognize.

With slow, deliberate movements, Corydon tugged the pullover from his britches until the tail hung free. He crossed his arms over his chest, took hold of the shirt's hem, and pulled it slowly upward and over his head. He stood there with the shirt clutched in a fist at his side for a moment then let the garment drop. He flexed his pectorals—first one then the other.

Rosalyn sucked in a slow breath, for the breadth of Corydon's chest started an ache between her legs and caused her knees to grow weak. Up close, that hunky body was a sight to behold. A thick pelt of dark, wiry hair matted his upper chest from collarbone to just above the diaphragm, covering his manly breasts, and then tapered down the middle in a crisp line that dipped below the beltline of his britches. His chest hair looked as though it had been lovingly crafted upon Corydon's body by the hand of a brilliant artist. The wiry curls spread out along each side of the middle part of his rib cage less thickly than on his upper chest only to call attention to the hard striations of muscle that ridged his abdomen. Unaware she did so, Rosalyn licked her upper lip then curled her tongue downward to wet the lower one.

Corydon put his hands to his belt and slowly drew the end from the leather keeper, pulling back until the silver grommet came free of the metal tongue. Casually, he used the thumb of his other hand to move the metal tongue out of the way so he could ease the belt from the buckle. With infinite slowness, he tugged the black leather strap from the belt loops at his waist, doubled it once over his right fist, then with the metal tang in his left hand, hunkered down before Rosalyn, looped the belt over her head and pulled her toward him.

Rosalyn was mesmerized by the handsome face looming toward her. The belt dug lightly into the muscles of her neck as he drew her forward but she was unmindful of any discomfort. Her gaze was locked on the full lips only a few inches from hers. She put her hands up to cup his and shivered as the crisp hairs on the back of his hands tickled her palm.

His mouth settled lightly upon hers, his tongue slipping gently past her lips. His teeth nipped at her bottom lip, her chin. When he moved back she groaned deep in her throat, for his kiss was intoxicating and she required more.

Coming to his feet, the Captain of the Imperial Guard draped his belt over one bare shoulder then placed his hands at the button of his fly. Still holding Rosalyn captive with his gaze, he began to work his way through the pearl studs that held his britches closed.

"How many of us do you want at a time?" he growled as the last stud pulled free of its buttonhole.

Rosalyn's gaze dipped to the V of that opening and swallowed hard. The crisp curls that drew attention held her spellbound and she could barely breathe much less talk.

"Two?" he whispered as he eased the waistband of his britches down his lean hips. "Three?"

Completely aware of the clean male smell that clung to him—cinnamon oil and leather and a faint muskiness that set her blood to simmering—Rosalyn felt an ache in her breasts and loins that made her squirm on the cushion.

"Four?" he queried and the britches went lower. Just a glimpse of the pale glistening head of his cock was revealed and Rosalyn felt sweat forming on her upper lips.

"Five?" His voice was deep, passion-filled, and sent quivers down her spine.

He wore no underwear and that did not surprise her in the least. A man as sensual as Corydon Lesartes would want nothing to come between him and the abrading fabric of his britches. As that garment slid slowly, enticingly down his hips, his cock sprang free.

Had she thought Jubil and Keltyn greatly endowed? Her mouth sagged open at the sight of Corydon's fleshy sword, for surely no woman could accommodate such a stiff organ. Thickly veined and pulsing with a life of its own, the man's cock put a shudder of alarm through Rosalyn's chest.

"It will fit," Corydon told her. "I can guarantee it will."

She slowly lifted her gaze from that delicious instrument of pleasure to look up into Corydon's face. Never had a man looked so inviting to her. It was more than just the smoldering look in his amber eyes or the full lips and deeply cleft chin. It went beyond the seductive slant of his eyebrows that were perfectly formed and just full enough for her tastes. His cheekbones were high and set into a gently oval face that bore a hint of beard even this early in the day. A regal nose that was neither too long nor too broad hinted at a heritage beyond the typical peasant.

"Perhaps only one at a time?" he questioned her and reached up to drag the band from his hair.

Lust drove straight through Rosalyn as his bound hair came undone. It was long—just past his shoulders but not quite long enough to reach his nipples—and thick as he shook it free. It was a dark brown with golden highlights running through the wavy strands. Released from its restraints, it fell about his head in layers that looked as though the hair was windblown.

"By the goddess," Rosalyn whispered and had to swallow the drool that formed in her mouth as he stepped out of his britches and stood before her in all his male glory.

Corydon gave her a moment to pass her intense attention over his naked body. A slight smile tugged at his lips. Lazily he blinked, his breathing calm and steady though his cock leapt with every breath he took.

"Get up," he ordered and held out a hand.

Rosalyn placed her hand in his and allowed him to draw her to her feet. She felt as though she were locked into a delicious daydream.

The other men came closer. Their eyes were hot, their bodies hard as steel and pulsing with need. They watched as their leader put hands to the beautiful woman standing before them and kept silent.

Corydon took hold of Rosalyn's bodice and rent the fabric down the middle, exposing the creamy lace of her camisole to their view.

Rosalyn's eyes grew wide and she started to put her hands up but Corydon would have none of that.

"Jubil," he said. "Hold her arms behind her."

Never one to question his Captain's orders, Jubil hastened to do as he was told. He gently but firmly took hold of Rosalyn's arms and drew them behind her, the action causing her breasts to thrust forward.

"You have ruined my gown," she protested, a vein throbbing at the base of her throat.

"I'll buy you a dozen gowns," Corydon countered.

As Jubil held her arms, Corydon ripped Rosalyn's gown all the way to the hem. The silk fabric clung only to her left shoulder. "Owun, give me a knife," he ordered.

Rosalyn tucked her lower lip between her teeth as Owun supplied a wicked-looking weapon that was used to cut away the remaining hold her gown had upon her person. The garment slid into a silken pool at her feet.

Sliding the blade gently between her breasts, Corydon slit the camisole from bustline to crotch and peeled it from her like the skin of a luscious peach.

Standing there before the men with only her stockings, Rosalyn felt a deep blush envelop her body.

Corydon took the belt from his shoulder and passed it around her waist. He ran the end through the buckle and pulled the belt tight. "Too tight?" he asked.

Rosalyn licked her lips. "No."

He tightened the belt around her a bit and cocked a brow.

"No," she said, barely able to breathe, for her nether regions felt heavy and full and in need of administering to. It was the throbbing between her thighs that made her sag against Jubil's hold.

"Can't remain standing, milady?" Corydon asked as he buckled the belt. He looked to Jubil. "Lay our lady down, warrior."

Whimpering like a frightened child, Rosalyn was pulled to the floor where Brion had kicked cushions to bear her weight. She felt the coolness of the cotton against her back and rump and realized Jubil had squatted down behind her so that her head now rested in his naked lap. She could feel the pulse of his staff along her shoulder and moaned.

Squatting down at Rosalyn's feet, Corydon slowly and with infinite care rolled the stockings down her legs. He let his hand linger on her right ankle, rubbing it with both his hands. "Keltyn, take hold of her left ankle," he ordered. "I will take this one."

Keltyn dropped down beside his friend.

"Spread-eagle her," Corydon said.

They pulled her legs apart so that she was open for all to gaze upon the dampness between her thighs.

Jubil's hands were on the side of her face, holding her head steady. In tandem—at some unseen, unheard command from their leader—the twins stretched out perpendicular to her, each with a breast to fondle and suckle, an arm to anchor to the floor.

"Oh, my god!" Rosalyn gasped as tongues laved her nipples and lips drew upon their fullness. She was spread-eagled beneath six glorious men who were turning her body into one massive quiver of sheer lust.

Brion settled between her legs, paused above her with his hands braced to either side of her waist. He bent forward and dragged his tongue over and around her navel, probed the deep indention with his tongue then slid that wet muscle down her belly until his mouth closed around her clit.

Bucking beneath the hold that pressed her to the pillows, Rosalyn opened her mouth to cry out but Jubil slid his palm firmly over her mouth. She gave him a stormy look but he simply smiled and shook his head.

The wondrous spiral of Brion's tongue flicked at the tender bud of her clitoris and sent shudders through Rosalyn's legs. The man knew what he was about for his tongue darted into her, probed there, swirled in another place—each motion perfectly timed and done with just the right amount of pressure. He lapped at her dewiness, suckled her nether lips, nipped at her quivering thighs then sat up to thrust first his index finger, then his middle finger, slowly and with infinite care. In and out the stiff appendages moved—slowly and expertly delving into her moistness and going deeper with each thrust. When he turned those fingers so that his palm was facing upward and the tip of his middle finger pressing firmly upward she groaned so loudly all the men chuckled.

"Me thinks the lady doth like what you are doing there, Bri," Jubil stated.

"She has yet to experience the whole of it," Brion replied as he moved his thumb back and forth over her swollen clit.

Her hips squirming upon the pillows, her heels digging into their plumpness, Rosalyn closed her eyes, dragging breath through her nostrils in short and shallow bursts. The twins were torturing her breasts with dual sensations from gentle hands that fondled and knowing tongues that licked. When they removed their mouths from those glorious orbs, they used soft pinches and the rolling of turgid nipples between thumbs and forefingers to cause a delirium of passion to flood Rosalyn's straining body.

"She is a delightful handful, eh? Only one of us should have her," Keltyn said softly. He looked at Corydon. "Will you take the pleasure, milord Captain?"

Corydon nodded. He was enflamed with lust, his cock as hard as he could ever remember it being. Never had he enjoyed the delights of a woman in tandem with his men. Though often encouraged to take part in one of the mindless orgies after a battle, he had forsaken such temptations and gone off on his own, finding a woman with whom to share his desires—quietly and away from the others. Not even during those times when he and his men brought a "friend" to share the third Windsday meeting with them did he pay any attention to what was going on upon the other cots.

Now he thrilled to watching Timun and Owun suckling Rosalyn's breasts. He felt passion flowing through his veins as Jubil bent forward to plant soft kisses on her forehead and cheeks, replacing his hand with questing lips that drew upon hers and muffled the sounds of her ardor. The sight of Keltyn beside him massaging a slender, shapely leg and sweet little turned-up toes set his own hands into motion so his actions mirrored Kel's. Brion's soft murmurs as he thrust his fingers in and out of Rosalyn's wriggling body added spice to the moment and when Brion turned his hand over and insinuated a thumb into the lovely woman's anus, Corydon could not help but laugh at the squeal that was half-smothered beneath Jubil's knowing mouth.

"She is almost ready, Cory," Brion said, looking back over his shoulder.

"Finish her," Corydon ordered. "Then we'll start again."

Smiling gamely, Brion bent forward and with his fingers inside Rosalyn's cunt and ass, pressed his mouth over her clit and began to tease that swollen nub.

Rosalyn jerked against the men holding her. She was in thrall to the marvelous sensations rocking her body, unable to free herself from strong, firm hands belonging to handsome, powerful men. Her gaze went from one attractive man to the next and when she finally found

Corydon's hot eyes she felt the ripples of her release itching their way to the surface.

Corydon wrapped his fingers around her toes and massaged deeply, arching her foot up and down as she went rigid, her hips nearly off the pillows as she came. Her grunt of completion made each of the men grin but they did not release her. Instead, they exchanged places, not giving her time to scoot away from them.

Keltyn and Brion each claimed a breast.

Owun and Timun took possession of her long legs and began working on her toes, suckling each in turn.

Jubil had positioned himself between her legs and it was his hot mouth that sucked away the passion juices that flowed unchecked from her slit.

Corydon was holding her head and when he bent down to claim her lips, he drew from her the sweetest of sounds—the murmur of surrender that every man longs to hear from his woman.

"She's claimed him," Owun said.

"Aye and he's claimed her," his twin agreed.

His kiss was long and hard and possessive. It took possession not only of her mouth but her heart and soul and body, as well. It placed upon her his stamp of ownership. It was a knowing kiss that sealed the bargain between them, for her tongue slipped out to accept his and draw upon it with a tenderness the warrior found intoxicating.

Trained well in the art of lovemaking, Jubil worked his magic deeply and well into Rosalyn's damp orifice. He plunged hot fingers deep inside her then withdrew them, held her gaze then slipped the slick fingers into his mouth to suck away the juice.

Rosalyn shivered at that brazen, carnal act. The mouths drawing on her nipples, the teeth nibbling at that swollen tips, and the firm pressure of the twin massagers working her toes pushed Rosalyn over the edge and before she knew what was happening, fell headlong into another climax that left her gasping for breath.

"Take her, Captain," Jubil said in a harsh, authoritative voice. "Let her know what it feels like to be your woman."

Jubil stood and stepped back as Corydon came to stand between Rosalyn's widely spread legs.

"Hold her head," Corydon ordered. "Her hair is in her eyes."

Jubil hunkered down once more and put his hands to Rosalyn's forehead, pushing away the damp hair that was matted to her cheek. He smiled down into her eyes as she gazed up at him with lust-slacked eyes that were heavy-lidded and slightly glazed.

"I've heard he is a swordsman of note, milady," Jubil told her. "His cock is sought after far and wide."

Corydon dropped down to his knees between her legs and ran his hands over her belly, his lips twitching as her flesh trembled at his touch. He trailed the backs of his fingers up the inside of her thighs then turned his hand to smooth his palm down the silken tops. He put his hands on the juncture of her thighs and used his thumbs to spread her apart, gently using his thumbnails to traverse the valleys of the outer lips of her vulva, softly scratching that sensitive area where many women seemed to always itch—first up and down together then in opposite movement.

Rosalyn was on fire with passion. The sweet sensation of Corydon's thumbs dragging along her outer lips made her start to pant. She was sweating under her arms, along her upper lip, in the folds behind her knees. Her entire body was trembling.

"What you need," Corydon said gruffly, "is a good fucking, milady."

He bent forward, slid his palms under her ass, and lifted her cunt to his mouth. Stretching his long legs out behind him, he fastened his mouth over her nether lips and commenced to suckling her as though he were a newborn at his mother's teat.

Whimpering with need, Rosalyn dug her fingernails into the palms of her hands and would have hurt herself had Keltyn and Brion not prevented her from doing so by threading their fingers through hers. Their lips were on her breasts, drawing from her little groans of pleasure as they nibbled and suckled. Neither felt the strong grasp of her hand upon theirs for they were lost in the moment.

Owun and Timun were suckling her toes.

Jubil was once more kissing her with an abandon that set her senses to reeling. It seemed each of them was suckling some part of her anatomy in chorus and the heady sensation rocked Rosalyn's core and sent her crashing through a crystal barrier that brought shards of tinkling sounds strumming through her brain.

"Now," Jubil suggested.

Corydon pulled himself up and over her and pressed the full weight of his manly body upon hers. He was looking down into her eyes, holding her with the force of his personality, his authority. His cock was wedged between her spread legs and pressing urgently against the core of her.

"Do you want me?" he asked in that gruff, wolf-like voice that sent shivers down her spine.

Rosalyn licked her dry lips. "Aye," she managed to answer.

Corydon cocked his head to one side. "Are you sure?"

"D-damned sure," she stuttered.

All around her the men chuckled but it was one deep sound of laughter that she heard the clearest. His body weight was delicious pressing down on her. The feel of it was so thrilling, so satisfying, she wanted to remain beneath him forever. His chest hair was prickling at her sensitive nipples. Now Keltyn and Brion were holding only her wrists pinioned to the soft pillows as Owun and Timun restrained her ankles.

"Think you can accommodate all of him, milady?" Jubil asked, drawing her eyes up to him.

"I can damned well try," she said through clenched teeth.

"Well, let's see if you can," Corydon declared as he reached down to position himself at the juncture of her thighs.

His shaft was like steel as it pressed into her. Smooth and hot and slick with the seepage of his own fluids, he pushed gently into her until he was seated as far as he could go—pressing tightly against her womb. He stilled with his huge cock sheathed within her velvety folds and fused his gaze with hers.

"Lie still," he said for she had started to writhe beneath him.

It took every ounce of Rosalyn's self-control to do as he bid. She lay there with that enormous weapon lodged deep within her and felt the throbbing of the engorged blood along its wicked length. She could see another vein pulsing in the thick column of Corydon's throat and the two were flowing in unison. He was pressed up against her womb and the thought caused a deep clenching sensation in her lower belly.

"Have you got your money's worth yet, wench?" Corydon asked, his eyes never leaving hers.

"No," she said. "I want to feel you come. Then I'll be satisfied."

Corydon's eyes widened. The first thrumming of his release was building in his balls and he was having trouble remaining still. Sweat was pouring off his body, dripping down his chin to land upon her chest. His hands went under her, lifted her hips as he pushed himself up on his knees.

"Let her go," he ordered and almost instantly Rosalyn's legs came up and wrapped around his waist, her arms grasping at his broad shoulders. Her hands dug into his powerful shoulder muscles then slid down to the straining biceps that felt like granite beneath her small hands.

Pumping into her as though she were a fire he needed to put out, Corydon slammed his pelvis against hers. The slap of their lower bodies was loud in the room. Rosalyn was sliding back and forth as he thrust deeply into her but she held on to him, squeezing her legs tighter around his waist.

Corydon was grunting brutally with each stroke. The pressure was building inside him and when it broke free, he growled—that sound coming from the very depths of his chest.

Rosalyn, too, voiced her release, shrieking in wild abandonment as the climax shot over her in wave after wave of delicious pleasure. Between the heavy weight of the handsome man atop her and the restricting pressure of his wide leather belt around her middle, she had journeyed to the very top of carnal enjoyment and was slowly sliding down the opposite side.

Lying there panting, neither Corydon nor Rosalyn was aware of the other men in the room. Neither saw the five men discreetly turn aside to rid themselves of the hard erections that had grown painful over the last two minutes. Neither heard the groans of satiation that came from the men as they took care of the matter in hand.

Corydon was sprawled between Rosalyn's sweet thighs, his head pillowed on her chest. Her fingers were running through his long hair—pushing it back from his sweaty forehead, tugging an errant strand from his eyes. She had released her hold on his waist and her legs were stretched out alongside his, the toes of her left foot lazily stroking his ankle.

"I could get used to this," Corydon whispered in a sleepy voice.

"That might can be arranged, milord," she whispered back.

A light knocking at the door made each of them lift their head toward the sound.

"That will be Davon," Rosalyn said, putting a hand to her mouth to stifle a yawn. "No doubt your meal has arrived, gentlemen."

Jubil snatched up his britches and hopped into them, almost losing his balance a couple of times before dragging the garment up his hips. He padded to the door and opened it a crack.

The shorter of Rosalyn's guards was framed in the narrow opening. "Your women are here with the food."

Jubil nodded. "Give us a moment," he said and shut out the scowling, savage face of the guard. He looked around. "That man isn't a happy soldier."

"Brothers rarely are when their sister does what they think she shouldn't," Rosalyn said with a giggle.

Corydon blinked. "Brothers?" He moved off her and sat up to run a hand through his tousled mane.

"Davon and Lyle," she said. "Davon is the oldest and by far the most dangerous despite his size."

The men looked at one another, concern wrinkling their handsome faces.

"Don't worry," Rosalyn said, stretching. "They are well-behaved for the most part."

Heavy footsteps on the stairs alerted the men to the impending arrival of the Sisters from Hell—Helia and Audra.

"Here," Keltyn said as he walked over to Rosalyn. "We don't have any gowns available but you look to be about Timun's size."

Rosalyn took the britches and shirt extended toward her and sat up. She poked her dainty feet into the britches legs and then lay back, lifted her hips and wriggled into the tight-fitting garment.

"Oh, I like the feel of these," she said, sitting up again.

The men were staring at her lush breasts and felt a moment of disappointment as she flung Timun's shirt around her and stuffed her arms into the sleeves. They watched as she buttoned each button then sighed when her sultry charms were no longer in view.

Corydon was standing off to one side, dressed once more—as each man was in one stage of dress or another—and was watching Rosalyn knotting Timun's shirt at her waist. "You're still wearing my belt," he reminded her.

"And I will continue to do so until you come to fetch it back from me," she said saucily.

"Where?" the men asked in unison but were not rewarded with an answer for there was another—more forceful—knock on the door.

Jubil opened the door and stood aside as the Sisters from Hell as well as Davon and Lyle came in carrying trays laden with succulent-smelling food. Helia and Audra didn't even glance at the men and barely noticed Rosalyn. They took their trays to the low table and set them down. Without a word, they turned and left the room.

Davon put down the heavy platter of roast duck he carried then looked over at his sister. His eyes narrowed. He straightened, glanced around the room and when he spied her torn gown, a muscle began working in his cheek.

"I am well and very content, Davon," Rosalyn said as she reached up for Keltyn to take her hand and help her up.

"It is unseemly what you are wearing," Davon grated through tightly clenched teeth.

"Then go find me a gown," Rosalyn said in a flippant tone.

"I'll go," Lyle volunteered. Though his face held no expression, his eyes were blazing hot as he shot Jubil a look as he left.

Davon folded his arms over his chest and glared at his sister.

"You are welcome to join us for the noon meal," Keltyn suggested but looked away when Davon turned a narrow-eyed glower his way.

"Davon?" Rosalyn asked in a soft voice. "Would you please leave us alone?"

Blowing out a harsh breath through his nose, Davon spun on his heel and left, his boot heels hard on the stairs as he stomped down them.

"Are we going to have trouble with him?" Jubil asked.

"No," Rosalyn said on a long sigh. "But I most likely will."

Corydon stepped up to her and reached out to lightly grip her chin, turning her face up to him. "In what way will you have trouble with him?" he demanded.

Rosalyn put a hand to his cheek. "Have no worries on my account, milord," she soothed him. "Davon will bluster and pout but he would rather cut off his own hand than raise it to me."

Corydon studied her face, searching for the truth behind her beautiful violet eyes. "You swear he will do no harm to you, milady?"

"On my honor," she replied and her fingers closed around his strong wrist. She lowered his hand to her breast and molded it around that lush globe. "I have chosen you."

Corydon's left eyebrow crooked upward as he fondled her breast through the fabric of Timun's shirt. "Chosen me for what?"

She simply smiled at him then turned to look at the glorious repast laid out on the table. She moved away and went to the table, dropping down gracefully upon one of the cushions.

"I'm hungry," she said.

The men took the cushions that had been used for Rosalyn's makeshift love bower and placed them around the table once more, sitting down to begin filling a plate for her.

Besides the succulent roast duck, there was hot, crisp asparagus, beets pickled with cucumbers and sliced onions in a sweet oil sauce, roasted apples with warm caramel sauce dripped over them, a bowl of mixed salad greens with cherry tomatoes, pepperoncinis, black olives and crumbles of goat cheese and drizzled with oil and vinegar, crusty bread hot from the oven and a variety of cheeses and fruits that boggled the mind and astounded the eye.

Brion poured chilled wine for each of them and brought it to the table.

Salivating, the men and Rosalyn began eating. They talked about current events and were surprised to find the beautiful woman as savvy concerning politics and local affairs as were they. Her intelligent discourse was a pleasant surprise for normally the women they brought to their clubroom had little in the way of brains inside their lovely heads.

"To my way of thinking," Rosalyn said, "Master Reynolds should be asked to vacate his office." She waggled a duck leg to underscore her point. "He's been in his position far too long."

"Precisely!" Keltyn agreed. "The man is an arrogant ass. Doesn't he realize the populace is tired of his highhanded tactics?"

"Aye!" Rosalyn said. "I feel the same way!"

Corydon leaned back on his cushion and swirled the ruby contents of his wine goblet. He was listening closely to Rosalyn's opinions. The woman was a veritable fount of knowledge about many current events and to listen to her speak was both entertaining and enlightening. Obviously she was well-bred and well-read as well as beautiful. For the first time in his life, he contemplated taking a wife. Looking at her over the rim of his goblet as he took a sip of the heady plum wine, he felt good about the decision he was attempting to make.

"Well, this has been great fun," Rosalyn said. She wiped her lips daintily with a linen napkin. "But Davon will be chomping at the bit and wanting to get home before the noon rush."

"Where exactly is home?" Brion asked for them all.

Rosalyn opened her mouth to speak but a forceful knock came at the door and she pressed her lips together in a woebegone smile, cocked her head to one side and shrugged in what was obviously a "see, what did I tell you?" way.

Owun got up to answer the door. He barely had time to step aside before Davon pushed his way into the room.

"It is time to leave!" the burly man snapped. He didn't wait for his sister to speak before going over and extending his hand to her.

Rosalyn sighed loudly then took his hand. She smiled sweetly at her brother but said nothing as he led her to the door.

"When will we see you again?" Keltyn asked.

"When you see her!" Davon threw back at him and escorted his sister from the room. He closed the door with a loud slam.

The other men turned to Corydon. "We don't know her last name!" Timun spoke for them.

"We'll find her again," Corydon said, draining his goblet. He put it down then dug into his pocket to pull out the sack of nine hundred quesons Davon had given him. He put the sack on the table. "Shall we play for our earnings, gentlemen, or do we disburse them evenly among us."

"Only you serviced her," Brion protested. "By right, that pot should go to you."

"We all serviced her," Jubil disagreed. "If anything, we should divide the pot between us."

"Why not make it high card?" Keltyn suggested. He pushed aside the dishes in front of him and produced a deck.

"High card wins the pot and the next meeting with our lady!" Brion amended.

"The lady is mine," Corydon said in a steely tone of voice that brooked no argument. "The pot?" He shrugged. "We'll cut for it."

Brion expertly shuffled the cards then placed the deck in the center of the table. "Timun, you go first."

Drawing the warrior of love, Timun felt fairly confident, but when his twin drew a warrioress of pleasure, the young man's expression fell.

Keltyn drew next and frowned as a ten of clubs destroyed his hopes.

Likewise Brion and Jubil were removed from the competition, for one drew a three of trees and the other a six of wells.

Corydon smiled. "Want to make a side bet that I will draw the highest card?" he asked.

Brion snorted. "What makes you think you will?"

"Rosalyn was destined to be mine. The gods would not let me lose."

Jubil rolled his eyes. "Arrogant prick." He nudged his chin toward the deck. "Aye, I'll make a side bet with you. I'll double the pot if you draw the winning card."

Corydon met and held each man's gaze in turn and they all agreed they would meet Jubil's wager.

"All right," Corydon said and casually reached out to take the top card from the deck. Without showing it, he brought it to his chest and held it.

"Let's see!" Jubil demanded.

"If the card is a High King or a keep, the gods have put their stamp of approval on my decision," Corydon said.

"What decision would that be?" Brion asked.

"That I should ask the lady to Join with me."

The men's mouths dropped open.

"You?" Brion gasped. "Marry?"

"Owun is going to win the pot with his queen," Jubil complained. "There's nothing for our glorious leader to worry about. Him marry? Poppycock!"

"Rosalyn's cock it will be," Corydon said and slapped his card down on the table. The High King peered back at them with a smug look.

"By the gods," Keltyn whispered.

Corydon leaned back and folded his arms over his chest. "The gods have decided, my friend."

"But you don't even know her last name!" Jubil exclaimed. "You know nothing about her!"

Corydon shrugged. "By the end of the week, I'll know all there is to know about our luscious Rosalyn."

# Chapter Two

But a week came and went and even with his network of knowledgeable spies, Corydon had not been able to find out anything about the beautiful Rosalyn. No one in the marketplace knew her and even after a door-to-door search of the village, his men could turn up no clue to either her identity or whereabouts. No one admitted seeing her or her formidable brothers.

It was a despondent Corydon Lesartes who left the Windsday Club's meeting room two weeks later. The others had long since gone back to either the barracks or their individual quarters and had left him alone to stare broodingly into his goblet of wine. With dejected footsteps, he descended the stairs and turned to lock the door.

"Have you missed me?"

Corydon spun around to find Rosalyn coming out of the dark shadows at the end of the building. Her brothers flanked her but stayed where they were when she came forward.

"Where have you been?" Corydon asked and shot out an arm to grab hers and pull her to him. His heart was thundering in his chest and he held her head to his breast.

"I'm here now," she answered. "That's all that matters."

He pushed her back from him so he could look down into her lovely face. "I thought I had lost you."

Rosalyn smiled. "Never, milord. I chose you. Remember?"

"But…"

"Here," she said and reached into her pocket to draw out a slip of paper. She tucked it into the pocket of his shirt. "There is my address. Be there first thing tomorrow morning."

"Rosalyn, I…"

She cut him off with slender fingers laid across his lips. "Be there," she repeated then pulled away, evading his questing hand.

Corydon stepped forward, intending to go after her, but Davon blocked his path.

"You'll do things by her way or not at all," the angry warrior announced. His hand went to the dagger at his belt. "Is that clear?"

Corydon looked beyond the man standing in his path and frowned sharply. Rosalyn and Lyle were nowhere to be seen. He had no choice but to jerk his head once in agreement.

Davon locked eyes with Corydon for a moment more then turned and stalked off into the shadows.

* * * * *

Corydon had not slept well the night before. Not even bothering to undress, he had flung himself upon his cot and had stared for most of the night at the delicate handwriting on the slip of paper Rosalyn had stuffed into his pocket. He alternately found himself heading for the door to scope out the address on the paper and flinging himself back down, angry that he had such little self-control all of a sudden. Dawn had found him bleary-eyed and nervous as he tore out of his rumpled clothes and sponged himself off before dressing in a freshly pressed lawn shirt and leather britches.

The street written on the paper was on the far side of the village, away from most homes and establishments. He had to hunt for the address—passing the right door three times—before he realized he had arrived at his destination. With his palms sweating and his heart thundering in his chest, he marched up to the door and rapped quickly.

"She will be mine," he kept repeating to himself as he heard footsteps approaching the door. "She will be mine and no other's."

Instead of Davon, whom Corydon expected to open the door, it was Rosalyn herself. She smiled at him and stepped back, bidding him enter.

The room was bright and airy with the morning sun pouring in through a wide bank of windows. An ornate dining table that would seat a goodly crowd was set with very expensive china and crystal goblets. A large, beautiful bouquet of fall flowers was arranged in an artfully crafted centerpiece. Along one wall were six ornately carved doors—three to each side of a sideboard that held silver chafing dishes, steaming and emitting fragrant smells that made Corydon's stomach growl.

"Are you expecting company?" he asked, frowning.

"No," she replied. "Just you."

Rosalyn stepped up to him and slipped her arms around his neck. "I've waited two long weeks for you, my love." She pressed against him. "Did you miss me?"

"Aye," he said, gruffly and slid his arms around her waist to hold her to him.

Rosalyn stood on her tiptoes and took his face in her hands to bring his head down to her. The instant her lips touched his, Corydon was as hard as a rock. He groaned low in his throat and swept her up in his arms.

"Where?" he asked.

"The far right door is my room," she said.

He carried her to the door and kicked it open then pushed it shut with his heel. The room smelled of gardenia as he carried her to the sumptuous bed that sat between two high windows. Laying her down upon the plush fur coverlet, he started to undo his shirt but she sat up.

"No," she said, sliding off the bed. "This time you lie down, milord, and I will do the stripping."

Corydon grinned. He jumped up on the bed and lay down on his back, putting his hands behind his head.

Rosalyn shook her head. "We'll do this my way," she said and reached out to pull his right arm from beneath his head. Stretching it to the top of the headpost, she retrieved something from below the top of the mattress and lifted it.

The click of the handcuff startled Corydon and his eyes flared. He jerked against the bond and would have snatched at it with his free hand but Rosalyn was up and over him, straddling his chest and grasping his left arm to pull it up to the headpost. She was stronger by far than he would have thought for he could not break free of her tight hold.

"Wench, what are you about?" he demanded, unaccustomed fear sending warning tremors through his belly and tightening his balls.

"I chose you," she said. "You have nothing to worry about, milord. Just lie here and enjoy us."

"Us?" he questioned, his voice unsure.

He barely felt the restraints being slipped around his ankles as Rosalyn scooted down the bed.

"You and I were destined to be one, milord," she said. "Perhaps we'll wed or perhaps we'll remain lovers without the benefit of Joining. Who knows? For this day and for always, though, only I will know the sweetest of your stalwart cock sheathed within me, but…"

Corydon heard the door open and lifted his head to see who had entered. He feared seeing Davon and Lyle standing there, revenge peppered in their steely eyes. But that was not who was coming toward him.

His mouth dropped open. His heart skipped a beat and his cock leapt.

"Welcome to the Thorsday Morning Club, Captain Lesartes," the tallest of the five naked women who had just entered welcomed him. "You're in for a grand good time."

## About the author

Charlee is the author of over thirty books, the first of which are the WindLegend Saga that began with WINDKEEPER. Married 39 years to her high school sweetheart, Tom, she is the mother of two grown sons, Pete and Mike, and the proud grandmother of Preston Alexander and Victoria Ashley. She is the willing houseslave to five demanding felines who are holding her hostage in her home and only allowing her to leave in order to purchase food for them. A native of Sarasota, Florida, she grew up in Colquitt and Albany, Georgia and now lives in the Midwest.

Charlotte welcomes mail from readers. You can write to her c/o Ellora's Cave Publishing at 1337 Commerce Drive, #13, Stow, OH 44224.

## Also by Charlotte Boyett-Compo:

Desire's Sirocco

Longing's Levant

# Manacles of Love

Elizabeth Lapthorne

*Dedication*

For My Martha, who always puts up with my shit, no matter how drama queen-ish I get. And who seems to make me smile even when I just want to shake my fist at the Guy Up There (okay, so maybe they're not *all* idiotic, moronic imbeciles…)

With love.

# Chapter One

*The year 2201*

Ma'ra stood in the doorway of the seedy bar. Smoke she didn't want to identify curled upward toward the stained ceiling from numerous spots around the dimly lit room. She mightn't officially be on duty but as she had learned time and again the hard way, a merc never really seemed to know how to switch off.

Now that she thought about it, that had been one of Steven's biggest complaints about her at the conclusion of their brief affair. Her self-realization on this matter had been a strong reason behind her not contacting him this time around on her short stay.

Resting her hand on her small tazer, she swallowed as she recalled the other reason for not contacting her ex-lover. She might need some help dealing with the man she hunted tonight, yet what she had planned was borderline legal no matter which angle you came at it from.

It also fell into the category of being completely and utterly *illegal* in a number of ways you could think of.

Ma'ra straightened her spine, determination etched upon her face.

Elise might be delicate, she might be young and practically unable to take care of herself alone, yet she was still the only blood kin anywhere in this universe Ma'ra had. She had been tempted long before now to let Elise stand on her own two feet and learn some things the hard way. Yet she always remembered the kinship between them, and once again saved Elise from her own actions. Ma'ra took her responsibilities seriously, no matter how she longed otherwise.

Elise bitched about Ma'ra cruising off to other planets and galaxies constantly, but she never complained about the healthy share Ma'ra always gave her of her credits.

Ma'ra smiled wryly. Elise might whine, but she definitely knew which side her *pan* was buttered on.

Ma'ra stepped slightly aside as the door behind her opened and let in yet another scantily clad escort. Feeling pity well up inside her, she resisted the impulse to turn the barely pubescent-looking young girl aside, fill her hands with credits, and tell her to head back home and return to her parents and studies. Even though the new regulations for escorts made the legal age of consent seventeen, Ma'ra had never been able to stomach the youthfulness of such escorts.

But knowing that to hand the child credits and try to bribe her to head back home would cause nothing but scorn from the girl, Ma'ra sighed sadly and turned to focus on the other side of the smoky bar. The chink of light from the opened door helped Ma'ra catch sight of her quarry.

Paul Sullivan.

The name sent a shiver down her spine, and not because of what she had planned for him on the brief trip over from Elise's tiny apartment, where she had left the girl wallowing in her tears

The man was easily over six feet tall, built solidly and definitely made to last in whatever endeavor he had planned. Dark blond hair framed his face, cut simply and grown long in the back. Ma'ra knew from half-listening to Elise's stories and sigh-filled tales of lust he tied it back when he worked.

Paul sat with a group of other men playing a game of cards, his muscular frame bunched into the seat and currently at ease. Ma'ra staked out a small table and chair and ordered a coffee. She needed to watch him, to gauge her moment. She wanted him inebriated enough for her plan to work, yet sober enough that he could still move under his own steam.

She was strong, certainly stronger than many women, yet not even she could carry Paul without arousing suspicion. She doubted he would go willingly with her, drunk or sober, if she gave him even a hint of her true agenda.

Ma'ra smiled at the waitress and idly paid her, keeping her attention focused purely on Paul. He seemed to be drinking blue vodka at an alarmingly steady rate. Either he was attempting to drown his sorrows, or simply throwing his money away.

In less than half an hour, he had lost a staggering amount of money and had put away the best part of a bottle of the expensive liquor.

As he staggered to his feet, rambling incoherently about finding himself a willing escort, he snickered and jeered with the men around the table, then wove unsteadily to the bar's doors.

Ma'ra stood silently, watching each step Paul made and making sure no one was paying attention to the drunken man. As he started singing a bawdy tune, he pushed open the doors, and Ma'ra breathed a sigh of relief. Hurrying after him, it took her less than a dozen paces to catch up with him.

Palming her tazer and hoping to take him by surprise, she pressed it to his carotid artery.

"Get into the red cruiser just up ahead," she softly murmured into his ear. She felt a spurt of panic as he turned around, looked rather soberly into her face, and then jerked in surprise.

"Ma'ra!" he hissed. "What the devil do you think you're doing? Didn't Elise tell you—?"

Ma'ra cut him off, not wanting him to say anything and maybe deplete her courage.

"Shut the hell up and do what I say or I'll turn this beam to its top notch and to hell with your chances."

They had stopped walking when he had recognized her. Standing on the filthy sidewalk in one of the seediest areas of the city Ma'ra felt for the first time that night the chill edge to the wind.

Seedy would be a generous description of the street and entire neighborhood they stood in. A hovel or grotto would be a more accurate description. It was only a slight step up from the worst side of the small city.

Ma'ra waited while Paul looked over her face and then focused on the steady hold she had on her small tazer. Size didn't always account for power these days, and they both were well aware of it.

From what Elise had hinted, Paul no longer worked for the Legal department in crime prevention anymore, but he still retained the knowledge from his more than twenty years in the Force. They both knew he hadn't a hope if she was serious.

Thankfully for her, neither of them could be totally certain just how pissed she truly felt at the moment.

Mumbling again, Paul climbed into her car, letting her open the door for him and slamming it shut behind him. Ma'ra quickly ran around the cruiser, letting herself in the driving side.

As she slammed her own door shut, she took a deep breath.

Unfortunately for her, that breath included a lungful of the smell of Paul. Salty masculinity, the faint scent of pine, which she always assumed was his aftershave. A single potent breath of Paul and already her pussy was heating, creaming for him and in anticipation of what she had planned.

She couldn't afford to get distracted until they were back at her lodgings!

"I am assuming good old Elise has completely overreacted once again. Let me guess, she comms you just as you come back from your two-year stint and she starts bawling her eyes out. 'It's just not fair,' she wails. 'He's such a bastard,' she cries. What dastardly deeds has she lain at my door this time?"

Ma'ra felt a second's pause. Elise had always turned on the tear works whenever something didn't go her way. As children at a birthday party once, when Elise had felt Ma'ra had taken the bigger slice of cake, she had thrown a tantrum, earning herself *two* slices of cake. When Ma'ra came home with a perfect score on her math quiz, Elise cried until her parents had rewarded her, their own daughter, as well as the poor, orphaned cousin.

*No!* Her mind screamed. She would not fall back onto their childish quarrels. This time she had seen the evidence. Someone *had* withdrawn all Elise's funds, and Paul now had thousands of credits worth of new car, new lodging, new everything and had been thrown out of the Force for corruption.

It was all she needed to know to revenge poor Elise.

Ma'ra turned to him, surprised how small and cramped her cruiser seemed with them both in the front seat.

"Look, Ma'ra," he continued. "I don't have time for this shit, fun as it may be. I've got work to do—"

Again she cut him off, not wanting him to make her question her cousin once again.

"Elise told me how you were thrown from the Force for corruption. So shut the hell up, I'm not listening to you."

"Ma'ra—"

Deftly, knowing one wrong move or the slightest second of hesitation and he would disarm her and she'd be in a whole lot more trouble than simply questioning whether her cousin was lying to her or not, Ma'ra brought her tazer up and zapped him.

She had been hoping to be able to hit the main nerve on his neck. But in the cramped quarters of the car, with both their senses heightened, she knew she might miss, and she truly didn't want him hurt. So instead she pressed the small tazer into the side of his belly. There was barely any softness there either, but it was the safest place for her to reach and still have a hope of knocking him out.

She had set the tazer before entering the bar, not wanting to have to fiddle with it later. She had *very* carefully calculated from Paul's size and strength how much would knock him out, without hurting or damaging him. She might want her revenge, might want to sate herself and her curiosity about him, but she didn't want to possibly burn him or give him a scar.

Paul slumped back in the seat, the boneless flop of his body showing her she had accurately calculated the necessary strength of force.

Leaning over him, she felt for his pulse, checked his breathing and made sure there were no burn marks on his skin. Only a slight redness on the spot where she had zapped him remained. He was fine.

Smiling, replacing the tazer in her pocket, Ma'ra started up her cruiser. She wanted to have him in her lodgings and properly contained before he awoke. For three years now she had fantasized about this man, and tonight she would have a small taste of those dreams.

Tomorrow she'd have to turn him in, not that it would necessarily make a difference if the Force was truly riddled with corruption. But for tonight he was hers and hers alone.

# Chapter Two

Paul opened his eyes to a sore neck, a dull headache, and a vision he had dreamed about for years. Ma'ra stood over him, her black merc gear bulging in all the right female places.

Her shoulder-length red hair was released from bondage, allowed to curl free in its natural windblown look. Her large bust was almost within range of his mouth and tongue. The front of her shirt gaped, allowing a tantalizing glimpse of the heaven that awaited him.

Paul cast his eyes down, reluctantly, away from the healthy show of cleavage. Seated as she was, he couldn't see her ass, and he felt a keen disappointment. The imitation leather pants cupped her cheeks in a way that had every man panting and wanting to grab the flesh encased in her uniform.

Paul recalled the first day her younger cousin, Elise, had introduced them. Paul had known Elise had a childish crush on him. Even at twenty-three Elise was more girl than woman. He had been humoring the kid, not wanting to upset or offend her by being vocal in his nonsexual interest in her.

Aside from his desire to not upset her, his work often brought him into contact with Elise, a legal transcriptionist. Until he had been introduced to Ma'ra, there seemed no point in being rude to the girl or more firm than necessary.

Yet the instant he had seen Ma'ra he had wanted to bed her.

Badly.

With Elise hovering over them, laughing and chatting, he had never had a chance. Elise with her clingy, adoring looks had obviously staked a claim—no matter how false—and Ma'ra had set off for parts mostly unknown quickly afterwards.

Which left him with his erotic thoughts, his cheap escorts, and law enforcement partners.

And his dreams.

His highly erotic, XXX-rated dreams.

Frowning, feeling a pang as Ma'ra sat down next to him on the bed, Paul tried to get his wits in order. Not only shouldn't Ma'ra be here on the bed with him, but he was supposed to be on assignment.

*Assignment!*

The word reverberated around his skull, causing the dull ache to recede and the memory of the pub, the sting, the undercover assignment he had been cultivating for over the last six months all came clearly rushing back into focus.

*Damnation!*

Squinting, wanting to focus his groggy attention, he remembered how tonight was supposed to be the start of the end. For months he and the Force had been carefully laying the groundwork, faking his court-martial for corruption, his lavish lifestyle and his integration into the seedy underworld. For more than six months he had been living a constant lie, determined to get every thought away from Ma'ra and bury himself in his work.

He had been doing splendidly until tonight. Tonight the plan had been for him to be contacted outside the bar by the network he wanted to infiltrate. Instead, he had been dumbfounded to have Ma'ra stick a tazer in his neck.

He had been astonished to see her on that dilapidated street, creeping up behind him. He hadn't been as inebriated as he had been acting. Most of the alcohol had been slipped down his sleeve in the old sleight-of-hand maneuver he had perfected, but also he had taken a shot to dull the effect of the small amount of liquor he had to consume. He might smell drunk and appear drunk, but his head had been perfectly clear.

He had been so stunned by Ma'ra's surprise appearance he hadn't hesitated to enter her cruiser. He hadn't wanted to draw attention to himself, but more, he hadn't wanted to draw unneeded attention to *Ma'ra*.

Sitting upright, he gasped as his hands *clanged* against the metal frame of the bed.

"What the hell!" he exclaimed, completely astounded to see a pair of manacles surrounding his wrists.

Pulling at them, unbelieving, he turned back to the red-haired witch on his bed. Looking about the room, he realized it wasn't his bed, this wasn't even his quarters!

"Where the hell am I and what do you think you're doing?"

He gazed at Ma'ra as she stood, brushing imaginary lint from her imitation leather pants.

"I brought you here to get a few answers."

Paul raised an eyebrow and lay back in the bed. No way was Ma'ra going to get a rise out of him.

"You been reading my diary, Ma'ra? You must have skimmed the best and kinkiest parts. It's supposed to be *you* chained to the bed, not me. Word-activated, I assume?"

Paul grinned. The flush creeping over Ma'ra's features, the flush of what he knew to be part embarrassment, but also part arousal, made him hot.

When she nodded, he knew it was in response to his latter question, not the former baiting.

"I'm not here to fulfill your kinky fantasies, Paul. I'm here to get Elise's money back. She informed me on my return how low you've sunk. How you've been court-martialed for corruption, how you stole all her credits and have been living the high life. And no, I didn't instantly believe her, but she showed me the press releases and her e-bank statements. One massive withdrawal of all her funds. So I'll leave you to think about how to explain all that to me, and when I come back you'd better be ready to return her money, or you'll regret it."

Paul raised his eyebrow in the mocking manner he knew steamed her.

"Going to torture me, darling?"

"If I need to," she replied smartly enough to make him laugh. "You're the one who brought up sexual fantasies. I bet you never thought you'd be the one losing control. I'll make you beg for release, until you'll be ready to give me anything, let alone returning the credits you stole from Elise."

Her throaty, husky promise to make him beg made his laugh die in his throat. That was the voice he'd dreamed of, fantasized about, jerked off to more times than he could count.

Before he could think of a witty reply, a fantastic comeback, she turned, swung her luscious ass, and walked out of the room.

Paul sat back and breathed deeply. Closing his eyes, he thought of the small tidbits of information Elise had let drop now and then about her older cousin. Ma'ra had turned thirty earlier in the year, the perfect age for his own thirty-six years. Mentally filtering through all his information, he remembered Elise mentioning how Ma'ra often kept the same three or four passwords.

*"Oh, she never had the best of memories, keeps the same couple and just rotates through them. That way she always can guess what her password is, even if she can't remember it."*

Twisting his head so his voice carried the word clearly to the manacles, he tried his hardest to remember the three words Elise had listed off to him.

"Shakespeare," he said clearly, waiting.

Nothing happened. Paul frowned, disgruntled. The famous playwright, a favorite read they both shared, was the one that came to mind the easiest. They both had a weakness for the tragedies the man had written many centuries ago. He frowned again, racking his brain. Suddenly he remembered something both Elise and Ma'ra had told him back on their first meeting.

*"Pathetic but true," she had smiled as she said to him. "My first lover bought violets for me on one of our initial dates. I've had a weakness for them ever since."*

"Violets" he said clearly, his voice ringing with his conviction.

The manacles shuddered and opened, releasing his arms.

Paul sat up in the bed, feeling more comfortable than he had in ages. Picking up the heavy metal cuffs, he held them in his hands, testing their weight. Ma'ra would never believe he would work them off, let alone turn the tables on her.

The surprise he envisioned on her face, quickly followed by the mental image of him snapping the manacles over her wrists and binding *her* to the bed, had his erection lengthening like never before. Ma'ra manacled to the bed. Completely at his mercy. Open to his every desire and fantasy.

Paul shifted as his pants became way too tight.

Even the thought that he had unknowingly warned her of what would now be coming had him growing harder. He had told her how he had fantasized about their positions being reversed, fantasized about it on more than one occasion.

The heat simmering in his blood at finally being able to bring this particular fantasy to life had him groaning at the pressure now building in his cock.

Smiling his joy, he crawled off the bed. He needed to think of something else or he would come in his pants before Ma'ra returned. Standing, stretching his legs, he brought the cuffs near his mouth.

He needed to change the lock word—a simple enough task—and hopefully good enough to get his mind out of his pants and return some of his blood back into his brain and away from his erection.

The cuffs were standard issue. Many mercs, and everyone on the Force, knew how to use them.

Paul grinned. He could cuff her and have his wicked way with her, let his fantasies come true. She had called him kinky? She had no idea *just* how kinky he could be.

But what to change the lock word to?

Paul wrinkled his brow in thought. Something she would never think to say, some word he could pleasure her through and never have either of them cry out.

His face lightened, his smile came back. He had the perfect word.

"Lock word change to…" he started in a clear voice, certain of what he was doing.

In the empty bedroom, he stated the one four-letter word he felt certain neither of them would utter.

That done, he dropped the manacles onto the bed. Paul turned around and began to search the room. He wanted to be fully prepared when she came back, not only to manacle her to the sturdy bed, but also to start his "*kinky*" fantasies.

Just the mental picture of those kinky fantasies has his cock getting harder and hotter.

His smile, not to mention other parts of his anatomy, grew broader at the thought.

# Chapter Three

Ma'ra pressed her forehead against the cool imitation glass. She had purposely chosen the peaceful scene of a rainforest to be shown through the "window". Somehow the thought of having a scene of the beach or a trickling river did nothing to help soothe her. Only the forest managed to help her clear her mind.

And what an image she tried desperately to clear.

Paul, chest straining, legs spread, manacled to her bed

Never had she thought to have such...well, outré fantasies!

She had never been one to subscribe to bondage fantasies or romances. Never had she admitted to *anyone* about having the remotest interest in being bound or tying a man to her bed.

Yet when it came to Paul, the thought of having him at her mercy, being able to take her time to touch, to taste, to do anything and everything she wished held immense appeal. More appeal than she ever had imagined.

So intoxicated by the thoughts rushing around her head, in fact, that she felt it necessary to come out here into her main living area and set her screen to the soothing images that always made her feel peaceful and at ease. To take steady, deep breaths so she wouldn't simply pounce on the poor man and eat him whole.

*Mmmm*…her mind purred, locking for a moment on the vision of her eating his enormous staff. Fiercely she pulled her mind from the image. She was supposed to be here to get *rid* of those sorts of images!

*What you really should do,* insisted her damnable conscience piping up with its own opinions, *is take him straight to his bosses on the force and to hell with this revenge. Surely putting in an official complaint and request for reimbursement with his superiors would be enough for an inquiry. Elise can track her own damned money from there!*

Ma'ra sighed.

The problem with that route, she informed herself, would be she would never be able to seduce Paul, never again get the chance to touch or taste him.

*That* thought was enough to shut her conscience up immediately.

For over two years now she had run and hidden from the man her cousin had staked out as her own. Never mind the fact Paul was blatantly not interested in Elise, had indeed turned down her cousin's overtures for months. The mere fact Elise had claimed him first meant Ma'ra could look but never, ever touch.

And that was what rankled. Why the hell couldn't she touch, if just for once? Elise had taken dozens of lovers while Ma'ra had been off keeping herself busy. Obviously the girl hadn't completely forgotten Paul, yet no one would ever know of this one night.

Thinking about the time she was wasting, Ma'ra shut the screen down and straightened her spine. She had chosen this route, damned if she would turn aside now.

Paul lay waiting on her bed, albeit *manacled* to said bed, and the thought of the delicious meal he presented to her was more than enough to have her breathless with excitement. Her pussy throbbed with the blood rush, and her nipples were erect and scratching against the lace of her bra.

Who needed a fit of conscience when one had a willing stud manacled to the bed?

She had never even thought to have a man, this one in particular, bound and at her mercy. The myriad of things she could do, that she *wanted* to do, to this man had her steps hastening back to her sleeping quarters.

She paused outside her bedroom. Fluffing her hair, she then smiled at her idiocy. Who *cared* what her hair looked like? *She* was in control here!

Pressing the discreet button, she watched the door swish open, a smile of anticipation on her mouth.

She stepped into the room, satisfaction seeping into every inch of her body.

Until she realized no one lay on her bed.

Her mouth opened, an unformed query on her lips. The feeling of a hard, warm masculine body pressing against her back took her by surprise. Before she even thought to articulate one of the many questions floating in her mind, she found herself turned and walked backwards toward her bed.

"Paul!" she managed, not even certain if she were upset, angry or just plain befuddled.

In quick, concise movements he pressed her down so she fell on the bed. The warm yet solid feel of manacles closing over her wrists had her gasping in shock.

"How the hell—?" she started to shriek in a completely embarrassing manner as he began to strip her shirt and pants, bra and panties from her body. He ended up tearing the delicate lace of her bra and her thin merc shirt to remove them from her arms, the rip of the fabric stunning her as nothing ever had previously.

She never wore shoes inside her quarters, and for a fleeting moment wished she had the barrier of them to protect her feet which itched to kick him.

She felt such shock, was overcome by confusion of things not being what she had anticipated. She would never feel genuinely threatened by this man, even manacled to her own bed. Yet as her mind processed the shock of having the tables turned so easily on her, she felt her pussy dampen with heat and dew. She gasped, both with her desire and the surprise still firing her system.

Her gasp turned into a moan as Paul's lips pressed down on hers. Warm, smooth lips, too seductive by half. His kiss felt even better than she had imagined. He felt like heated silk running over her lips, inviting her to temptations untold.

He pulled himself up and away from her and she bit her lip. Even so, a whimper escaped and she chastised herself severely for it. Deciding to finally take the offensive instead of merely reacting, she cleared her throat.

"I take it you worked out the lock word?"

She swallowed as Paul smiled toothily at her. *Man, he could tempt a nun to sin!* She tried to hide her expression as he began to pull off his shirt. Sculpted abs and then a smooth, tanned chest that made her mouth water were revealed.

Ma'ra wondered where her wits had gone. She lay naked and bound on her own bed, where less than five minutes ago she had been congratulating herself on capturing and keeping under control the man who now shed his clothes onto her floor.

"You really should find new passwords, Ma'ra my dear," he chided gently, making her face flush.

"I'll make sure the next time I set the lock words to find a particularly obscure one. Now that you've had your fun, would you mind releasing me before you make your already deplorable situation worse?"

Ma'ra knew her chances were futile, yet the grin, the possessive gleam in his eye told her more clearly than any words just how fruitless those chances were.

"Now, now. You were all willing and ready to seduce a bound captive. I think it's only fair that I return the favor. Besides, darling, I *did* warn you all my fantasies revolved around your gorgeous self being the bound one, not I."

Ma'ra struggled as he spoke and began to shed his pants, even though she knew wriggling out of the manacles would be useless. Many stronger beings than she had struggled with them. Nothing ever broke free from these damned things. It was why she had chosen them in the first place.

"Look, Paul—"

Ma'ra groaned as she felt heated, naked flesh rub against her own. She didn't understand how this situation had flown out of her control so quickly. She couldn't believe her body would turn traitorous and be creaming so wildly at the thought of Paul being able to do anything and everything to her. Yet the simple fact was she felt wildly excited, more turned on than she had ever been before.

She knew a large part of it hung on the fact it was Paul in control. Paul's flesh she felt next to her own, Paul's skin skimming along her own, Paul's massive erection pressing against her thigh.

"Just let me live this fantasy, Ma'ra," he cajoled, his sexy, husky voice crooning to her as if she were a scared little animal. "I can explain everything tomorrow, once we've both sated ourselves. It's obvious we both have the same fantasies."

"I seriously doubt it!" she cried out. She couldn't tell if she felt anger or helplessness, all she felt was the heated blood running through her system, making her hornier than she had ever felt before. "I have *never* fantasized about being bound."

Ma'ra wriggled as Paul crawled onto the bed on his hands and knees. The shoulder-length mass of his hair fell down to caress her skin. The simple act alone had her squirming in delight.

Looking up, determined to plead her case, Ma'ra felt herself drown in the warm brown pools of his eyes. She had always had a weakness for his eyes, thinking of them as molten chocolate. Good enough to swim in forever.

Ma'ra groaned and gave up the struggle as Paul started to string kisses down her neck, nipping and laving seductively as he journeyed across her skin.

"Paul," she moaned, unsure exactly what she asked for.

"You know," he started, stringing kisses between the erotic pull of his words, "your skin is as soft as satin, and tastes just like you. Salty, sweet, and very feminine."

"I'm a merc," she ground out. "I'm never feminine."

Husky chuckles emanated from his mouth, sending shivers along her nerves as he rumbled against her skin.

"You have a chest men dream about, skin as soft as a baby's. Your wit is sharp, and you can handle yourself. You're the stuff of wet dreams, my dear."

"If I can…uh…handle myself—please don't stop that!—then why am I bound to my own bed, being ravished?"

Ma'ra tried not to whimper as Paul pulled away. When he spread her legs, she felt a moment's panic.

"Oh yeah," he ground out, looking with a strange mix of desire and jealousy at her pussy, "wet and creaming, just the way I wanted you."

Paul dipped down for a moment, unable to help himself. Ma'ra felt electric currents pass through her body as he swiped a long, slow lick of her lips. Her *lower* lips.

Somehow, his tongue managed to cover and hit every nerve, every point of screaming, straining flesh that so desperately wanted to be touched. The low, almost pain-filled moan that fell from her mouth came as a shock.

Paul sat back on his haunches, looking incredibly like the cat who stole the cream. Which indeed he might be—if one considered a giant panther or leopard a *cat*.

Ma'ra realized she simply lay there, flat on her back, naked as the day she came from the womb, staring at the man who delicately licked her juices from his lips.

"You can handle yourself, my dear," he continued their conversation as if they had never stopped. As if he hadn't just done the most intimate thing any man had ever performed on her. "It's just I'm not convinced you can handle *me*."

Feeling her back arch as he relaxed once more between her thighs, Ma'ra kept her mind firmly on the conversation, not the shooting electric jets his touch caused her body to feel.

"I think I did just fine until you figured out the lock word."

The smug, utterly masculine smile he gave her set her teeth on edge, but made the fire in her belly burn hotter. How could this man possibly irritate her and turn her on simultaneously? Surely that was the biggest paradox in the galaxy.

*Men!*

As Paul slowly, reverently, took another lick of her flesh, causing her back to arch and her toes to curl, Ma'ra knew she was entering Big Trouble.

"Okay!" she called out. "I quit! What the hell do you want?"

"I just want you, darling," he purred against her pussy, making her close her eyes in the ecstasy. The vibrations from his words alone sent heat and desire spiraling through her system.

The meaning behind the words sent an entirely different kind of heat racing through her. If he truly were a panther, he seemed almost ready to pounce.

"I want you like this, open and spread before me, embracing my every lick and thrust. I want you to scream when you come, and I want you to call my name so loudly your bedroom walls tremble."

Ma'ra found herself panting at his words, at the graphic images they caused to form in her head. She could see every lick, every caress. She could see herself crying out and straining against his delicious body, *screaming* his name as she came in shuddering spasms.

She was no psychic, no seer, but damn, she had a feeling all those images, plus plenty more her brain *hadn't* seen, were about to truly occur.

In a split second, much like she made most of her decisions, Ma'ra weighed the pros and cons of her situation.

She didn't feel physically threatened by this man, she knew he would never hurt her. She had also lied when she stated she had never fantasized about being bound. It was one of those things a woman, and a merc in particular, never told or admitted to another living being.

She was a normal woman and of course she had dozens of fantasies. This just happened to be one she never thought to act upon in reality.

With those two most important pieces of information, she made her decision. She could take back control the following morning. Bring Paul in as she had intended, get Elise's money back, if indeed he had stolen any. The more she thought about it the less likely it seemed.

For now, she was going to be selfish for the first time in her life. She would take this night of passion and pleasure with Paul for herself, and return to the memories for the rest of her life.

She relaxed her body, took in a deep breath. She saw by the glint of knowledge in his eye that Paul knew she was handing over control to him, embracing their situation and time together.

"Go ahead, Paul. Let's see if you can *really* make me scream, or if your ego is just inflated like most men's."

The grin that came across his face looked so wicked, so knowledgeable she felt her heart race. He was every bad-boy fantasy she had ever held, every wet dream, every erotic fantasy a girl could ask for. The fact he used to be on the Force, on the Good Guys' side just made him that much more seductive.

And just for tonight, he was *hers*. Completely. Unequivocally. Totally hers.

"You know what you're saying, my Ma'ra? You'll give control completely over to me?"

"For tonight, sure. You've made some pretty impressive promises, Cowboy," she taunted him with her old nickname for him. A Lone Ranger of the Law, he had once described himself to her. She, and not Elise, had caught the old-fashioned book reference. Since then, she had taunted him with his self-description of a cowboy. Until now, she had been too angry, too upset with him to relax and poke the beast.

"Then let's make some of those promises reality, my dear. Starting with *this*."

Ma'ra arched up from the bed, biting her lip in refusal to scream this early in their game.

Paul had ducked his head back down and now licked and tongued her in earnest. She had thought him proficient at eating her earlier. *This* was consuming her, not just delicately nibbling. His tongue laved her, lapped up her juice and then speared inside her pussy, creating more juice to come from her.

Ma'ra pressed her pussy into his face and moaned for more.

She wondered for a split second if she should have dared the man to make her scream. Then the intense pleasure, the utter abandon and joy swept over her and she didn't care if she screamed herself hoarse. The pleasure was well worth the loss of her voice.

# Chapter Four

Paul lapped at Ma'ra and marveled that he had held himself back for so long. She tasted of ambrosia, the sweet, salty taste of women around the galaxy. Yet there seemed to be a musky undertone to her juices, a subtle flavor that was Ma'ra and hers alone.

He was no saint. He bedded women with frequency and great delight. He enjoyed their shapes, textures and most importantly of all, their screams of delight as they came. Rarely, however, did it become necessary to tie a woman down. The innate possessiveness of the act often had him dodging such requests.

With Ma'ra, it just seemed natural. Here was *his* woman, taunting and teasing him and simply begging for a delicious fucking. She felt ripe, fairly hummed with the desire to come over and over again. She consciously or subconsciously arched into his strokes, his lapping, his body, and practically vibrated with her need for him.

As she was far from ready to commit to him, to bowing to his cock and affection, the use of the restraints, manacles or no, seemed somehow so very *right*. For her own pleasure, for her own good, binding her and seducing her seemed like the best idea he had come up with in three years.

Paul lay back down, enjoying the heavenly feeling of resting between her spread thighs. He bit his inner cheek to assure himself he wasn't asleep and dreaming. Creamy, pale thighs spread wide, dew glinting on her curls, beckoning a man to his doom.

Lightly flicking her clit, enjoying the way it swelled and plumped out, begged for his tongue and teeth, Paul buried his mouth against her slit and thrust his tongue deeply inside her.

He lapped up her moans and jerky movements as much as her juices.

When she came, she cried out. Certainly not the *scream* of pleasure he was used to, but he would get them both there. With barely a pause for breath, shooting her a smug, utterly masculine look of pride and ego, he continued to pleasure her, playing with her clit and enjoying the feel of her. He fit three of his fingers inside and she whimpered from the full feeling, spiking his lust higher.

"I bet if I make you come again I can fit my whole fist inside you."

Ma'ra moaned, pressing her sweating head into her raised arms.

"Bet you can't," she teased, panting hard.

Paul merely smiled and continued to pleasure her, tease her clit and lap at her dripping pussy.

After her second orgasm, as he had guessed and gently taunted her, he fit all five of his fingers inside her wet, gloving pussy, yet still not his whole fist.

The sight of her body stretched wide, opened fully to him and his fingers, his will, enthralled him. He had never before wished to indulge himself in viewing his lover. Sure, he enjoyed watching their faces widen in joy and delight as they fucked themselves raw, yet there felt to be more with Ma'ra.

He enjoyed watching his fingers trail over her skin, enjoyed feeling her clit throb with its desire against his tongue. He enjoyed watching her body suck at his fingers as if it never wanted to release him.

He lost track of time, indulging himself. He touched, he caressed, he drove her wild and loved the flush of sexual heat heighten her color on her neck and upper chest.

Some time later, when he began to sweat and feel the pressure in his balls rise to an uncomfortable level, he knew he needed to buy himself just a little more time. Ma'ra certainly felt ready to embrace him deep inside herself, yet he wanted this first time, this most special time, to last.

Withdrawing his fingers, he smiled as she moaned.

"No! Please don't leave me here…"

"Shh," he soothed her. "I'm just looking for something more. What secrets does your dresser drawer hold?"

Scooting across the bed, leaning down onto the simple piece of furniture, he opened the top drawer, hoping to find something with which to extend their time just a bit more.

As the heavy drawer opened, his eyes widened.

*Well! Wasn't his Ma'ra full of surprises!*

He felt an evil, gloating grin cross over his face. Turning back to her, bound to her own bed and flushed with her sexual heat, spread and eager for his possession, he felt the rest of the night snap into place.

*Definitely full of surprises!*

# Chapter Five

Ma'ra mentally groaned as Paul opened her top drawer.

Fine, she might be a merc, but that didn't mean she didn't have sexual cravings like everyone else.

Two years ago when she had decided to go on "extended contract", she had known the chances of picking up even a half-decent lover were slim to none. In fact, she had known the chances of having real sex became almost nonexistent. One did not sleep with one's crewmates, and one did not ask one's captain or crew to stop off for a quick fuck to release the tension.

Instead, Ma'ra had chosen to become a connoisseur of sex toys.

And she had surprised herself by loving every minute of it. Every pit stop they had made, the crew got released for the day. Many of the men went to the bars, had a few beers and a few women. Most of the females joined the men in their pursuits—simply to prove they could.

Ma'ra felt confidant enough in herself and her own skills she didn't need to prove her balls, so instead she amused herself shopping for sex toys. After the first few items, she found she loved scrounging around, finding new and ever more exotic toys.

Even better was teaching herself how to use them and enjoy them.

As the months and years passed, she dragged the whole caseload of toys around with her. There was no sense in letting everyone else find out about her secret indulgence.

Yet now that she had moved home, however temporary it might prove to be, she had unloaded her big case of toys and placed them in her top dresser drawer, as any self-respecting woman would.

Watching Paul, openmouthed in his shock and sifting through the toys, did strange things to her.

He picked up a life-like jelly Elephant Man Vibrator and held it out for her to see, shock and disbelief etched on his gorgeous face.

"You *use* this thing? And were complaining about my fist? Darling, this is bigger than both my fists together!"

Before she could respond he had turned back around, replaced it with a shake of his head, and continued his search.

Face masks, more manacles— "Shakespeare" he said, confidence and absolute knowing shone in his eyes as he watched her and not the manacles as they opened as if by magic. She resolved to *really* change her lock words. Other assorted paraphernalia were shuffled around as Paul scrounged in her most private drawer.

"Aha! Absolutely perfect" had Ma'ra straining to see what he had found that so captured his attention.

He turned around and crawled back onto the bed to her. Whatever he had found, they fit in his big, closed palm.

"Nipple and clit clamps," he gloated, opening his hand.

Ma'ra felt the blood drain from her face. Her body flushed, hot and then icy cold.

"Those aren't regular—"

"I know *exactly* what they are, and shame on you, young lady, for never telling me about your fascination with sexual aid toys. We could have had this party long before now."

Ma'ra took a deep breath.

*He knew what they were. And he obviously knew how to use them. Oh man, she was in deep shit.*

Ma'ra watched warily as Paul flicked the discreet switch on the small clamps. There didn't outwardly appear to be any change in them. Yet Ma'ra knew, and obviously Paul also knew, he had set the clamps revving.

Ma'ra arched her back as Paul took one of her nipples wetly into his mouth. Heat surrounded the bit of flesh, ignited the fire already consuming her body. The sucking pressure his mouth created, the heat and intensity of her secret vice being known—and so effectively used!—had her creaming like fury.

She whimpered as the heat of his mouth left her, and then cried out as he closed the small clamp bitingly around her erect nipple. For a moment, a lightning arc of pain consumed her, and then the pleasure crashed over her, nearly causing her to come yet again.

The clamp warmed her cold nipple. It felt different from the encompassing heat of Paul's mouth, yet warmth still closed over her erect teat.

Ma'ra gasped for breath.

And then the tiny jolt of electricity had her arching in pleasure again.

She opened her eyes, not knowing when she had closed them, as she felt the now-familiar heat of Paul's mouth close over her other nipple. Her clamped nipple throbbed in time with her pumping blood. The tiny, erratic electrical pulses turned her on even more than the wet heat of his mouth.

Ma'ra closed her eyes again, the pleasure driving her insane. Paul's mouth sucked better than the suction pump she had tried months ago, the wet, slurping noises adding to the intimacy of the act. When he pulled his mouth away, she braced herself.

And so, of course, he surprised her and returned his mouth to her nipple.

Ma'ra moaned, the eroticism of the act spiking her temperature even higher.

The clamp felt almost sentient in its working. The harmless, pleasurable electric jolts were sporadic, holding to no set rhythm, no pattern she found. It mingled heat with a sense of suction, interspersed with the tiny jolts that had her creaming and begging for Paul's thick, hard cock.

"I need you inside me," she panted. Paul simply grunted, his eyes gleaming his wicked amusement.

In the space of a heartbeat, he pulled himself upright, placed the clamp on her nipple, and moved himself down between her thighs.

"Oh no," she panted, "not my clit. I'll come."

"That's the general idea, my dear," he returned, smugly male.

The second his mouth closed over her throbbing erect clit, she screamed. Both nipple clamps sent their erotic jolts, and the heat and pressure on her clit had her screaming her orgasm.

Just like he had promised.

But it didn't seem as if he gave a shit he had done what he promised. The man had a glint in his eye, a wicked knowing that he had not even *begun* with her just yet.

Panting, Ma'ra prayed for strength, for endurance, for a chance to return even half of this erotic teasing before the night was over. Ooh, she'd make him pay. She'd *make up* a lock word, one he would never find out and she would never remember. She'd keep him bound to her bed for the rest of their lives, and she'd tease him until he begged her for release.

*Yes,* she thought, as another orgasm ripped through her, leaving her panting for breath. *She would pay him back for every gasp, pant and orgasm. And when they both lay completely sated and totally exhausted, she'd figure out whatever it was she had meant to find out.*

That thought returned a tiny bit of her brain capacity. Hadn't there been something she wanted?

As another orgasm ripped through her she decided to let it go. Whatever the hell it was, her mind was in no shape to try and work it out. Frankly, she couldn't care less.

She'd think later, when her body didn't feel like it was on fire and her clit and nipples didn't positively ache with desire and unspent lust.

Yeah…later.

# Chapter Six

Paul wished to hell his little wildcat had mirrors on her bedroom ceiling. Never having been very into voyeurism himself, he had never fully appreciated the necessity of mirrors to aid sexual gratification.

Yet lying between his Ma'ra's spread thighs, sucking on her clit as if it were a child's sucker, he couldn't do this and fully appreciate the expressions crossing her face. Couldn't sit back and enjoy her body, bound and spread, nipples clamped enticingly, a veritable offering for his body and eyes.

*Yep, definitely need to add a few strategic mirrors around the place. Then I can do this and pause intermittently to watch the show.*

For a woman with hundreds of credits worth of sexual toys, manacles, plugs and enough other items to keep a man busy for months, he certainly felt surprised not to see mirrors lining the walls and ceiling of her bedroom.

Even while he wished this, a part of his mind felt relieved. If he could fully see her face, could taste, touch *and* see her reactions simultaneously, then more than likely he would have come before now himself.

And for the first time since his youth, *not* inside a woman, as well! How degrading. He hadn't done that in—what?—twenty years?

Instead, he nibbled and laved, thoroughly enjoyed bedding the one woman he seemingly couldn't get out of his mind. This night of fantastic, blow-your-mind sex might be enough to get her out of his system. But as the minutes and hours clicked by, he felt increasingly certain that one night of pure mind-blowing pleasure mightn't be enough.

As he wrung one more orgasm from Ma'ra, heard her voice begin to croak with weariness, he knew this first bout was coming to a close. His balls positively felt blue with the strain of holding back, and if he put this off much longer he *would* be disgracing himself.

He had thoroughly loved watching her come multiple times, but as he flicked her clit again and she flinched, he knew the time was ripe for him to finally enter her.

Kneeling on the bed he bent down, resting the very tip of himself in her entrance. He felt her juices running over his cock, felt his pre-cum pearl on his tip.

Gently, reverently, he pressed his lips softly against hers.

"Are you okay with this?" he asked softly. Much as he had fantasized about this for three years, much as he might tease and taunt her, he would rather walk into an ice-cold shower and jerk himself off—multiple times—than take her by force.

Wearily, Ma'ra opened one beautiful eye. Wariness lay deep within.

"Is this a trick question?"

He smiled, and then laughed.

"Of course not, I just want you to take some responsibility for tonight."

"Well, duh. Have I been screaming the place down?—okay, don't answer that," she grumbled as he laughed, scattering kisses down her nape. "Yes, I'm fine with this, if you *don't* thrust inside me any second now I will personally think up some evil revenge and not rest until I have you begging for mercy…"

He loved the catch in her voice, the way he so overwhelmed her she lost her train of thought. She groaned in the abject pain of pleasure as he thrust himself balls-deep inside her, gloving his aching shaft just like he had dreamed of forever.

He paused inside her, wanting to catch his breath, desperate to hold onto his control. Yet the warmth of her pussy, the sucking walls and sheer exhilaration of hearing her scream his name, begging him for release, tried his patience like never before.

He withdrew slightly and then plunged back inside her. He held tightly to his desperate need, but only through sheer force of will. Having Ma'ra finally scream for him, scream with joy and sexual abandon, was definitely the thing wet dreams were made of.

Now he just needed to hear her shout out her orgasm once again before he burst inside her.

Touching her, he sensitized her to all the nuances of her body and his where their naked skin met. Surreptitiously he flicked both nipple clamps, setting them on to high.

Ma'ra groaned with the extra stimulation, raising her hips completely off the bed and widening her legs to let him in deeper, further.

Paul withdrew to his very tip, taunting and torturing them both.

"Paul..." she cried out, begging without even needing to say the words.

He reached down one hand and in a quick, concise movement removed the clit clamp. Ma'ra screamed, the loss of the stimulation accentuating the heated, driving thrum of both their pulses and pleasure.

Wanting this last ride to last forever, he thrust himself back inside her to the hilt, wishing he could push himself even deeper inside her.

He held her hips steady, angled them just how he loved, determined to give them both the time of their lives, so neither one ever forgot this night.

He wanted to make this last, but a man only had so much self-control.

Plunging deeper and deeper, faster and faster, he set a hard riding pace. Ma'ra started to pant, to cry out his name. He felt her losing control and unraveling.

"Oh yes, Paul, keep that...right there...oh man, how can you feel this good? Oh yes, love, harder, *harder...*"

In his red haze of passion and lust, only when he felt her arms creep around his back, nails digging into his skin and pulling him even closer to her, did he realize she'd said the lock word.

Even in his raging rut, with his cock mere seconds from bursting, he felt himself freeze.

She'd called him *love.*

# Chapter Seven

Ma'ra barely remembered the words that had fallen from her mouth, so desperate had she been to feel him sinking deeper and deeper inside her.

Yet she wasn't so far gone that she couldn't remember calling him her love.

Not the smartest thing she had ever done, but damned if she would admit that now. All she wanted was to come once more, the glimmering, shimmering edge of the world's biggest and best orgasm just lay on the horizon, and damned if she would let him stop now and *talk about their feelings*.

A girl had to have priorities.

"We can talk about your choice of lock words later," she insisted, grabbing his delectable ass and digging her nails into him, marking him. "Right now, you have promises to keep, Paul, and I will do massive amounts of damage to you if you don't finish this right now."

Thankfully, he snapped right back to attention at the small sting of her nails and her tilting of her hips. His iron-hard cock sank another unbelievable inch into her, and they both groaned.

"You're so right," he groaned, pressing his lips against hers. "Talk later."

She kissed him, grateful and mildly annoyed at the same time. She wasn't stupid, despite how she had acted in the last few hours. She knew he must have chosen the word *love* because he hadn't expected either of them to say the word throughout the course of the evening.

It only stung a little bit.

Anyway, the incredible pleasure his chest, arms, lips and cock gave her more than made up for the slight bit of feminine affront.

More quickly than she could have imagined, his touches and kisses heated her up once again, and they both stood on the razor-sharp edge of release. Her nipple clamps were truly astounding, working much more effectively than they ever had in the silence and sanctity of her quarters on board the cruisers.

The fact she had a real-live man and iron-hard—yet still impressively warm—cock between her thighs might have something to do with it.

"Come on, baby," she heard Paul murmur enticingly, "scream for me one more time when you come."

"I don't think..." she panted, closing her eyes. The small glare of her lamp, barely any light at all, was nevertheless enough for her to be sensitive to, with all her senses heightened and on red-hot alert.

"Of course you can," he insisted. How the hell he knew what she was saying was well beyond her.

"I mean," she panted, trying to express herself between gasps and moans, "I don't think I can scream... Ooooh myyyyy..." She couldn't help herself. Throat raw, eyes squeezed shut, back and neck arched she felt her fingers dig even harder into his back as one mother of all orgasms ripped through her.

She heard that white buzzing noise inside her ears, signifying everything inside her had momentarily shut down. She couldn't hear herself, having no idea what noises she was making or even if she was making any at all.

Light crashed behind her shut lids, she swore she saw the stars and a huge lightning display going on behind them. She felt her pussy clamping down on Paul's shaft, and then she felt him coming, convulsing between her tightening walls and erupting.

It was the biggest, most intense thing she had ever felt, and she barely even made out what was happening. Everything seemed to shut down and speed up at once.

What seemed like hours, but probably was only seconds later, her hearing returned and she opened her eyes. She heard the sounds of both their panting breaths, and as she felt her muscles unlock and she fell back into the mattress, loosening her grip on Paul.

He fell half on top of her, half next to her.

She tried to gather her wits, tried to catch her breath and say something witty. The only thing she could think of was *Wow*, and somehow that seemed a little too high school for such an incredible moment.

"Wow," Paul said beside her. She turned to him, certain his shocked face must reflect much like her own. She smiled, and then snickered.

"You took the word right out of my mouth," she sleepily complained. All that pent-up energy, annoyance and disappointment had washed away with the multiple orgasms. She had always known men got tired after sex, yet she personally felt like she had run a marathon.

"That wasn't all I took out of your mouth," he cheekily commented, moving one sluggish hand to remove her nipple clamps.

"Great investment," she idly commented. "Can't wait to use those again," she said, wondering where the hell the words were coming from. The husky, raw timber to her voice also felt new and strange. Amazing how gravelly a voice sounded after half a dozen screaming, mind-numbing orgasms.

Paul scooted over the bed, dropped the clamps into the still-opened drawer and switched the lamp off.

"We'll catch a nap," he insisted, spooning her from behind, "then talk."

"Talk," she drowsily repeated, the word ringing a bell somewhere deep in her brain. "I did want to talk to you about what went on and Elise…"

"Shh…" he soothed. "We'll talk when we wake up. I promise."

Ma'ra heard him but only from far away, she had already fallen asleep.

# Chapter Eight

Ma'ra woke up to the most delicious sensations. A man, hot and aroused, lay between her thighs. He licked and nibbled her stomach, her belly button, her nipples and her clit.

She moaned, shifting her legs apart to give him better access.

As he thrust deep inside her, she came fully awake.

"Paul," she cried out, opening her eyes.

"Who else?" he teased, stroking deep inside her. Ma'ra moaned and let her hands rest on his chest, playing nimbly with his hair and nipples.

"What happened to talking?" she murmured, obviously not complaining.

"This is your wake-up call," he insisted huskily. Ma'ra smiled.

"Best wake-up call I've had in years," she assured him.

Slowly re-exploring each other, they made casual, relaxed love. Taking their time, touching and tasting, Ma'ra felt a thrill of desire as she flipped Paul onto his back and straddled him.

"My turn," she insisted, laughing.

Paul smiled indulgently. "Go ahead," he insisted, "try your best."

Ma'ra enjoyed riding him, set the pace at a leisurely stroll. As they both became hotter, more out of control, she worked herself faster and harder upon him, driving them higher.

As they both crested together, crying out in tandem, Ma'ra felt a smile of satisfaction cross her lips as she fell down on his chest, limp and sated, sweating.

Giving them both a moment to catch their breaths, she idly traced patterns on his chest, playing with a nipple.

"You won't get any answers if you start up again, sweetheart."

Rolling from him, regretting the loss of his body contact, Ma'ra sat cross-legged on the bed.

"Okay," she said, running a hand through her messy curls. "Start at the beginning and we'll work from there."

Rubbing a hand over his face, grimacing at the need to "talk", Paul pulled the sheet over his naked lower half.

Setting himself up on the pillows, he looked at the ceiling and began to talk.

"There's always been the drug runners and the escort pimps. No news there. But last year a new, far more organized circle set itself up. Very quietly, very discreetly. By the time the Force cottoned on to it, the organization was flourishing and couldn't easily be stomped out. So they needed a couple of volunteers to infiltrate."

Ma'ra felt her heart sink. Even on this tidbit of knowledge, she guessed much of the rest.

"Oh shit," she commented, knowing what was to come. Paul met her eyes, his steady, serious, and completely truthful.

"I volunteered. I can't give details, love. You know the rules better than that. Suffice to say Elise didn't appreciate my non-communication, in fact my complete disappearance from her life. I've never been serious about her, never tried to lead her on. You know that, but I did play the game a bit with her and her ego suffered. The Force leaked the fake court marshaling, the corruption, the whole kaboodle. I assume when you returned Elise decided to try and milk it for what it was worth."

Ma'ra felt a flush creep up her neck, desperately wished to pull up some bedclothes herself.

"So I made a gigantic fool out of myself?"

Paul smiled, the rakish, boyish grin that never failed to melt her.

"And then some, love," he laughed. "Last night was supposed to be the start of the end. Instead of some sleazy intermediate contact, I got pulled up by you, and very grateful I am about it."

Ma'ra frowned.

"I ruined your setup?"

Paul waved a hand dismissingly.

"Not in the least, there's always tonight. Probably you'll be written off as some escort picking up for the evening. No harm, no foul."

Ma'ra shrugged, not really knowing what to say.

"So you'll go back tonight."

For the first time Paul looked deeply into her eyes. She hoped he couldn't see her soul, her wanting and need. She could always go back out into space for another couple of years. Last night's memories would more than last a while.

Before she even finished the thought, she had been rolled underneath Paul's warm, erect body.

"I know that look, and no way are you jetting off again. This should only take three, maybe six months tops to finish up, and then I'll move to desk duties. No way are you running from me, lady."

Ma'ra frowned.

"You'd hate desk duties."

Paul shrugged. "Well, normal duties then. No more undercover stuff. I was just passing the time until you got back, anyway."

Ma'ra looked deep into his eyes, thinking. Elise would certainly be peeved, but she'd get over losing out on Paul. He had never been interested in the first place, and only nerves and uncertainty had kept Ma'ra away previously. All that seemed to have changed.

She smiled.

"Half your appeal last night came from being disreputable," she laughed. "I rather liked the appeal of the good guy turned bad."

Paul nuzzled her neck, pushing her hair gently aside.

"I'll be as bad as you like behind closed doors," he insisted. "We can go through that drawer full of your naughty toys. After I finish this case. You can wait?"

She smiled, feeling happy and light for the first time since before she left on mission.

"Yeah, I can wait. Three months, six tops, huh?"

"At the maximum," he promised, bending down to kiss the juncture of her neck.

"Mmmm..." she murmured. "And when do I have to drop you back at that sleazy pub?"

"Mmm..." Paul nuzzled, glancing a look at his timer. "About four, maybe five hours."

"Excellent," she gloated, pulling him closer.

"Hang on," he insisted, urgency in his tone. Ma'ra frowned and sat up and he climbed over her and off the bed.

When he opened her bedside drawer, she felt her blood tingle and her palms begin to sweat. What toy did he have in mind now? She had a softly padded flogger she had been hanging onto until she found a partner to try it out with, and then there was the Elephant Man Vibrator...

Paul pulled something small and black out, enclosing it mostly in his palm. He climbed across and sat on the bed, fairly glowing with excitement.

Ma'ra frowned and looked down as he opened his palm.

A small black bullet-shaped item lay in his hand, bumps and ridges and nodes all over it.

She recognized it instantly.

*The Galaxy's best and most-used butt plug vibrator for women,* its title proclaimed.

Ma'ra felt herself creaming.

"Five hours, huh?" she smiled, scooting for some lubricating jelly.

"At the least," her lover promised.

# Epilogue

*Six months later*

Ma'ra sat in her favorite comfy chair and read the most recent news release. Paul lay zonked out in their bed in the next room, exhausted from the blitz of media rounds and finishing up paperwork and filing.

*"Local force hero not corrupt!"* the front scan of the release screamed.

Ma'ra snorted.

*Idiots!*

Skimming the article, she smiled at the mesh of fact and fiction, secretly relieved the whole mess was over. The ring was busted, the organization taken apart painstakingly slowly, and the galaxy was right once more.

Oh, and she and Paul were heading off into parts unknown for a much deserved break and R&R.

Ma'ra smiled.

Elise had finally admitted to Ma'ra's less than pleasant pushing to having withdrawn her own funds in a haywire building blitz that had crumpled, leaving her creditless. Grudgingly, Ma'ra had loaned her enough to keep the wolves at bay until Elise's own job paid her enough to get her solvent again.

As Ma'ra had figured, Elise hadn't been impressed at her and Paul getting together, but the kid could deal. Elise was keeping busy with three lovers, one full-time and one part-time job. The kid had plenty on her plate already. She could get over her and Paul as an item.

Besides, Ma'ra had bigger fish to fry.

Like the gigantic barracuda currently snoring on her bed.

Ma'ra stood up and walked to her small rucksack.

Unzipping it, feeling a thrill of ecstasy run through her, she rifled through the butt plugs, clamps, vibrators and tiny felt whips until she came to the brand new pair of manacles.

This time she was prepared.

This time she had asked the teenaged male salesclerk to pick a lock word.

The man had smirked in a knowing way, a way much too old for his supposed eighteen years. He had insisted some device from many centuries ago called a *Chastity belt* was her best bet for a word.

Men had seemingly forgotten about them, from the description the kid had given, with good reason! But she had been promised no modern man would think of the word, let alone think about it in the concepts she had running through her head.

Ma'ra padded silently on bare feet into her small sleeping quarters on her ship. There, exactly where she had left him sprawled enticingly, was her man.

His chest, tanned and naked, beckoned her. His legs were spread, his cock half hard. His arms, thankfully, were already raised above his head. The man was a picture of elegance and masculinity.

Exactly how she wanted him.

Carefully carrying the manacles, Ma'ra stripped off her pants and shirt, glad she hadn't donned any underwear.

Climbing onto the bed and over him, she easily straddled the gloriously naked man. Taking his warm arms into her hands, she kissed his parted lips as she maneuvered his hands toward the headboard.

"Mmm…" he huskily moaned, half asleep still. Ma'ra continued kissing him as she closed the manacles around his wrists, chaining him to the bed.

"Huh?" he queried, waking up.

"My turn," she softly insisted.

His eyes opened, warm chocolate brown, annoyance and desire both reflected in them.

"Ma'ra," he warned, but she just chuckled and slid down his body.

"You never let me taste long enough," she complained. "Never let me take my time. You always take over. So I want my turn at my own leisure," she insisted, licking the tip of his engorged cock.

"Oh woman," he groaned. "You're going to pay for this one."

Ma'ra chuckled as she began to suck on him in earnest.

"I look forward to it, but for now, you're mine."

"Wrong," he insisted. "*You* are *mine*."

Ma'ra laughed around his now fully engorged shaft.

"Same thing," she murmured, enjoying the vibrations of her words around his cock. Tonight might be her turn, but they had the rest of their lives to bicker for dominance.

She looked forward to the challenge.

## About the author

Elizabeth Lapthorne is the eldest of four children. She grew up with lots of noise, fights and tale-telling. Her mother, a reporter and book reviewer, instilled in her a great appreciation of reading with the intrigues of a good plot.

Elizabeth studied Science at school, and whilst between jobs complained bitterly to a good friend about the lack of current literature to pass away the hours. While they both were looking up websites for new publishers, she stumbled onto Ellora's Cave. Jumping headfirst into this doubly new site (both the first e-book site she had ever visited, as well as her first taste of Romantica ™) they both devoured over half of EC's titles in less than a month. While waiting for more titles to be printed (as well as that ever-elusive science job) Elizabeth started dabbling again in her writing.

Elizabeth has always loved to read, it will always be her favourite pastime—she is constantly buying new books and bookshelves to fill—but she also loves going to the beach, sitting in the sun, eating nachos with her best girlfriends, having coffee (or better yet, CHOCOLATE and coffee) with new friends and generally enjoying life.

She is extremely curious, which is why she studied science, and often tells "interesting" stories, loving a good laugh. She is a self-confessed email junkie, loving to read what other people on the EC board think and have to say, she laughs often at their tales and ideas. She recently has developed a taste for the gym. She's sure she read somewhere it was good for her, but she is reserving judgment to see how long it lasts.

Elizabeth welcomes mail from readers. You can write to her c/o Ellora's Cave Publishing at 1337 Commerce Drive, #13, Stow, OH 44224.

## Also by Elizabeth Lapthorne:

Behind the Mask anthology

Lion In Love

Payback

Rutledge Werewolves 1: Scent of Passion

Rutledge Werewolves 2: Hide and Seek

Rutledge Werewolves 3: The Mating Game

Rutledge Werewolves 4: My Heart's Passion

Rutledge Werewolves 5: Chasing Love

# The Ellora's Cave Library

Stay up to date with Ellora's Cave Titles in Print with our Quarterly Catalog.

# Lady Jaided Regular Features

## Jaid's Tirade

Jaid Black's erotic romance novels sell throughout the world, and her publishing company Ellora's Cave is one of the largest and most successful e-book publishers in the world. What is less well known about Jaid Black, a.k.a. Tina Engler is her long record as a political activist. Whether she's discussing sex or politics (or both), expect to see her get up on her soapbox and do what she does best: offend the greedy, the holier-than-thous, and the apathetic! Don't miss out on her monthly column.

## Devilish Dot's G-Spot

Married to the same man for 20 years, Dorothy Araiza still basks in a sex life to be envied. What Dot loves just as much as achieving the Big O is helping other women realize their full sexual potential. Dot gives talks and advice on everything from which sex toys to buy (or not to buy) to which positions give you the best climax.

## On the Road with Lady K

Publisher, author, world traveler and Lady of Barrow, Kathryn Falk shares insider information on the most romantic places in the world.

## Kandidly Kay

This Lois Lane cum Dave Barry is a domestic goddess by day and a hard-hitting sexual deviancy reporter by night. Adored for her stunning wit and knack for delivering one-liners, this Rodney Dangerfield of reporting will leave no stone unturned in her search for the bizarre truth.

## A Model World

CJ Hollenbach returns to his roots. The blond heartthrob from Ohio has twice been seen in Playgirl magazine and countless other publications. He has appeared on several national TV shows including The Jerry Springer Show (God help him!) and has been interviewed for Entertainment Tonight, CNN and The Today Show. He has been involved in the romance industry for the past 12 years, appearing on dozens of romance novel covers and calendars. CJ's specialty is personal interviews, in which people have a tendency to tell him everything.

## Hot Mama Cooks

Sex is her food, and food is her sex. Hot Mama gives aphrodisiac a whole new meaning. Join her every month for her latest sensual adventure -- with bonus recipe!

## Empress on the Mount

Brash, outrageous, and undeniably irreverent, this advice columnist from down under will either leave you in stitches or recovering from hang-jaw as you gawk at her answers to reader questions on relationships and life.

## Erotic Fiction from Ellora's Cave

The debut issue will feature part one of "Ferocious," a three-part erotic serial written especially for Lady Jaided by the popular Sherri L. King.

# COMING TO A BOOKSTORE NEAR YOU!

# ELLORA'S CAVE 2005

## BEST SELLING AUTHORS TOUR

# Why an electronic book?

We live in the Information Age—an exciting time in the history of human civilization in which technology rules supreme and continues to progress in leaps and bounds every minute of every hour of every day. For a multitude of reasons, more and more avid literary fans are opting to purchase e-books instead of paperbacks. The question to those not yet initiated to the world of electronic reading is simply: *why?*

1. *Price.* An electronic title at Ellora's Cave Publishing runs anywhere from 40-75% less than the cover price of the exact same title in paperback format. Why? Cold mathematics. It is less expensive to publish an e-book than it is to publish a paperback, so the savings are passed along to the consumer.
2. *Space.* Running out of room to house your paperback books? That is one worry you will never have with electronic novels. For a low one-time cost, you can purchase a handheld computer designed specifically for e-reading purposes. Many e-readers are larger than the average handheld, giving you plenty of screen room. Better yet, hundreds of titles can be stored within your new library—a single microchip. (Please note that Ellora's Cave does not endorse any specific brands. You can check our website at www.ellorascave.com for customer recommendations we make available to new consumers.)

3. *Mobility.* Because your new library now consists of only a microchip, your entire cache of books can be taken with you wherever you go.
4. *Personal preferences are accounted for.* Are the words you are currently reading too small? Too large? Too...**ANNOYING**? Paperback books cannot be modified according to personal preferences, but e-books can.
5. *Innovation.* The way you read a book is not the only advancement the Information Age has gifted the literary community with. There is also the factor of what you can read. Ellora's Cave Publishing will be introducing a new line of interactive titles that are available in e-book format only.
6. *Instant gratification.* Is it the middle of the night and all the bookstores are closed? Are you tired of waiting days—sometimes weeks—for online and offline bookstores to ship the novels you bought? Ellora's Cave Publishing sells instantaneous downloads 24 hours a day, 7 days a week, 365 days a year. Our e-book delivery system is 100% automated, meaning your order is filled as soon as you pay for it.

Those are a few of the top reasons why electronic novels are displacing paperbacks for many an avid reader. As always, Ellora's Cave Publishing welcomes your questions and comments. We invite you to email us at service@ellorascave.com or write to us directly at: 1337 Commerce Drive, Suite 13, Stow OH 44224.

ELLORA'S CAVE
ROMANTICA PUBLISHING